HARDWICK HEATH KILLER

An absolutely gripping crime thriller with a massive twist

MICHELLE KIDD

DI Nicki Hardcastle Series Book 3

JOFFE BOOKS

Joffe Books, London
www.joffebooks.com

First published in Great Britain in 2024

Cover art by Nick Castle

ISBN: 978-1-83526-556-7

CHAPTER ONE

Thursday 7 March 2019
11.10 p.m.
Hardwick Heath, Bury St Edmunds

The rope creaked, the body swinging in the strengthening wind.

PC Jim Parker angled his torch up towards the man's face. He'd seen a dead body before — several, in fact — but never one quite like this.

He was sure that the man was dead.

The head lolled a little to the side, a pair of unfocused eyes staring vacantly into nothing. He was dressed in a dark blue hooded jacket and a pair of dark jeans. Even in the surrounding gloom, PC Parker noticed the fresh-looking mud stains to both knees and around each ankle. A pair of dirty white trainers with their laces untied encased the man's feet as he dangled.

The constable took another step forward, at the same time pulling his radio towards him.

The call to the duty sergeant at the station was brief. Any unexplained death would be treated with caution until proven otherwise — PC Parker knew the drill well enough.

With reinforcements on the way, he stood back to wait, careful not to encroach on the scene any more than he already had — *just in case*.

The couple who had made the unfortunate discovery were waiting further back in the shadows of the trees. PC Parker had taken their details and impressed upon them the need to remain close by, at least until the duty sergeant arrived. They'd seemed reluctant, and a little uncomfortable at the prospect, but they appeared to be doing as they were told. For the moment.

Parker briefly asked himself who on earth would choose a night like this, with an amber weather warning in place, to take a walk in the woods.

But he had more pressing things to worry about than the two potential witnesses.

He swung his torch up towards the hanging body once more. Although he was as sure as he could be that no life coursed through the man's veins, he needed to cut the poor sod down.

It was then that he saw the note poking out of the man's pocket.

* * *

College Lane, Bury St Edmunds

Nicki Hardcastle heaved the holdall onto the kitchen worktop and sighed. The trip hadn't been as fruitful as she'd hoped, and now all she had to show for it was a bag of dirty washing — and one that needed dealing with before going back to work in the morning.

Work.

As a detective inspector with the local police force, Nicki was never really *not* at work — at least, that's what it felt like. Even when on annual leave, she would invariably keep in touch with her team via text or email — more often than not it would be both — asking for updates on any number of the investigations that were currently weighing down her already overcrowded desk.

She found it hard to switch off. So, most of the time, she didn't bother.

Sighing once more, she started pulling clothes from the holdall and transferring them into the waiting washing machine. If she didn't do it now, it would be another unwanted task to face in the morning. And she didn't want to think about the morning.

Just then, she felt something soft brush against her legs. Glancing down, she spied Luna, her Russian Blue cat, weaving her way around her calves, mewing softly.

"Hey, sweetie, did you miss me?"

Nicki bent down to give the cat a tickle under her chin, feeling Luna's soft purr beneath her fingers. Luna then extracted herself from between Nicki's legs and trotted over towards her food bowl, sitting down by its side and casting a mournful look in Nicki's direction.

"Of course you didn't miss me," smiled Nicki, reaching for a packet of Luna's favourite food. "All you're interested in is that stomach of yours, isn't it?" She tipped the contents of the sachet into Luna's empty bowl and then turned back towards the pile of washing. Her heart sagged — and not just because of the dirty laundry.

She'd had such high expectations of the trip. A feeling that at last she would find the answers she'd craved for so long — an end to the incessant nightmare that crowded her thoughts on an almost daily basis. Benedict had told her to be cautious and not to get her hopes up, as they really didn't have much to go on — but although she'd tried, she couldn't help it.

Deano.

Now she knew her brother was alive, she wouldn't rest until she found him.

Alive.

The word seemed so alien to her. She still couldn't quite believe she was saying it at all. For the last twenty-two years she had been swamped by the competing emotions of guilt and grief. Both feelings had been ingrained in her day-to-day life for so long, walking hand in hand like Siamese twins, that they had become a part of her.

As the years rolled by, she, like everyone else, had assumed that Deano was dead. What other explanation could there be? Disappearing from the fair that cold November night at just five years of age, how could he possibly still be alive after all this time? After all the efforts so many people had made to try and trace him, to try and find him, to try and bring him back to his family — there could be no other explanation.

Deano was gone. Deano was dead.

Except that he wasn't.

Thanks to Benedict Thatcher and his dogged perseverance in uncovering the truth — well, as much of the truth as they knew at this stage, which wasn't much — she now knew that Deano was alive.

Nicki still had no real idea where Deano had been all this time, or how exactly he had come to be taken from them in the first place — he was literally there one minute, gone the next. But those were details that could wait. For now, all she could focus on was finding her baby brother. The trip to Carlisle had been the first step. Benedict had traced Annette and Larry Browning to the cathedral city in Cumbria — but any excitement or elation she might have felt had quickly evaporated when the lead came to nothing.

Annette and Larry Browning.

Nicki had tried to picture in her mind what type of people would abduct another person's child — *another mother's child* — and then bring them up as their own. For that was what the Brownings had done with Deano: plucked him from the fairground like a ripe plum and then disappeared with him into the night. Their selfish act had deprived Deano of his real family, and had plunged the Websters into a lifetime of pain, guilt and recriminations from which they would never truly recover. From that moment on, Nicki's life changed forever.

After learning that her brother was still alive, Nicki had initially felt some form of gratitude towards the couple — maybe even a degree of warmth. They had obviously loved and cared for Deano, treating him as if he were their own, but over the last couple of months that feeling had morphed into one of anger, and then a sharp-edged hatred. The loss of Deano still felt as raw as the moment it had happened. Finding out about Larry and Annette Browning had merely deepened the pain.

Nicki popped a detergent capsule into the machine and stifled a yawn. The drive back from the north had tired her out, and all she wanted to do right now was sleep. As the thought of rolling into bed filled her head, she heard her mobile chirp. Pulling it from her pocket, expecting it to be Benedict, she saw the caller was one of her detective sergeants. Frowning at the time, which was coming up to midnight, she slammed the washing machine door closed and accepted the call.

"Roy? Is everything OK?"

CHAPTER TWO

Friday 8 March 2019
12.20 a.m.
Hardwick Heath, Bury St Edmunds

"You did the right thing." Nicki followed Detective Sergeant Royston Carter's narrow gaze.

The body was now lying on the muddied ground with no signs of life. PC Parker had been joined by several more of his uniformed colleagues from the Neighbourhood Response Team, and a section of crime scene tape was in the process of being secured to two neighbouring fence posts.

"Are we sure it's a crime scene, boss?" Roy's brow creased, his face pensive. "I mean, I may have overreacted . . ."

Nicki gave a curt shake of the head. "Not at all. Like I said, you did the right thing, calling it in like that. Parker did the right thing, too."

As soon as the duty sergeant had taken PC Parker's call, she had attended the scene to be apprised of what he had found — or, at least, what he *thought* he had found. It didn't take long. DS Carter was the on-call duty detective that night and the next call made its way to him.

"We have to err on the side of caution with something like this — and, by all accounts, you're not the only one here to think it looks a little suspicious."

Both Nicki and Roy's attention turned towards Dr Carolyn Mitchell, who was ducking beneath the police tape and heading in their direction. She nodded at the two paramedics who were still standing by, their resuscitation skills not needed tonight. Despite the dark and stormy night, Nicki could see the look of concern on the pathologist's face as she approached.

"Hey, Nicki. How's things?" Carolyn 'Caz' Mitchell was the lead pathologist at the West Suffolk Mortuary and she knew Nicki well, both inside and outside of work. Pulling her elasticated cap from her head, she let her chestnut red hair tumble onto her shoulders.

"All good, thanks, Caz. What do you think about this?" Nicki gestured towards the body lying a short distance away.

Caz's gaze flickered back over her shoulder for a second or two before returning to land on DS Carter. A small smile twitched at the corner of her mouth. "Your man here made a good call."

"It's suspicious, then?" Nicki's eyebrows hitched. "You don't think it's a suicide?"

"Suspicious enough for me to tell you that you'll probably need to dig a bit deeper on this one." Caz began walking in the direction of where she'd left her car, gesturing for Nicki and Roy to follow. "Of course, it could still turn out to be a suicide — but it doesn't have all the obvious signs that I would expect to see if it was. I'll know more about what we're looking at once I get him examined."

"Murder?" Nicki's eyebrows went a notch higher.

Caz shrugged. "That's for you guys to determine. All I can tell you is whether or not he died by his own hand. There's no question that life is extinct so we'll leave the body in situ until the scene has been processed by forensics."

Nicki pulled out her phone, thinking she may as well get the ball rolling. "Thanks, Caz. And thanks again to you, Roy — good shout. Well done."

If it hadn't been so gloomy in this part of the heath, Nicki and the pathologist might have seen DS Roy Carter's cheeks darken a little, and the light in his eyes begin to dim. "It was nothing," he eventually managed, his voice distant. "It was the uniforms who noticed something wasn't quite right. They should get the credit, really. I just confirmed their suspicions, that's all."

"Well, whatever happened, it was spot on." Nicki started walking towards her own car, parked a little further away. "Let's get out of this wind and back to the station — get this investigation underway before we call it a night."

If she had taken a moment to look back over her shoulder, she might have seen the detective sergeant's eyes stray back towards the sad discovery among the trees behind them. And if she had, she might also have seen the haunted expression that followed.

* * *

He knew he hadn't been seen. The heath was usually deserted at this time of night, the last weary dog-walkers long since headed for home; *if* they had been out at all. The storm that had battered the country for the last few days seemed to have kept most people off the streets, which made his job all the easier. And the particular section of woodland he had chosen had no houses or any other buildings nearby, so there was no one to twitch their net curtains and wonder what he was doing. He gave a self-satisfied smirk. Nothing and no one would have seen him.

The lad wasn't particularly heavy, but getting him strung up like that had been more awkward than he'd imagined. After two botched attempts, he'd started to wonder if the idea had been such a great one after all. It wasn't like the police were going to be fooled for long — they usually weren't, as a rule — but if it could take the heat off him for a short while, then it was worth the gamble.

It would give him time to think.

When deciding what to do with the body, he had very quickly come to the conclusion that he wouldn't bother trying to bury it — shallow graves were always found, weren't they? It was always some dog-walker, some jogger, some annoying do-gooder poking their nose in where it wasn't wanted. Unearthing even the most careful of disposals — or so the glut of CSI programmes on TV would have you believe, anyway.

But if he made it look realistic enough, he might just get away with it — for a while, at least. It was worth a shot, anyway.

On the third attempt he'd managed it.

Backing the car up beneath the tree, he'd used the bonnet to help him heave the body up. It was a good job he was strong. He had already tied the noose around the lad's neck and calculated how much drop he needed — he'd done his homework. It was surprising what you could find out when you looked hard enough.

The branch had creaked ominously under the weight when he let the body take the strain, but it had held firm.

Now back home, away from the darkness of the heath, he felt a strange sensation ripple beneath his skin. Taking a life had come surprisingly easily to him.

But, then again, he'd done it before . . .

The actual act of killing hadn't really registered all that much at the time — he was surprised how strangely cold and detached he'd felt; as if he wasn't really there. Wasn't really *in the moment*. He'd certainly felt no emotion, that was for sure — other than anger, maybe. Anger that had been building for a while now. And tonight it had overflowed.

There was something in addition to the anger, though — he could recall a strange feeling of delight at watching the life finally ebb from someone else's eyes. It was an odd sensation — unexpected, but not entirely unwanted. And now he thought about it, he was sure he'd read somewhere that the eyes were the last to go — the last of the senses to leave the body in death.

The heart and lungs would eventually fail, the blood then cease to flow.

But the eyes.

The last to go were *always* the eyes.

He grinned. Didn't executioners say that when the guillotine sliced its way through the condemned man's neck, separating his head from his body in one swift movement, that somehow the eyes still blinked?

The thought made him smile again.

CHAPTER THREE

Friday 8 March 2019
Bury St Edmunds Police Station

It was early, just after seven thirty, but nobody seemed to mind. Mugs of coffee were being handed out where required, although more would no doubt be needed before the day was out.

Nicki put her mug down, took a marker pen and approached the first empty whiteboard. "You'll all no doubt be aware of what happened overnight." Taking the lid off the pen, she proceeded to write 'HARDWICK HEATH' in capitals at the top of the board. "The body of a young male was found just after eleven p.m. last night, hanging from a tree in a secluded, wooded area. Although we don't yet have conclusive confirmation, we are treating the death as unexplained at present."

Nicki flashed a look in the direction of DS Royston Carter, who was seated towards the back of the incident room. "Roy and I attended the scene last night and . . ." She paused, noting that the detective sergeant didn't look like he had slept much, if at all, in the intervening hours, his eyes glassy and somewhat unfocused. Unable to fully catch his gaze, she carried on. "According to the attending pathologist, the body didn't have the usual hallmarks that would be expected of a suicide, but seems to have been made to look like one — including a handwritten note in his pocket. We'll have a copy of it in due course but, Roy, I know you took down a note of what it said."

Roy pulled out his notebook. "I took a look at it while waiting for everyone else to arrive. It was a simple piece of white paper, tucked in the front pocket of his jeans. In block capitals it said '*SORRY. EVERYTHING IS JUST TOO MUCH TO STAY HERE. LIFE IS JUST TOO HARD. I LOVE YOU ALL.*' I didn't take it fully out of the pocket in case it disturbed evidence of some kind."

Nicki faced the whiteboard and tacked up a series of crime scene photographs. "Thanks, Roy. So, this is all we have for the moment. Faye and her team have spent the night there, and will be carrying on their investigations this morning. She will no doubt let us have a video of the scene and any other information as soon as possible." Nicki knew the experienced crime scene manager well, and was satisfied the examination of the heath would be in very safe hands. Faye Armstrong was nothing if not thorough. "And the post-mortem is scheduled for later today."

She turned back to face the team and tried to give Roy an encouraging smile. Joining them only last October, he'd settled in well, quickly becoming one of the best officers Nicki had ever had the pleasure of working with. Playing a key role in the Lucas Jackson investigation had earned him a fractured cheekbone, cracked ribs and a concussion in the process. Today he was sharply dressed in a well-cut suit; Roy was always immaculately turned out, no matter what time of day or night it was — or whatever horrors he might have witnessed just hours before.

Next to Roy sat DS Graham Fox, another officer Nicki held in high regard, though maybe not always as immaculately turned out as his colleague. Graham sported more of a crumpled look: shoes that could do with a polish, and a shirt that had only had a brief acquaintance with an iron. If anyone commented on his creased appearance, he would merely grin and say that it was 'shabby chic' rather than just 'shabby'.

The two of them had had their moments over the last year or so. Fox had veered off the rails a little after the breakdown of his marriage, when his attention to the job had suffered. But he was back to his best now, for which Nicki was grateful. He, too, had played a crucial role in the search for Lucas Jackson, putting his life on the line in its closing stages. At one point Nicki truly thought she had lost him — but, in true Graham Fox style, he'd pulled through with his usual grit and determination. And probably a good dose of stubbornness, too.

DS Fox had recently dispensed with the walking cane he had been forced to use while recovering from his injuries, but he still kept it propped up in the corner of the incident room as a reminder of how something so simple had helped in the capture of the Trophy Killer just a couple of months before. Although he no longer needed it to help him walk, it was clear that he couldn't quite bring himself to part with it.

Seated at the front were two detective constables who made up the rest of Nicki's team. DC Matt Holland and DC Duncan Jenkins. Both were astute and hardworking officers whom Nicki knew she could rely on.

There was one other officer, however, who was missing from the team today. DC Darcie Butler was on leave, having taken her sister, Amy, to a spa retreat to celebrate Amy's thirtieth birthday. Darcie was a rising star in Nicki's eyes, certainly on a path to greater things in the future. Nicki, for one, couldn't wait for her to get back.

"While we wait for any further information to come in, let's start with the usual actions. Duncan, can you look at any CCTV from around the heath. There aren't any cameras on the heath itself, but check surrounding streets. I've asked the officers conducting house-to-house nearby to look for any doorbell cameras." Nicki leaned against a table close to the whiteboard, picking up her coffee mug once again. "We need to ID our body as a matter of priority. Maybe we can see him, or whoever brought him there, getting in or out of a vehicle close by?" Duncan nodded and pulled out his notebook. "Fingerprints have been taken to see if they flag up on the system — we'll keep our own fingers crossed on that one. Matt, can you liaise with Missing Persons? Just on the off chance." The officer nodded and drained his mug.

Nicki turned towards DS Fox. "Graham. You were in early this morning — anything you can tell us about the couple who found the body?"

Fox consulted his notebook. "Just before eleven o'clock last night, Adam Spencer and Molly Thorne were walking through that particular section of woodland on the heath—"

"An odd time of night to be taking a walk," commented DC Jenkins. "Especially as the weather was none too special. Most sensible people would've stayed indoors."

"Indeed," replied Fox, a smirk forming on his face. "Let's just say they were searching for a secluded spot where they wouldn't be interrupted. The weather none too high on their list of concerns." He paused, the smile developing. "Adam and Molly are both married — but not to each other, if you catch my drift. Anyway, they were both suitably embarrassed and asked that we be as discreet as possible in dealing with their statements."

Nicki felt her own smile twitch behind her mug. "Well, we're not here to judge. What people choose to do in their spare time is none of our business. Even if they do choose the worst night of the year in which to do it."

"They've provided prints of their footwear so they can be eliminated from any found at the scene." Fox closed his notebook. "That's about it as far as they're concerned. They didn't see or hear anyone else on the heath. Unsurprisingly, it was deserted."

Nicki nodded. "The area around the body was muddy from the rain — forensics might be able to pull something out for us, but I'm not too hopeful." After taking another mouthful of coffee, she continued, "As mentioned earlier, the victim's death is being treated as unexplained for the time being. The handwritten note found in his front pocket will be sent to the lab just as soon as the post-mortem is concluded, and we'll get a copy. Hopefully there'll be something more on that later today."

"If it's not a suicide then someone went to a lot of trouble to make it look like one," added DS Fox.

"Indeed. Which leads me on to the rope." Nicki pushed herself up from the table and approached the whiteboard again, tapping one of the crime scene photographs that showed the body lying beneath the tree, rope still in situ. "The rope will also be sent to the lab once the post-mortem is complete. But in the meantime, let's see if we can't do a few preliminary checks as to what type of rope it is, where it might be purchased, that kind of thing. Roy? Can I leave that one with you?"

Roy nodded. "Of course."

"Right, for the moment that's all we can do. If you need me, I'll be in my office." Nicki made a move towards the door. "I also need to go and brief the DCI on last night. Let me know if you hear anything on the fingerprints."

* * *

West Suffolk Mortuary

Caz hadn't planned to work today, but she'd known as soon as she left Hardwick Heath last night — or, more accurately, in the early hours of this morning — that she couldn't hand the case over to anyone else.

The body lying before her on the cold mortuary examination table looked to be in the region of twenty to twenty-five years of age. There was an innocence about him, an angelic quality that tugged at the heart strings. This was someone's son. Maybe someone's brother. Someone's lover. Whichever way it turned out — a tragic suicide or otherwise

— it was yet another young life wasted; another painful hole ripped into a grieving family that would never heal, no matter how much time passed.

And what if it *was* foul play?

Caz's chosen profession exposed her to the cruellest and most warped ways that human beings could hurt each other, and it never got any easier to deal with, no matter how many times she saw it. Not only was the life of the young man laying before her wasted, but the life of whoever might have put him there was also ruined. In situations like these, there was never just the one victim.

With a sigh, Caz started the recording device above her head and pulled the light in closer. "Today is Friday the eighth of March 2019, and we have the body of a Caucasian male — age estimated to be between twenty and twenty-five years. Height one hundred and ninety-one centimetres, weight eighty-six kilos."

Each item of clothing had already been carefully photographed then removed from the body, bagged up and suitably logged. The note from the victim's pocket had been photographed, swabbed, then bagged separately. With the young man's body now lying face up on the examination table, under the harsh overhead lighting, his skin took on a ghostly, bleached white tone.

"Externally, the lower body is in good condition. Bruising of varying degrees and ages are visible on both lower legs, muscle and skin tone is otherwise good. No open wounds or signs of recent injury." Caz side-stepped slowly along the edge of the table. "Turning to the upper body, there are two areas of extensive bruising to the left flank, and one further area on the lower back." As gently as she was able, Caz rolled the body onto one side to expose the lower back and left flank, stepping aside to allow the mortuary technician to complete a series of close-up photographs. "The injuries look relatively fresh, certainly within the last forty-eight hours, and appear to have been made by some sort of physical force. Either punching or kicking, or maybe falling against a hard surface."

Caz lowered the body back to the table and continued. "Both arms show evidence of healed wounds on the inner side of each forearm. Possible self-harm, but none are recent." More close-up photographs were taken while Caz took a step back, her gaze travelling up to the poor man's face.

DS Carter's instincts had been spot on. Nothing so far was screaming suicide to her either.

The rope was still wound around the young man's neck. Caz leaned in and began to gently tease the knotted threads apart. They came away relatively easily — it wasn't a traditional hangman's knot — and Caz was soon able to pull the entire length free. The mortuary technician was standing by with a plastic evidence bag, as Nicki would want the rope sent for analysis as soon as possible, but as she dropped it inside, Caz made an observation. To her, at least, the rope looked relatively new, even after being out in the wind and rain. Maybe whoever used it had bought it recently — and with a specific job in mind.

Caz shuddered and turned back to the examination table. If she'd had any doubts about it being a suicide before, they were being redoubled now. Admittedly, each case was different, but there were common signs to look out for when dealing with a death by hanging. Usually, the rope would cut into the skin around the neck as the noose tightened. Abrasions would be extensive and an unmistakable discolouration would then follow. Depending on how long the body had been hanging, the skin beneath the rope may also have started to break. In addition, the face would become distorted and bloated as the blood and oxygen supply was cut off. The lips might swell, the tongue loll to one side, and micro haemorrhaging would appear in both eyes. Occasionally, the force would be great enough to damage the larynx, or even the cervical vertebrae. At the point of death, the victim often lost control of their bladder and bowels.

None of these outward signs were present on the table before her.

The rope had left some markings to the neck, but nothing as extensive or deep as would be expected if this was a true death by hanging. The man's face was a little discoloured, but there was no obvious bloating. No lip or tongue swelling. There was a mild degree of haemorrhaging and petechiae in both eyes, and a blue tinge around the lips, but nothing yet to support the suspicion of suicide.

Caz reached for her scalpel and wondered what the internal examination would reveal.

* * *

2 Old Railway Cottages, Dullingham, Nr Newmarket

Benedict Thatcher wasn't used to feeling this level of disquiet. Priding himself on having nerves of steel, the email had been both unexpected and unwanted.

A job.

In Benedict's line of work, a 'job' wasn't the usual nine to five that the rest of the population might envisage. There was no office, no desk. No factory or workshop. Benedict was a 'fixer'. If you had a problem, then he was the man to call. And while he would never claim that his methods always toed the line, legally speaking, his morals usually kept him on the right side of good and bad. Often he was just needed as the hired muscle — he had powers of persuasion that could break even the most ardent resistance. At other times it was his intricate knowledge of the dark web and all things technologically clandestine that gave him employment opportunities. There wasn't much he couldn't unearth given time and resources — and that included finding people who didn't want to be found.

For a fee, of course.

He could also make people disappear for an even bigger one.

With as many aliases and false identities as there were names in the phone book, Benedict Thatcher prided himself in remaining far below anyone's radar. He'd been off-grid since late last year, something his current employers were none too pleased about. They liked him where they could see him. When they couldn't see him, they got nervous.

He tipped the dregs of his cold coffee into the sink and tossed the half-eaten round of toast into the rubbish bin, appetite lost. Over the last couple of months or so, he'd got used to being around the house more, filling his day with the odd jobs that he'd neglected for far too long. Now he had the time to breathe, he found that he liked this slower pace of life.

But that had been before the email.

He wasn't stupid — he'd known this brief hiatus of calm couldn't last forever; he had just hoped it could have lasted a little longer.

If the tone of the email was anything to go by, he knew it was time to come in from the cold. The job they described wasn't particularly onerous — he'd pulled off similar ones in the past without so much as breaking a sweat. *That* wasn't the problem.

The real problem was the subject.

As soon as he had seen the name on the screen, his blood had chilled. His first instinct was to ignore it, pretend he hadn't seen it. Even delete it. But he knew that wouldn't be an end to the matter. It wasn't something they would let him run away from, off-grid or not. They would catch up with him sooner or later and the end result would be the same.

Pulling the laptop closer, he tapped out a reply to the email.

Understood.

It was all that was needed.

After hitting 'send', he deleted both the incoming email and the reply, just to be sure. Both had been encrypted and would have bounced around so many ISPs on their journey that anyone wishing to trace them would only end up tying themselves in endless knots, and by the end of it they wouldn't know which way was up or which was down. The message told him arrangements for the job would follow in due course, but Benedict pushed the thought from his mind.

Right now he had other, much bigger fish to worry about in this particular part of the ocean.

Mason Browning, for one.

Or rather, *Dean Webster*.

Benedict unlocked the back door and stepped out onto the small patio at the rear of the house. It was a quiet village, which was what had originally drawn him to buy the property, and at this time of the morning there usually wasn't a single sound to be heard. Today, however, the skies were a heavy grey, managing to squeeze even more fat raindrops from their bulbous clouds, and the wind was whipping through the trees, rattling rooftop tiles and battering fences.

Not being much of a gardener, Benedict kept his as low maintenance as he could — just some simple turf and a series of perennial bushes that lined the edges. But it wasn't his own garden that he felt his gaze straying towards.

The Browning family lived next door — at least, they had done until Larry and Annette had done a moonlight flit some two and a half months ago. Benedict hadn't had much to do with his neighbours until their unusual activity towards the end of last year had piqued his natural inquisitiveness — and, not long after that, he'd made the chilling discovery at the bottom of their garden. It had been entirely unexpected and shaken him to the core.

And that said a lot — for it took something very special to shake Benedict Thatcher's foundations.

In the days that had followed his discovery, it became apparent that the Brownings were not all they seemed to be — not even close. Benedict thought *he* was good at keeping secrets — in his line of work you had to be — but he had nothing on Larry and Annette Browning.

Tearing his gaze away, he pulled his phone from his pocket, his finger hovering over Nicki's name in his contacts list. He really should call her about the arrangements for the weekend, but each time he tried he found himself hesitating. They had got back from the north late last night, and he knew by the look in her eyes that she'd been disappointed they hadn't managed to track down her brother. It had been a long shot at best but, even so, he felt guilty that he hadn't been able to pull that particular rabbit out of the hat. Despite his talents, the trail had soon gone ice-cold.

In the end he made the call. It went to voicemail and he left a message.

Yes, I'll be there.

CHAPTER FOUR

West Suffolk Mortuary

Caz pulled the rubber apron free from around her waist and discarded her wellington boots. Pulling off the protective cap that kept her shock of chestnut red hair in place, she headed towards the sanctuary of her office. She needed a shower — something to wash away the stench of death from the morning's examination — but she knew Nicki would be waiting anxiously for her call.

Slipping behind her desk, she popped a pod into the coffee machine while grabbing her mobile with her other hand. She needed caffeine, and she needed it fast.

Nicki answered her call on the second ring. "Caz? Any news?"

Caz took the cup of scalding coffee from the machine and slumped down into her chair. "I've just finished with him. Poor bloke." She'd spent the last hour and a half dissecting the man's internal organs as carefully as she could, identifying and weighing each in turn. It was a macabre dance that she had played out many times before, but for some reason this one felt different. She wasn't sure why. Maybe it was because she was sure now that someone had tried to make it look like suicide, tried to make it look like the poor man himself was to blame. It didn't sit easily with Caz, so she had taken her time with him; treated him with the respect that had so callously been denied him in death.

"It wasn't suicide." Caz got straight to the point. "It was made to look that way — crudely, I might add. But the poor sod didn't hang himself." She heard a sharp intake of breath on the other end of the line.

"Cause of death?"

"Asphyxiation — but manual, not by hanging. There was a small head wound, maybe enough to incapacitate him but it certainly didn't contribute to his death. Plus, an open wound to his left cheek, maybe from a kick or a punch. Some degree of haemorrhaging in both eyes, supporting asphyxiation. There was some blunt force trauma to the lower back and left flank — but again, not enough to contribute to the cause of death."

"So someone strung him up *after* he was dead?"

Caz took a sip of her coffee while nodding. "That's about it in a nutshell."

"You have any idea as to the time of death? Even a rough window?"

"My estimate would be not too long before he was strung up. Definitely some time yesterday evening."

"Anything else of note?"

"There was some evidence of possible previous self-harm markings to each forearm — some healed wounds — but nothing to suggest it was recent. We'll do the usual post-mortem bloods and toxicology. I've taken some skin scrapings and clippings from his nails — the usual — just in case he fought back. His clothing was quite heavily mud-splattered — it's all bagged up ready for your forensics team."

"Thanks, Caz."

"I'll put it all in a report and let you have it as soon as I can. I'll also send you a picture of the note found in his pocket."

Caz ended the call and leaned back in her chair, bringing the coffee mug to her lips. She could feel the caffeine sparking electricity through her bloodstream, but also found it swirling uncomfortably in the pit of her empty stomach. Whoever it was out there on her examination table, she had done her best by him. She just hoped it was enough to help uncover the truth.

* * *

Bury St Edmunds Police Station

Nicki placed the phone down amid the mess that masqueraded as her desk. The five days she had taken to travel north with Benedict in search of Deano seemed to have heralded the onslaught of an avalanche of new cases needing her attention — and each and every one was stacked up before her.

But there was only one case that she really felt able to focus on right now: last night's body in the woods.

She hoped for the young man's sake that an ID was forthcoming soon — that some family member, some loved one somewhere would come and reclaim him. Lying unnamed in a chilled cabinet, lost and forgotten, wasn't where anyone should end their days.

The preliminaries were underway now that they knew with some degree of certainty that they were looking at a wrongful death — maybe even murder. Faye and her team were still at Hardwick Heath processing the scene, as much as they were able to in weather like this, and would most likely be there for the rest of the day.

But Nicki had been in the job long enough to know that the heath wouldn't be the scene of the poor man's demise. The woods were just some macabre stage — the actual crime scene, where the man had met his death, could be anywhere.

An ID would point them in the right direction, or at least give them something to work from.

Bloods and fingerprints had been taken for analysis, so for now it was just a waiting game. Matt had got back to her quite quickly to say that there were no likely matches with

Missing Persons, although they would continue checking. So it was unlikely the ID would be coming from there.

Stacking the newly acquired cases to the side, promising herself she would give them the once-over later, Nicki pulled towards her the only other file that filled her thoughts. It was an investigation that had drained her and the rest of her team, both physically and mentally, and had reached its conclusion just over two months ago.

The Trophy Killer — at least that was what the media had dubbed him.

Although the killer was now behind bars awaiting trial, the case wasn't yet closed; far from it. With the unnervingly gruesome discovery that there were potentially another nineteen victims out there somewhere, the case was ongoing, and would be for some time. Due to the numbers involved, the investigation had been handed to a specialist unit with experience of handling cases of this magnitude. For once, Nicki wasn't disgruntled at an investigation being taken away from her — if anything, she had actually welcomed handing over the reins on this one. The time she had spent hunting the Trophy Killer had sapped her of every ounce of energy; she hadn't anything left in reserve to hunt for another nineteen victims. But she still kept the file on her desk as a reminder of how precious life was — how the actions of one person could affect so many.

Nineteen more victims. It made her shudder.

Setting the file aside, her thoughts turned to the coming weekend. Her parents were coming for Sunday lunch, her father due to play a round of golf with the DCI in the morning. The more she thought about it, the more surreal it all felt. She hadn't seen her parents in . . . so long she couldn't quite remember. But the thawing of relations over the festive period had been followed by a tentative '*you should come over for lunch one Sunday*' . . . and now it was here.

Sunday.

She hadn't yet thought about what she was going to cook — maybe that was her way of saying that she wasn't quite sure the grand reunion would actually take place. Benedict's voicemail from earlier confirming that he would be there had gone some way to settling the butterflies waging war in her stomach — but only a little.

She pushed thoughts of Sunday to one side and let her eyes sweep the desk once more. Most of the cases adorning it could wait — but the discovery last night on the heath could not. The first forty-eight hours in any investigation were the most important. She wondered if she really had the time to entertain her parents when there was so much needing her attention here. Usually, she would work on through — evenings, weekends — throwing herself into the case until it was solved.

Her eyes flickered towards her mobile phone. She still had time to cancel. They would understand, surely? Her hand gravitated towards it. But before she could cement her decision, there was a brief knock at the door and DS Fox's head appeared around the frame.

"Boss? We've just had a hit on the fingerprints."

* * *

Guildhall Street, Bury St Edmunds

Sir Cecil Pemberton didn't usually set foot in the town centre if he could help it, content to live his days like a recluse within the walls of Pemberton Hall. There wasn't much you couldn't get delivered these days if you tried hard enough. But the bank had insisted he attend in person — something about authenticating his identity, which couldn't be done over the phone or online. If he didn't, access to his bank account would be frozen.

It was for his own protection, apparently. The fight against fraudsters.

It was an irritation he could do without, but not one he could avoid. He had asked for the earliest appointment they had, hoping he could be in and out before the good people of

Bury St Edmunds had finished their cornflakes and noticed that he was out and about on their streets — but the only appointment they could offer him today was midday, which didn't really suit him at all.

For that reason, he was already irritated.

He also hadn't slept much, which didn't help, and the weather was atrocious. He'd considered cancelling the appointment, but knew he would only have to make another one and go through this whole charade again. Best to get it over with.

At least the wind and rain would keep most people safely tucked up in their houses, and he wouldn't have to deal with their snide looks and catty comments. He was well aware of the hostility the vast majority of the town seemed to feel towards him; he'd received enough hate mail to realise that quickly enough. No one ever wrote to him to congratulate him on anything good he might be doing, or pass on any kind words — it was all hate, hate, hate. To begin with, he had notified the police each time a particularly spiteful missive came flying through the door — but lately he just burned them in the fireplace, watching the angry words curl up and die in the flames. He got the distinct impression that he wasn't exactly top priority when it came to police investigations.

That was something else that irritated him.

Part of him couldn't really blame them, he supposed. His own father, Sir Alfred Pemberton, had lived quite happily at Pemberton Hall, '*cheek by jowl with the locals*,' the old man had described it — he would even frequent the town pubs and stand a round of drinks on occasion, much to the joyous amusement of the regulars. But his father had died some months ago and Sir Cecil was the resident of Pemberton Hall now.

And times had changed.

He didn't want to mix with the locals. He didn't want to sit next to them in a poky pub and listen to their incessant whining. He was nothing like them — *any* of them — and he had no intention of pretending otherwise. So, yes, he understood perfectly well how they might feel towards him. When news reached them that he was intent on selling off swathes of land around Pemberton Hall for development, everyone was instantly riled. But it was *his* land. That was what most of them forgot as they waved their homemade placards in his face and shouted obscenities.

It was *his* land to do with as *he* pleased.

His father would be turning in his grave, he knew that, but it caused Sir Cecil little concern. They had never seen eye to eye, not even on his father's deathbed, so he wasn't going to start pretending otherwise now.

Making his way towards the centre of town, he didn't see the fist coming, just felt it clock him on the side of his chin, below the left ear, leaving a sharp sting in its wake. Not quite forceful enough to knock him from his feet. Sir Cecil whirled round to find an empty pavement behind him.

"What the . . . ?"

He instinctively felt his jawline for a wound but found none. Blinking rapidly, slightly stunned, he stumbled on in the direction of the bank.

The second blow landed on the back of his head, causing him to lose his footing this time and stumble towards the gutter. Miraculously, though, he remained on his feet. Turning around, again he saw that the pavement behind him was empty. He felt his scalp and winced as he found the open wound, a small smear of blood left behind on his fingertips.

"Who is this?" he shrieked. With his words disappearing along the empty street, he thrust his hands into his coat pockets and resumed his stride. He needed to get to the sanctuary of the bank, and fast.

He should never have come.

He didn't see the foot darting out from a side alley until it was too late. It connected with his ankle and sent him flying headfirst onto the pavement. He was unable to pull his hands from his pockets in time, so the full force of the tumble was borne by his nose and forehead. He both heard and felt the sickening crunch, then the pain that followed. He could hear someone behind him, maybe more than one, but his eyes were so full of stars by now that he couldn't focus.

Several swift kicks to his side followed, plus more to his lower back. There was a dampness, and what he guessed was someone's spit landing on his exposed cheek.

Then there was nothing.

Scrambling to his feet, he stemmed the blood pouring from his nose with a handkerchief and hurried back the way he had come. The bank could bloody wait.

He hated this town.

* * *

Bury St Edmunds Police Station

Everyone's eyes were trained on the whiteboard.

"Calvin Shaw." Nicki wrote the name beneath 'Hardwick Heath' on the board. "We now have a positive ID of our discovery last night. Fingerprints were a hit. Graham — what can you tell us about that?"

DS Fox pulled a sheet of paper from his desk. "Only brief details at the moment, but our victim, Calvin Shaw, was arrested last summer after an altercation broke out in the town centre, just outside the Grapes."

"Do we know what type of altercation?"

"Well, looks like one that involved the consumption of too much beer by the sounds of it, boss. Not sure what sparked it off, but he lumped another young lad and put him in hospital. Then he took a swing at one of the officers trying to restrain him. Charged with common assault — received a fine. Can't see that he's come to our attention since."

"Do we have an up to date address for him?"

"Last known address is in the town. I'll do some checks, see if that's still current."

"OK — well, assuming it is, we'll head out there later. While we're out, I want to know all there is to know about him — especially any next of kin. They'll need to be informed as a matter of urgency. I'm keeping details brief for the media at the moment — and definitely not informing them of the ID at this stage — but you know what they can be like, and no parent should ever get to hear of their child's demise via newsprint." Nicki stepped away from the whiteboard. "And keep looking at the CCTV around the heath — we can add in the streets around his home address now, too. And the rope — I still want to know what type it is and where someone might get hold of it."

Quiet murmurings filled the incident room as Nicki headed towards the door. As she passed his desk, her eyes came to rest on Roy's hunched figure. "On second thoughts, why don't you all step outside for a while. Take a lunch break and go and get yourselves some decent coffee to see you through. Maybe some snacks. Roy and I just need the room to ourselves for a while."

The rest of the team didn't need asking twice. As they all headed for the door, Nicki crossed over to the hot water urn. She called back over her shoulder, "Graham? I'll see you out by the car in half an hour."

When the door of the incident room had closed behind her departing team, Nicki dumped a teaspoon of coffee into each of two mugs while eyeing Roy who had by now appeared at her side. "You OK?"

The detective sergeant avoided her gaze. Instead, he took hold of the mugs and set about pouring hot water into each.

"Fine, boss."

Nicki nodded but she was no fool. She handed Roy the carton of milk. "Couldn't help noticing the look on your face at the scene last night — and in the briefing earlier. You need to talk about anything?"

Roy's hand hovered over the mugs as he deposited a small splash of milk in each. Eventually he gave a quick shake of the head. "It's fine. It just wasn't a particularly pleasant thing to see — someone strung up like that."

Nicki took hold of the coffee mugs and crossed over towards a vacant desk. She gestured to one of the chairs. "It's just us in here now, Roy." She took a brief glance over her shoulder at the empty incident room. "You don't need to pretend in front of me." *I can see it in your eyes*, she wanted to add. Nicki was an expert in keeping things hidden; locked away out of sight. She could recognise it a mile off in others, too — sometimes it was just like looking into a mirror.

"If there's something about this case that's going to affect you — more than it usually would — then I need to know, sooner rather than later." Nicki paused, seeing the haunted look on the detective sergeant's face intensify. "It won't go any further," she added, slipping into the vacant chair next to him. "Just between us."

Roy took hold of his mug, staring down into the murky brown liquid. When it came, his voice was one notch above a whisper. "I don't know if you remember but, when I first started here, I told you about . . ." He paused and cleared his throat. "I told you about a close friend that I'd lost."

Nicki nodded, recalling the conversation in the Nutshell. "Yes, I think you said an overdose?"

Roy sank further back in his chair. "It was a little more than that in the end. It was back when we were both in college, both just starting out, not really knowing what we wanted to do with our lives. He was . . ." Another pause. Another cleared throat. "He was my best mate — star pupil. Top of everything — straight As, the works. A hit with the girls, too." A small, sad smile crept onto his lips as he cast his mind back. "He was even better at football than I was." Voice hitching, a darkness clouded the detective sergeant's eyes once more. "He was my best mate, and I never saw it. I never saw it coming."

Nicki let the silence deepen, resisting the urge to fill it. Eventually, Roy continued.

"I was the one to find him — at home, in his bedroom. He'd taken a massive overdose — enough to do the job anyway — but he'd made doubly sure by hanging himself with a belt."

Nicki drew in a sharp breath. "My god, Roy. I'm so sorry. I had no idea."

Another sad smile crossed Roy's lips as he took a hesitant sip from his mug. "No reason why you should. It's not something I talk about. I just don't know how I missed it. Surely there would have been signs? Something I should have seen?"

Nicki could see the raw guilt still etched into his face. "Are you all right?" She leaned across to place a hand on the detective's forearm, giving it a squeeze. "Staying on this investigation, I mean? I can put you on something else. Believe me, I have more than enough other cases that could do with an extra body or two." She thought back to the files currently littering her desk.

Roy smiled gratefully, but shook his head. "I'm fine. I'd like to stay on this one. I might not have been able to help Ellis, but maybe I can do something good here. Make up for being such a shit friend before."

"You couldn't have known, Roy." Nicki returned the sad smile. "As heartbreaking as it sounds, often those that are closest are the last ones to see anything. It's just the way it is. It doesn't mean you weren't his friend. Try not to beat yourself up about it."

Roy sighed, looking unconvinced, but his tense shoulders relaxed a little. "He was the reason I joined up, you know? Ellis. The reason I joined the police."

Nicki nodded. "I remember you saying that it wasn't a family tradition."

"I made the decision pretty much right there and then, standing in Ellis's bedroom. I felt the dead weight of his body as I cut him down. I knew instantly that he was gone; that there was nothing I could do to bring him back. I'll never forget the look in his eyes — the way his face was contorted in so much pain. It barely even looked like him." Roy breathed in a shuddering breath. "No one knew where he'd got the drugs. He wasn't a habitual user as far as we knew — but maybe we didn't know him as well as we thought. I made a vow right then, as I watched them carry his body out of the room, that I'd do something good with my life. Something to help others. It was too late for Ellis, but . . . I'll never forget what I saw that day."

Nicki started to nod once more. "Which was why you knew something looked off at the scene last night." Suddenly it all started to make sense. "Why you suspected that it might not be suicide?"

"It took me back to that day. All I could see was my mate. And that . . . *that* on the heath last night just looked all wrong." Roy gestured over his shoulder towards the white-board and Calvin Shaw's sparse details. "I can remember Ellis's face as clearly now as it was back then. It's never left me, not for a minute. And this Calvin? He looked nothing like that — not even close."

"Like I said at the time, Roy, it was a good call. If you ever need to talk about anything, my door is always open. And if the case gets too much, you can always step aside. Just say the word. No one needs to know why." After a couple of sips, Nicki abandoned the coffee she hadn't really wanted in the first place and stood up. "I'd better get going. I need to do a few things before Graham and I head over to Calvin's home address." She made a move towards the door. "But the minute this all gets too much, Roy, you come and find me."

CHAPTER FIVE

Melrose Avenue, Bury St Edmunds

Calvin Shaw lived on the first floor of a group of well-main-
tained flats on Melrose Avenue. A quiet part of the town, it
wasn't somewhere Nicki or anyone from her team were called
to very often. She led the way up the short concrete pathway
towards the communal door that was already open. A lone PC
stood on the front step, moving to the side to let Nicki and DS
Fox inside. Unsure if they were looking at a potential crime
scene, both of them donned protective gloves as a precaution.

A small entrance hall led towards a narrow set of stairs
which took them up to the first floor. Calvin lived in the flat
towards the rear of the block. The landlord had given them
a master key, which Nicki used to unlock the sturdy UPVC
front door to flat three.

They both hesitated on the threshold. Between them
they had visited enough crime scenes to recognise one
instantly from the smell alone. Instinctively they took in deep
breaths, but no instant scent of death rushed up to greet them.
According to Caz's phone call after the post-mortem, there
was no major external loss of blood contributing to Calvin's
death, so they weren't expecting to walk into a bloodbath

— instead there was a heavy silence in the air that only death could bring; a hollow, empty feeling. It was almost as if the flat knew that its occupant wouldn't be returning.

Calvin lived alone, so they weren't expecting anyone else to be inside the flat, but Nicki announced their presence just the same. "Hello? Anyone home?"

The silence continued.

Nicki led Fox through to the living room directly ahead. A well-loved, sagging sofa hugged a side wall, facing a cheap wooden unit that housed a 64-inch TV and surround-sound system. A games console rested on a footstool. On the sofa itself was a plate, decorated with a handful of crumbs and pieces of dried-up cheese, an empty, crumpled can of cola by its side.

"His last meal." Fox gestured towards the plate and can. "Poor sod."

Nothing in the sparsely furnished living room looked to have been disturbed. It really did just seem as though Calvin had paused his game on the PlayStation, finished his cheese sandwich, and left the flat — fully expecting to return.

A bunch of letters and junk mail sat on the windowsill and Nicki made her way towards them while DS Fox headed in the direction of Calvin's bedroom. There was the usual abundance of flyers for pizza and Chinese takeaways, an offer for full fibre broadband, a variety of charity bags, and a card for local gardening and tree-cutting services. There was also a booking confirmation for a pair of festival tickets for later in the summer, some utility bills, and several letters with 'return to sender' written in large capital letters across the front.

"Boss? You might want to see this."

Nicki dropped the letters back down onto the window-sill and turned to where Fox was hovering in the doorway to the bedroom. He gestured for her to follow him back inside.

The room was small — only enough space for a single bed, a slim wardrobe and bedside table. The covers on the bed were askew, the door to the wardrobe wide open. By the side of the bed was a leather holdall.

"What does that look like to you?" Fox picked up the holdall in his gloved hand and placed it on top of the bed.

Nicki peered inside. There was a bunch of underwear, a few T-shirts, a clean pair of jeans and a small collection of toiletries. "Looks like our man was going away for a few days."

"Precisely." Fox caught Nicki's eye. "If we needed any more confirmation that this was no suicide, boss, then I think we've just found it. To my knowledge, no one intending to take their own life packs a bag first."

* * *

Pemberton Hall

Sir Cecil poured another generous measure of brandy from the square lead crystal decanter. He knew he probably shouldn't but after his experience in the town earlier, he felt like he deserved it.

His nose had eventually stopped bleeding, and he'd found a small first-aid kit to dress the scrape to his forehead. There was a small cut on the back of his head, but it hadn't bled so much and was just throbbing now. As was his jaw, where the first punch had landed.

How dare they target him like that? In broad daylight, too, when all he was doing was going about his lawful business — and minding his own. It was precisely the reason why he despised them, the great unwashed. All it made him want to do was press ahead with selling off his land — the quicker the better.

He had reported the assault to the police as soon as he had returned to Pemberton Hall, for all the good it would do. He could tell from the tone of the voice on the other end of the line that they weren't particularly interested and his complaint would be placed at the back of a very long queue.

Wincing, he brought the brandy glass to his lips. He ought to phone the bank to rearrange his visit, but the mere thought of having to make the return trip into town someday soon made him grimace. His nerves were on edge, making him fidgety, and he hadn't been able to settle since returning.

He wasn't a great one for television — far too many trashy reality shows for his liking, plastic people living plastic lives. He'd put on some music — some of his favourite Bach — but even that had begun to grate on his ragged nerves after a while.

He knew what the real problem was. It was *here*; it was being in this house. When his father had died several months before, Sir Cecil knew it was inevitable he would end up moving back into Pemberton Hall permanently, as much as the thought dismayed him. That's what happened in families such as theirs. But it didn't make it any easier to swallow.

He didn't have many fond memories of the place — or of his father, if he were being brutally honest. He had lived at Pemberton Hall as a child, but there was never much love embedded within its walls. Not that he remembered anyway. Certainly no happy memories to take with him into adulthood, that was for sure. His father had been a distant man, somewhat detached from the mechanics of fatherhood. With Sir Cecil's mother dying when he was an infant, his father had employed a succession of nannies and governesses to take charge of his offspring. Looking back, life at Pemberton Hall had been reminiscent of something out of *Jane Eyre*. They'd all taken care of him right enough — the nannies, the governesses — they'd given him whatever affection they could in place of his mother, and he'd even grown to like some of them after a while — but it wasn't the same. They were merely doing what they were paid to do. And eventually he grew to resent it. He became defiant and rude — so much so that his father packed him off to boarding school when he was twelve; something that Sir Cecil was quietly thankful about, if the real truth be told.

But now he was here again.

Home.

When he'd first stepped back inside Pemberton Hall to tend to his dying father, he had felt all manner of memories instantly come flooding back, but the place itself still felt as cold and empty as it always had. He didn't envisage living at the hall for long — just enough time for a decent period of mourning after his father's passing — but a couple of his investments weren't doing as well as he'd have liked and he was in the unusual position of having to tighten his belt a little. Which was exactly how his accountant had put it to him.

Tighten your belt, Sir Cecil. Otherwise things could get choppy.

He had sold his luxury Mayfair apartment to keep the accountant happy, but knew that more was needed. Pemberton Hall was haemorrhaging money at an alarming rate — the cost of the repairs that were urgently needed were eye-watering to say the least.

Sir Cecil slugged back the brandy and poured another. His accountant had made some lurid suggestion that he make Pemberton Hall work for him — open it up to the public, he'd said. The very thought made Sir Cecil's skin crawl. People traipsing around his house? Bringing in all manner of muck and grime from outside? The grubby little fingers of children touching everything? The very vision made him shudder.

He would rather see the place crumble to dust than resort to that. But apparently that was what everyone was doing these days — even Buckingham Palace was open to the public now.

With his head now starting to throb in tandem with the pain from his nose, Sir Cecil decided to try and find some painkillers. He was sure there must be some in one of the bathroom cabinets — at least his father had left behind something useful.

* * *

Bury St Edmunds Police Station

Nicki waited for everyone to settle before picking up a marker pen.

"Let's recap on what we know so far. Calvin Shaw, aged twenty-two, lived locally on Melrose Avenue." She added the address to the whiteboard and tacked two small, square photographs to the side — one was a headshot, the other a copy of the handwritten note. "Identified through fingerprints which were on the system when he was arrested after a street fight last summer. The mugshot we have on file is also confirmatory of his ID. Graham and I visited his flat earlier today, where nothing looked disturbed or out of place. Essentially just a typical young man's flat. Not much by way of furniture. Seemed to live quite a basic existence by all accounts. Faye has arranged for whatever was there to be bagged up for analysis, but I'm not expecting much to come from it. All the same, we will need to have a look at it at some point, see if anything stands out as needing our attention. But there was nothing to suggest he met his killer there, so I'm confident that wasn't our crime scene. What we did note, however, was the lack of a mobile phone or laptop."

"I've tracked down the next of kin, boss." DC Matt Holland consulted his notebook. "Parents are Michael and Heather Shaw and they still live in the family home on Seymour Street. Death message has been delivered in the last hour."

"OK, well we'll pop out to see them later this afternoon and ensure a family liaison officer has been organised. Any other updates while we've been gone?" Nicki looked expectantly around the incident room.

"Uniforms are starting to speak to the residents of the other flats, to see if Calvin had any visitors of note in recent days." DC Duncan Jenkins consulted his notebook. "And so far, the CCTV surrounding the heath hasn't shown much of use. Any roads with cameras are busy streets. If we're going to log and track every vehicle, then it's going to take some time. And more manpower."

"OK. Narrow the timeline to the hours immediately before our lovebirds stumbled across the body. Sunset was around six o'clock. I can't see our killer stringing him up in daylight, so focus on anything between six and eleven o'clock. It was a pretty horrendous night last night, so I wouldn't expect to see too many people out and about. Ask the uniforms doing the house-to-house around Melrose Avenue to be on the lookout for anyone with those doorbell cameras, too. Then check back with them to see if there's anything we can use."

Duncan nodded. "Will do."

"The formal post-mortem report came in by email." Roy tapped the screen of his computer monitor. "It's just as you outlined earlier — cause of death asphyxiation, but no signs of intentional self-harm by hanging. Might have been struck over the head, and there's a facial wound, too."

Nicki nodded. "We obviously need to go and speak to Calvin's parents. Graham, you and I will take that one. Caz has given an estimated time of death of sometime earlier that evening, due to the lividity of the body. In layman's terms, the poor bloke was strung up in the woods not that long after he was killed. Whoever did this would have needed a vehicle — I can't see them trudging very far with a dead body on their shoulders. Matt and Duncan, can you take a look at possible routes in and out of the heath with a car? Faye and her team are probably still there; they'll be looking for tyre tracks in the vicinity of the body. It was muddy but there might be something we can use."

Both Matt and Duncan nodded.

Nicki turned back towards the whiteboard. "It's no mean feat to get the body of a fully grown man up onto those branches. Although our victim wasn't unduly heavy, whoever did this would need some strength about them."

"Agreed." DS Fox stood up. "Shaw was roughly the same height and build as me. Maybe a little less around the middle, though." He patted his stomach.

"You and me both," grinned Duncan.

"What are we telling the media?" asked Roy, looking towards the whiteboard. "Are we releasing the name?"

"At the moment, we'll give them just the bare facts. Body found in the woods. Enquiries ongoing. Nothing more than that. The name will be released in due course, but I'm in no hurry. I'm certainly giving them no speculation as to foul play or anything else at this stage." She paused and caught Roy's eye. "Anything of any use on the rope yet?"

Roy turned in his seat. "I've started to take a look. The rope used to suspend Calvin's body is a strong, polypropylene variety that is widely available in just about any DIY store — and online, too." Getting to his feet, he stepped forward and tacked a photograph of a similar coil of blue rope to the board. "This image is taken from a well-known online retailer — it's identical to the one in the crime scene photographs. It's a very popular type of rope and can be used for just about anything, hence you can buy it just about anywhere. I've made a start on a list of local retailers, but I can't see that a trawl through each one is going to help us all that much. Although the rope at the scene looks new and unused, we've no idea how long our perpetrator might have had it stashed away somewhere."

Nicki nodded her agreement. "Could be both a waste of time *and* a waste of the limited resources that we have. For now, maybe just keep a list of any local stores that would stock it. We'll have to ignore online retailers as that's just too vast a task at the moment. Then park it — we might come back to it later."

Nicki tapped one of the other images on the whiteboard: the note found in the victim's pocket. "*This*, however, could be our biggest clue." *Our only clue*, she wanted to add. "The supposed suicide note. We'll take a copy with us when we go to see the parents — see if they can confirm whether the writing is Calvin's. I suspect it won't be, and therefore whoever wrote it is likely to be our killer."

"Are we going to use a handwriting expert, boss?" DS Graham Fox squinted at the whiteboard.

Nicki could see the pound signs escalating before her eyes. Such an expert would be costly to the investigation. Although the DCI had told her she could use whatever resources she needed to, Nicki knew that this always came with a caveat.

So long as it doesn't cost too much.

"Maybe. But a handwriting expert won't be of any use to us until we have some handwriting to compare it to, which as yet we don't. It's not like we can order everyone in the town to submit a sample for analysis. The lab is testing it for fingerprints, DNA, the works. We may get lucky." But Nicki didn't want to hold her breath. "Carry on as you are for now. Graham, I've just got to go and see the DCI — bring him up to speed — then I'll be ready to go and see the Shaws."

CHAPTER SIX

News about the body found on Hardwick Heath did nothing to dampen the disquiet settling in DCI Malcolm Turner's stomach. Although he had the greatest confidence in Nicki and her team — if anyone could get to the bottom of it, she could — he couldn't help but notice the tiredness in her eyes as she'd outlined the salient points to him earlier.

No, that wasn't quite right. It wasn't tiredness; it was exhaustion.

He knew Nicki had taken a few days off recently, and hoped she'd used it to whisk herself away somewhere to recharge her batteries after a busy few months. But by the looks of it, that hadn't been the case.

They had spoken briefly about the arrangements for Sunday. Turner knew what a big deal it was for her — he didn't need to see the wariness joining the exhaustion in her gaze to know that. He had been a friend of the family for as long as he could remember, and knew all about Nicki's brother's disappearance. And the subsequent fracturing of the Webster family. He supposed it was inevitable — experience something as traumatic as that and there would always be repercussions. Not many families became stronger as a result; most, like the Websters, just disintegrated and crumbled.

He was about to reach for the latest file to populate his in-tray when his mobile began to ring.

Hugh Webster calling.

Turner answered the call immediately. "Hugh? What's up? Not a problem about the weekend, is it?"

"No, the weekend is fine," replied Webster. "Anne and I are looking forward to it. I just hope we haven't put too much strain on Nicki. I know how busy she must be. I did suggest we could go out for a meal somewhere, but she insists on cooking."

"That sounds like Nicki. But I've just seen her — she's fine. She's looking forward to it, too." Turner wasn't sure that was the complete truth, recalling the look in her eyes when he'd mentioned the weekend. With the new case landing on top of an already heavy caseload, there was only so much one person could take. But Nicki was tough — she was a Webster, after all. "So what's on your mind? Worried I'll show you up on the golf course?"

Turner heard a faint chuckle on the other end of the line.

"No, it's not that. It's . . . well, I'm not really sure what it is exactly. But can I run something by you?"

"Sure."

"There have been a few rumours circulating — nothing too detailed — but I've been warned that several of my old cases might be being reviewed. It's a while since I retired, but it seems someone is dragging some of them out of storage and unpicking every decision I ever made."

Turner frowned. "That sounds unusual. What do you need from me?"

"Not much at present, but maybe just be my sounding board when I get further details? I'm sure it'll come to nothing — these things always do. But . . ."

"Consider it done. Like you say, it'll probably fizzle out and come to nothing in the end. We all make mistakes along the way, Hugh. We're not superhuman."

The conversation drifted back to the weekend and their respective golfing achievements, and once the call was ended, Turner placed his mobile on the desk.

Hugh Webster had been an exceptional police officer, and an even better detective superintendent. It didn't strike Turner that much could be found wanting in any of the decisions he might have made back in the day. *Exceptional and thorough* — that was Hugh Webster. Whoever was digging around wouldn't find much — Turner would stake his life on that.

* * *

Seymour Street, Bury St Edmunds

Heather Shaw was a slightly built woman, so much so that Nicki thought the stiffening wind that followed them in through the front door of the Shaw family home might knock her from her feet.

"Come through," she said, her voice as brittle as ice.

"Thank you, Mrs Shaw." Nicki dutifully followed Calvin's mother along the narrow carpeted hallway towards a door to their right. DS Fox closed the front door behind them and headed in the same direction.

The living room was light and airy — or at least it would have been if the heavy curtains shrouding the window had been pulled back, and the unmistakable weight of grief wasn't sucking the very oxygen from the air around them.

As Nicki and Fox entered, a man whom Nicki assumed to be Calvin's father got to his feet. He'd been sitting on a sleek-looking leather sofa, but now his hulking frame seemed to fill the room as he stood.

"No need to get up, Mr Shaw." Nicki gestured for the man to sit back down. "I'm sorry we've had to call on you both at a time like this but . . ." She paused and glanced towards Calvin's mother, who had moved to stand by her husband's side. "Anything you can tell us about Calvin would be really helpful to the investigation at this stage."

The investigation.

It all sounded so cold. So clinical. So cruel. They had just lost the most precious thing in their lives and already Calvin Shaw had been relegated to an '*investigation*'.

"It's OK — we understand." Michael Shaw's voice was deep and throaty. As well as being tall in stature, Nicki noticed he was broad, too, his forearms thick and muscled. His shoulders sloped down towards what was most likely a well-muscled chest beneath his thin V-neck jumper.

The contrast between him and his wife couldn't have been more apparent.

"Please, take a seat." Mr Shaw waved towards two armchairs that faced the sofa, their backs to the curtained window.

Nicki knew the death message, as it was colloquially called, had been delivered to Calvin's parents earlier that day. Despite several hours having now elapsed, she was pretty sure that time had stood still for the Shaws. Death had a habit of doing that to people — making each second feel like wading through treacle.

"Thank you. We'll try not to take up too much of your time." Nicki seated herself in one of the armchairs, Fox slipping into the other.

The room was tastefully furnished — pastels and warm hues surrounded them, with several prints of countryside landscapes on the walls. Any surfaces were clutter free — just a small glass of water and packet of painkillers on the low-rise coffee table. Nicki suspected something stronger might be required as the news about their son sank in.

"Mrs Shaw," began Nicki.

"Heather. You can call me Heather." Calvin's mother managed a weak smile as she pressed her hands together in her lap, a ragged tissue squeezed between her fingers. "Mrs Shaw sounds like my mother. And this here is Mick."

Nicki nodded. "Heather. We really are truly sorry for the news you received earlier today. I can only try to imagine what you must be going through right now." That wasn't strictly true — Nicki could do more than try. She *knew*. She could remember with startling clarity the police officers who'd filled the front room of their family home in Little

Wynham after Deano had gone missing. So many bodies in uniforms stifling the air, suffocating them, making it hard to breathe. But at least she now knew that Deano was alive somewhere — Mr and Mrs Shaw didn't have that luxury. Their grief would remain with them forever. "Could you start by telling us the last time you saw your son?"

Calvin's mother visibly flinched, but before she could even start to reply, her husband stepped in.

"I should tell you . . . well, *we* should tell you . . . that Cal wasn't my biological son. I'm not his real father — although I always treated him that way."

Nicki and Fox exchanged a quick look — it certainly wasn't information that had made its way into the investigation so far.

"I brought the lad up as my own," continued Mick. "But me and Heather didn't get together until Cal was almost two. When we married, Cal took on my name. It seemed the right thing to do. To all intents and purposes, I'm his father. I've never thought of him as anything other than my own son. But . . ." Mick Shaw's voice caught in his throat. "I thought you needed to know — in case it's a factor."

Nicki gave the man what she hoped was an encouraging smile. "Thank you, Mick. It's appreciated. Can I ask — before we talk about the last time you both saw Calvin — what kind of a relationship he had with his real father? Was he still in his life?"

Mick edged closer to his wife on the sofa, placing a steadying hand on hers. "I'll let Heather answer that one."

Calvin's mother stared down at the frayed tissue in her lap. "As far as I'm concerned, Mick is Cal's real father." As soon as the words had escaped her mouth, she flinched and drew in a sharp breath. "*Was* Cal's real father," she corrected herself, as fresh tears threatened to spill from her eyes. "Sorry, I'm finding it hard to . . ."

Nicki shook her head. "It's OK, Mrs Shaw. Heather. Take as much time as you need." Nicki could remember just how long it had taken her own parents to talk about Deano in the past tense.

"Cal's real father . . ." As Heather took in a shuddering breath, Nicki noticed the woman's husband giving her hand another tight squeeze. "I'm ashamed to say I don't know who it is."

It wasn't the answer Nicki had been expecting and she slid another sideways glance towards Fox, who was already scribbling in his notebook. "That's all right, Heather. You don't need to explain yourself to us."

"Cal never really asked about him, so . . ." Calvin's mother pulled her gaze from her lap and looked up towards her husband. "And when I met Mick, it didn't seem to matter." She paused, a brief dash of colour faintly staining her cheeks. "I had a one-night stand — well, several of them in fact. It could be any one of them. I'd gone off the rails a little at the time. It isn't a part of my life that I'm particularly proud of, as you'll understand. And I never told any of them about Cal — we didn't keep in touch."

Nicki thought back to when she had watched *Mamma Mia* with the girls a few weeks ago, sharing several bottles of wine while banging out the Abba tunes. Somehow, she didn't think Heather Shaw's experience was altogether the same as Meryl Streep's. She decided to leave that line of questioning there. "Let's go back to the last time either of you saw or spoke to Calvin. Can you remember when that was? Sorry, I know this might be difficult for you."

"I last spoke to Cal a couple of days ago." Mick Shaw released his grip on his wife's hand and instead placed an arm around her sagging shoulders. "I was arranging a job for him."

"A job? What kind of job?"

"I have my own building and removals company. We mostly do groundworks, maybe a bit of roofing on occasion. And also house clearances and removals. One of the houses I was working on — the site manager needed a plasterer on another development down in Hove. It was good money for a few days' work. So I put the work Cal's way."

Nicki remembered the half-packed holdall in Calvin's bedroom. "Was he planning to go away soon — to Hove?"

"I think so," replied Mick. "The job starts on Monday. I think he was planning to go down over the weekend."

"Is that something you did quite often? Arranged work for him?"

Mick shrugged. "I wouldn't say *often*, but if the work came up then I'd try to put it his way. I've never really stopped to think about it. He's got his own contacts in the trade but . . ." Mick broke off, casting a wary glance at his wife before he continued. "Cal had been a bit distracted lately."

"Distracted?" Nicki's eyebrows hitched. "How so?"

Calvin's stepfather ran a hand over his rough beard. "I don't know. It's hard to put into words. Cal was a good lad and good at his job but things had taken a bit of a slide recently. Like his mind was on other things. That's why I put the Hove job his way."

"Any idea what those things might have been?" Nicki's eyebrows went a notch higher. "We know about his arrest last summer."

Mick shook his head. "That wasn't like Cal. He wasn't a fighter. It was completely out of character for him to get caught up in something like that."

"Well, as far as we know, he hadn't been in trouble since." Nicki cast a glance at Fox who gave a confirmatory shake of his head. "Maybe he'd seen sense after that one arrest?"

Heather gave a faint rueful smile, her bottom lip quivering. "He told us someone had posted some comments on one of his business posts — on social media. Basically trying to say Cal wasn't good at his job, that he cut corners with his work. It wasn't true. He told me that was why he'd done it. He'd had too much to drink and saw the person in the street. He doesn't usually drink that much — like Mick said, it was completely out of character." Heather crumpled against her husband's shoulder, the tears now running freely down her cheeks. "The last time we spoke we had a falling out. We never made up. My last words to him were in anger."

* * *

Jeremy Frost slipped into the vacant chair opposite Neil Watson's desk. "It's an explosive story but I'll need to tread carefully."

Watson took hold of the sheet of A4 paper, his brow creasing as he started to read. A minute passed before he spoke. "You're not wrong there, Jeremy." The editor of the *Bury Gazette* tore his gaze from the sheet. "I take it you can corroborate all this? Officially?"

Jeremy nodded. "Absolutely. I've a contact in the local force up in North Yorkshire — well, he's retired now but remembers the case well. It's one hundred percent bona fide. I'm making some enquiries with social services too."

"What do you intend to do with it? What kind of story are we looking at?"

Jeremy had expected the question, and had been thinking about the answer all day. "I'm not too sure, if I'm honest. There are several angles I could take, but it's a story that has legs, I'm sure of it. We could argue that it's in the public interest, what with the current debate on the age of criminal responsibility. There's been a series of articles on the subject in the *Guardian* and the *Times* this week."

Watson made a face. "Public interest might be stretching it — but whatever you decide to do, you're right. You need to tread extremely carefully with this one. If what you say is true, then emotions could very quickly run high, and it wouldn't take much for them to boil over into something more toxic. The last thing we want to be accused of is inciting a riot or encouraging vigilantes to prowl the streets of our town." He raised a hand to silence the objections about to spring from the reporter's mouth. "I've seen it happen first hand, Jeremy. I'm not saying we don't run with it — it's a good story and one that could be a real scoop for us. *But*." A sigh crossed the desk. "Do your research, then do it again. *And* again. We can't afford for this to blow up in our faces. I want facts — and facts backed up with witnesses. You know the score." He handed the piece of paper back, discussion over.

Jeremy rose to his feet, glancing at the name at the top before folding and slotting the sheet into his pocket.

Scott Edgecombe.

It was too good a story to pass up.

* * *

Seymour Street, Bury St Edmunds

Nicki spied a fresh box of tissues on the windowsill. She quickly got up to grab them, passing the box across. "I'm so sorry, Heather."

Once Calvin's mother had got part way to composing herself, Nicki continued. "Calvin lived in a flat on Melrose Avenue. How long had he been there?"

"About eighteen months, I think. Thereabouts."

"And he lived alone?" Nicki couldn't remember seeing any evidence of a second person living at the address, but asked the question anyway. Both Heather and Mick shook their heads in response. "Any current girlfriend? Boyfriend?"

More shakes of the head followed. "Not that I knew of," replied Calvin's mother eventually, glancing up at her husband.

"Me neither," added Mick. "I can't say I ever saw Cal with anyone, if I'm honest."

"Friends?"

"Again, I . . ." Heather broke off. "I'm ashamed to say I don't really know who his close friends were anymore, not since he'd been living on his own. There used to be a lad he was friends with from school that he sometimes kept in touch with. Robert. Robert Cahill. But I don't know if they were still friends."

Nicki watched Fox dutifully write the name in his notebook. She turned her attention back to Calvin's parents. "We noticed there wasn't a mobile phone or laptop in his flat. I'm assuming he had a phone — what about a laptop?"

Heather nodded. "He had both. He had an iPhone — got it for his birthday last year. And we . . ." Her voice hitched as fresh tears spilled. "We bought him a laptop for Christmas."

Fox made more notes.

"And there's no chance that they would be here?" Nicki's eyes scanned the room. "He wouldn't keep them here for any reason?"

Heather merely shook her head.

"Mrs Shaw," Nicki's voice softened. What she was about to ask could very well tip the poor woman over the edge, but it needed to be done. She took in a deep breath. "I'm sorry to have to ask this but did Calvin ever suffer with his mental health?"

Heather looked up, eyes wide. "His mental health?"

Nicki nodded. "Was he on any medication, or . . . ?" She paused and cleared her throat. "Had he ever expressed any intentions to take his own life?"

If there had been any colour left in Calvin's mother's cheeks, it would have drained completely away. Instead, she merely swayed on the sofa. "Cal? Take his own life?"

Mick made another grab for his wife's hand, enveloping it in his bear-like grasp, his forehead contorted into a deep frown. "I thought . . . The police officers who were here before, when they told us what had happened — I thought they said Cal hadn't . . . that it had just been . . ."

"Made to look that way, yes," finished Nicki. "That's correct. I was just wondering if the person responsible knew something about your son that we didn't. Maybe that was why they thought to stage it as a suicide?"

Heather shook her head, rubbing at her wet cheeks with the fresh tissue. "No, not my Cal. He would never think like that, not my Cal."

Nicki thought about the reference to the possible self-harm marks Caz had mentioned after the post-mortem report, but decided Heather had been through enough. Although there was one more thing she needed to raise.

She pulled out a photograph of the note found in Calvin's pocket. "I'm sorry to ask you both this, but . . ." She handed the photograph across. "Can you confirm whether or not this is Calvin's handwriting?"

Heather's face paled even more as she took hold of it, her shoulders shuddering while her husband gripped her other hand. It didn't take long for both of them to shake their heads.

"No," Mick eventually answered. "That's not Cal's handwriting. He was left handed and always slanted his letters when he wrote in block capitals."

Nicki took the photograph back. "Thank you. We were sure it wasn't his writing, but we had to ask you to confirm. I'm sorry — again." After a few more questions about Calvin's regular hangouts, both Nicki and Fox got to their feet.

"Thank you for your time, both of you." Nicki placed one of her cards on the coffee table and tried the warmest smile she could muster. "I know it's tough for you right now, but if you think of anything else, just call me. We'll be in touch when we have any further news for you. But in the meantime, we'll be sending a family liaison officer over to see you this afternoon. It'll be a Detective Constable Gemma Huntley. She should be here any minute. Please use her. She will stay with you as long as you need her."

Nicki and Fox saw themselves out of the semi-detached house and both exhaled a large breath once they were back in the crisp March air.

"That was painful," grimaced Fox as they made their way towards Nicki's car. "Those poor people. I don't know how anyone can function after something like that."

I do, thought Nicki, as she unlocked the Toyota. *Autopilot takes over and you just exist. One hour lurches into the next, one day morphs into another. Before you know it, weeks have gone by. But nothing is ever the same again.*

CHAPTER SEVEN

Bury St Edmunds Police Station

"Heather and Mick Shaw — our victim's parents." DS Fox added the two names to the whiteboard. "Although, strictly speaking, Mick isn't Calvin's real father."

"Are we going to push them on the identity of the real dad?" Roy looked up from his computer screen.

"Heather said she didn't tell any of the prospective dads of their impending fatherhood, so . . ." Nicki could only shrug. "She seemed genuine, if a little embarrassed. Let's park it for now. I'll ask Gemma to dig a bit deeper on that — see what she can find out. She should have arrived at the Shaws' house by now. Depending on what she finds out, we might come back to it."

Roy nodded. "What do we know about the stepfather?"

Fox stayed by the whiteboard. "Age forty-five. Has his own building and house removals business. Cared for the lad from a young age, brought him up as his own. But . . ." Fox hesitated. "He's a big man — and we're looking for a big man."

Nicki agreed. "He's well over six feet and clearly works out. We were only saying before how much of an effort it would take to get a body strung up like that. But . . . I don't know. He seemed genuinely upset."

Fox shrugged. "Just putting it out there."

"It's certainly something we need to bear in mind. But let's come back to the stepfather another time. I'm more concerned that we don't have Calvin's phone — it wasn't found on his body or at his flat. And the parents are sure it isn't with them. They've given us the number — I want it tracked. Let's see if we can find out where it's been, and maybe where it currently is."

Matt raised a hand. "I'll get onto that one, boss. And while you were out, me and Duncan had a quick trip out to the heath. There aren't that many ways to get in and out of there with a vehicle. Not legally anyway. There's the car park just off Hardwick Lane, but that's been closed off for renovation works for the past fortnight. However . . ." Matt hitched his brow. "We took a closer look and saw some of the fence posts were loose — looked like someone might have removed them, then put them back in place. It's feasible they could have got past the cordon, then driven up to the scene. With the car park shut like that, it's doubtful anyone else was there. The perfect spot, I guess. The crime scene investigators say they will keep looking out for tyre tracks."

Nicki nodded her thanks and took another look at the relatively sparse details populating the whiteboard. "To all intents and purposes, Calvin Shaw seems to have been a law-abiding citizen. That one arrest and conviction for assault last summer doesn't seem to have been the start of anything. Are there any more details about that? Calvin's parents suggested that it was all down to some online posts someone had made about Calvin's plastering business. That he took offence to whatever had been posted, saw the chap responsible in the street and, after too much alcohol, decided to make his displeasure known using his fists."

Duncan raised a hand. "Not much else on the system other than the victim was a Scott Edgecombe. Calvin admitted the assault and the case was dealt with quickly. They didn't proceed with the attempted assault of a police officer."

Nicki took the marker pen over to the whiteboard again, this time adding '*Scott Edgecombe*' and '*assault*'. "It's probably nothing, but let's have it up on the board." While there, she tapped the image of the handwritten note. "Both Heather and Mick confirmed this wasn't Calvin's handwriting. So I'm even more convinced that this was written by the killer." She glanced at her watch. "OK. I'm going to go and make a few calls — touch base with Gemma and see if she's arrived at the Shaws' home. Let's get that phone tracked and keep wading through the CCTV."

* * *

Carnaby Close, Bury St Edmunds

Scott Edgecombe tucked the bag of newly purchased spray paints beneath the folds of his jacket and, head down, hurried towards the front door. People around here were far too nosy for their own good. Take that old woman from the flats opposite. There was barely a time of day when she wasn't twitching at her net curtains, flashing a disapproving look across the street in his direction.

Part of him wanted to go up to her front door and spray one of his best creations right in front of her, scare the living daylights out of the old hag. But he knew he wouldn't. Instead, he pushed open the front door and ran upstairs to his bedroom.

Throwing his gym bag onto the bed, he stashed the spray cans on top of his wardrobe, next to everything else he wanted to keep hidden. It wasn't strictly necessary — he had added a lock to his bedroom door some months ago to keep his mum from rooting around where she shouldn't. But you could never be too careful.

He kept the curtains of his bedroom closed, both day and night, so the room was always in a semi-darkened state. He snapped on a small bedside lamp to give it a faint, muted glow. He wasn't one for possessions — the trappings of modern life didn't really appeal to him; not like they seemed to do for everyone else. He wasn't interested in the latest games console or phone. His phone was at least four years old and still worked, which was good enough for him. He had a small TV mounted on the wall, but it was already here when they moved in, otherwise he might not even have bothered with that.

The wall opposite the shrouded window was bare. Originally there had been another large wardrobe and bookcase stretching right across, taking up every inch of space. Much to his mother's horror, as soon as they had moved in he'd dragged both down the narrow staircase, depositing them outside on the patchy grass by the path. Sticking a note on the front — 'FREE' — it hadn't taken long for them to disappear.

The bare wall that was left behind now sported his life's work, all twenty years of it. He wasn't sure what anyone else would make of it — but as he never invited anyone back to the house, he didn't care.

Everything that meant anything to him was on that wall.

To begin with it had just been the odd cutting from the newspaper about climate change. There was a young Swedish girl making waves about the impact humans were having on the environment, in particular the effect on the climate. Some of what she said really struck a chord with him, but in reality he just admired people who rebelled against the norm. He started to follow her in the news and on social media, and started collecting more and more information for himself.

Then he broadened his interests.

He soon found lots of other activist groups: animal rights, environmental concerns, racial equality. The list went on. All full of like-minded individuals; people who were passionate about their cause and would do anything to spread the word. Then there were the various wars erupting around the world — and the inevitable rebellions that followed.

As time went on, more cuttings started to pepper his wall space.

To Scott, it didn't particularly matter what the actual cause was. What mattered to him was the stand against authority. The stand against dictatorship and being told what to do by those above. He hated being told what to do.

And then there was Sir Cecil Pemberton.

The man's face stared out from the very centre of the wall. Scott felt the familiar stirrings of anger welling up inside. He grabbed a four-pack of cheap lager that was sitting next to the bed and broke one off. Cracking the ring pull, he took a deep gulp.

The landed gentry: that was what everyone called him. Born with a silver spoon in his mouth that most people hoped would choke him one day. The man had managed to create a furore around the town in recent months, planning to sell off large parts of his land for residential development.

Scott wasn't particularly bothered about the man building houses on his land, if the truth be told, but he'd got swept up and sucked into the debacle after chaining himself to the railings outside the local planning office late last year. He'd only gone along because it seemed like fun — and every kind of protest was fun in his book. Then someone had suggested he join in.

While they were waiting for someone to come along and cut them free and then cart them off to the police station, one of the protesters filled him in on the delightful Sir Cecil. By the time they were freed and shown the inside of a police van, Scott was fully recruited to the cause.

Draining the can, Scott reached for a second. He then grabbed one of the spray cans from the top of the wardrobe and returned to face the wall. With a sneer curling his lips, he painted a large red cross over Sir Cecil's face.

A cruel laugh bubbled up inside his throat as he cracked open the second can.

"Hope you enjoyed your trip, mate. That was just the beginning. I'll finish the job next time."

* * *

"I certainly feel there might be more to this than she's letting on." DC Gemma Huntley kept her voice low, eyes on the closed door of the Shaws' kitchen. She'd disappeared some minutes ago on the pretext of making another round of tea that everyone would only make a half-hearted attempt at drinking — but instead she had rung Nicki at the station. "Call it a hunch. A feeling. I haven't been here long but something is definitely not quite right."

"Just with the mother? Or is the stepfather on your radar, too?"

Gemma flashed another look at the closed door. "The mother mostly, but I'm not sure. Like I say, I haven't been here long. I'll try and talk to them both again — separately, though."

Gemma had just ended the call and turned back towards the long-since boiled kettle when Heather Shaw came through the door. Gemma silently slid her mobile back into her pocket, casting a smile over her shoulder. "Sorry, I've been an age. I was watching the birds outside on your bird table." She gestured through the kitchen window in front of her. "I've been thinking of getting a bird table myself for a while." She poured the hot water into the waiting teapot and considered now was as good a time as any.

"I know I've said it before, but how are you holding up?" Gemma watched Heather's bottom lip start to quiver. "It's not a sign of weakness to let the barriers down, you know." She gave what she hoped was an encouraging smile. From what she had managed to glean about the Shaw family in the ninety minutes or so since she'd been assigned to them, she had nothing but admiration for Heather. The woman hadn't had it easy. "Mick must be a tower of strength — losing Calvin like this must be devastating for you. For both of you."

Heather merely nodded, brushing the corner of her eye with the sleeve of her cardigan.

"And tell me to mind my own business — I really don't mean to pry — but is there any chance of reaching out to Calvin's biological father?" Gemma saw Heather flinch. She held up an apologetic hand. "I know. I know. I'm sorry, but it's just that he might want to know. About Calvin, I mean. Also, he might be able to offer you some additional support." Gemma knew she was treading a very delicate line. Heather had already vehemently denied knowing who Calvin's real father was — but there was something in her eyes that suggested to Gemma that she might not be telling the whole truth.

"I know you told us you don't know who the father is — one of four, I think you mentioned?" Gemma saw Heather's cheeks colour as she continued to avoid the detective constable's gaze. "There's no judgement here, Mrs Shaw. Really, there isn't." Gemma began loading up the tea tray. "All I'm doing is thinking about you. So, if you do know who it is — and if you have been in some form of contact over the years, even if sporadically — then maybe it's best to let them know what's happened. I think, if I was in their position, I'd want to know."

All Heather managed was a faint nod before she turned and backed out of the kitchen, the conversation — if it had ever been one — clearly at an end. Gemma followed on behind with the tray. She wasn't sure if she'd made any progress, but she felt now — more than ever — that Heather Shaw wasn't telling them the whole truth.

* * *

Carnaby Close, Bury St Edmunds

Lana Edgecombe had heard the door slam, but by the time she'd reached the hall Scott was almost at the top of the stairs — all she could see were the soles of his work boots.

Work boots. At least that suggested he'd been to work that day, which was something. She was sure the job was doing him good — giving him something to get up for, a routine to his days. And things had been going well for a while now, so much so that she had almost started to relax.

Almost.

When they had first moved into the house, the estate had welcomed them — the neighbours were friendly, even the old woman across the road could be pleasant on occasion. For a while she thought she and Scott had finally come to the end of a very long road, managing to emerge on the other side more or less intact. They fitted into their new surroundings and life looked to be on the up.

Then, slowly, things had started to change.

Scott had started to change. Staying out late, refusing to say where he'd been. He then fixed a lock to his bedroom door and snarled at her if she even came close. Some days he barely spoke two words to her. When their paths did cross — the occasional hurried meal at the kitchen table, or passing each other on the stairs — she noticed that look in his eyes again. It was a look she instantly recognised and one she'd hoped she would never see again. It was difficult to explain exactly what it was, but it resurrected so many feelings inside her — feelings she had worked hard to bury for good. And it left a churning sickness in her stomach.

It couldn't be happening again, could it?

Lana heard the bedroom door slam and the tell-tale sound of Scott's thumping garage music filling the house.

* * *

Seymour Street, Bury St Edmunds

After drinking the tea nobody had really wanted, Gemma had managed to get Mick on his own in the garden, suggesting they refill the bird feeders she had seen dangling from a wooden bird table through the kitchen window. The rain had let up and the wind was starting to die down a little. Calvin's stepfather had seemed grateful for an excuse to get out of the house.

"How did you two meet?"

Mick stared at the ground. It was a while before he spoke. "By chance." A faint smile teased his lips. "We were both in the supermarket. Heather dropped a carton of eggs on the floor — everything broke, there was mess everywhere. Cal was sitting in the trolley seat, bawling his eyes out. No one went to help her — people just looked the other way. I could see the sheer exhaustion in her eyes — and the embarrassment." He shrugged. "I wanted to help."

"A good Samaritan?"

Another shrug. "I'm not sure I'd call myself that. I could just see that she wanted the ground to open up and swallow her whole. We've all been there at some point."

"So, love blossomed over a pile of broken eggs?" Gemma smiled as she hung the bird feeder back on the bird table. "How old was Calvin at the time?"

"Around eighteen months, I think."

"That's a lot for someone to take on. A new relationship plus a young child into the bargain. Kids can be quite demanding at that age."

Mick's eyes flickered through the fading light, back towards the house. "Maybe. But he was a good kid — mostly."

"Mostly?" Gemma's eyebrows raised a little. "How do you mean?"

"Well, I don't have anything to compare him to. I never had any of my own."

"You and Heather didn't want to have any more?"

"We tried, but — you know."

Gemma nodded, even though she didn't really know at all. Children hadn't yet registered on her radar.

"It just didn't happen for us," he explained. "But it didn't matter. We were happy enough with Cal."

"And there was never any contact with Calvin's real father? He was never on the scene?"

Gemma detected a slight twitch, the muscles in Mick's jaw tensing. "Never. Heather told me she didn't know who the father was — and that even if she did she was sure they wouldn't be interested in Cal. It was all water under the bridge by the time we got together."

"And Calvin was never curious to find out who his real father was? I take it he knew it wasn't you?" Gemma handed the packet of bird seed back to Mick. "Sorry, I don't mean to be blunt."

Calvin's stepfather shook his head. "No problem. Cal knew I wasn't his father. We told him when he was old enough to understand."

"And he never asked any questions about who his father might be?"

There was a slight pause before Mick replied, but it was long enough to register with the experienced detective. "No," he replied. "Cal never asked either of us about his biological father."

Just then, the back door opened and Heather headed in their direction. As she approached, Gemma saw her tear-streaked face.

"Mrs Shaw?" she asked, concern in her voice. "Is everything OK?"

"When can we see him?" Heather's voice was weak. "When can we go and see Cal?"

* * *

Bury St Edmunds Police Station

"Calvin's phone was last active in the region of Melrose Avenue." DC Matt Holland tapped his computer screen with the end of his pen. "It would fit with his home address. This was yesterday evening, but since then there's been nothing. It's likely been switched off or out of battery."

Nicki sighed. The news on Calvin's phone didn't take them any further forward. "Anything else new?"

"I spoke with Faye and although there are some tyre tracks on the heath, they're not particularly good ones." DC Duncan Jenkins gave a shrug. "She's not hopeful they're going to give us much of a lead on the type of vehicle."

"OK. It was worth a shot." Nicki studied the white-board. "Calvin was a young man — let's do the usual social media trawls. Check what sites he might have been on, how active he was, and in particular who he interacted with. We know he attracted some hateful comments from Scott Edgecombe, which led to the assault last summer. But see what else you can find. Matt? You OK to do that side of things?" Nicki recalled how useful the searches through social media platforms had been in trapping the Trophy Killer last year. Matt nodded in response. Nicki then tapped a finger on the photograph of the fake suicide note.

"Do we have anything back from forensics yet on the note? I'm guessing it's too early and too much to ask that the killer left their fingerprints."

DS Fox looked at his computer screen again. "Nothing yet, boss."

"OK. Finish what you're doing. Some of us have had a very long day." Nicki looked meaningfully towards Roy, who was seated at the back of the incident room. "We'll call it a day and be back in bright and early tomorrow, yes?"

CHAPTER EIGHT

Carnaby Community Centre, Bury St Edmunds

"So, what do we do about it?" Morris Skinner looked expectantly around the room. He was tired. He wanted to go home. It was nearly seven thirty and his wife would soon have dinner waiting for him and maybe a glass of red wine too, if he was lucky. Although he took his position as chairman of the Carnaby Close Residents' Association seriously, he wasn't entirely sure how he had ended up spearheading their latest campaign. He agreed with the sentiment — he didn't want hungry developers tearing up the local countryside any more than the next person; developers building yet more houses that the locals could ill afford to live in — but he was *tired*. At sixty-two, he was looking forward to winding down — not being wound up, which was precisely what Erin Fletcher was currently doing.

Winding him up.

"You know precisely what we can do about it." Erin's voice rang out around the community centre. "You just don't have the balls to suggest it."

There were various ripples of agreement.

Morris sighed. *Why did they always think everything was down to him?*

"This is a collective organisation, Erin, as you well know. I have no greater say on anything than you do. Like everything we discuss here, each person has the right to speak — and in the end we take a vote on what we propose to do. It's not just down to me."

"So let's vote." Erin got to her feet and started making her way towards the front of the hall. A tall, slender woman, her long grey hair was pulled back into a solitary braid that reached her lower back. She was well known in the local community, and generally well-liked. Although retired, she volunteered at the local foodbank and also one of the charity shops in the town. She was wearing one of her customary hand-knitted cardigans, in a variety of rainbow colours, over a pair of patchwork denim dungarees. At sixty-six years of age, she wasn't your typical grandmother of four.

Morris sighed again, and rested back in his seat. He knew what would come next, as did each and every one of the sixteen attendees who had taken time out on this windswept Friday evening to attend the hastily arranged residents' meeting. Erin always had something to say, an opinion she wanted to share, and tonight looked like it would be no exception.

"Back in 1981 . . ."

Here we go.

Morris started thinking once more of the braised beef waiting in the oven at home, and the glass of red. But he opened a fresh page in his A5 notepad — no matter how tired he was, Morris Skinner was the chairman. And the chairman had a duty to take notes. It was a duty he took extremely seriously.

Another figure got to his feet. Dressed in dark-coloured overalls, the man gripped the back of the plastic chair in front of him. "We all know about your protesting exploits back in the Dark Ages, Erin, but the world has moved on since then. Chaining yourself to a fence and singing songs around a campfire doesn't get you anywhere these days."

Erin bristled as she reached the front of the hall and turned towards the seated audience. "I wasn't going to suggest that." She glowered towards Glenn Clifford, the man in the overalls; a man she knew well. Erin had been a fresh-faced twenty-eight-year-old in 1981 when she had joined the Greenham Common CND protest camp in Berkshire. It had been an exciting time, standing up against an authoritarian government, seeking solace among like-minded individuals. Peaceful yet provocative at the same time. She'd been thrown into the back of a police van on several occasions, spent the night in the cells once, too, but none of it had diminished her resolve or dampened her spirit. If anything, it had ignited it further. The camaraderie she had found around the campfire was something she would never forget, and had never managed to come close to since.

"Direct action is what is called for here," Clifford called out across the hall. "Direct and painful."

Morris found another sigh escaping his lips. Erin and Clifford often clashed heads at these meetings, and tonight looked to be no exception. His gaze drifted to the back of the hall where a group of five youngsters had slunk in just after the meeting had begun. The group weren't regular attendees of the monthly residents' meetings, but Morris knew who they were. Or at least he knew their faces. He guessed they were in their late teens, maybe early twenties; young men with nothing else to do on a wet and blustery Friday night. Their names cropped up from time to time, mostly in connection with some sort of fracas or other on the estate. They were well known for hanging around on street corners, spraying their graffiti tags on just about every available outside wall space they could find. Especially that Scott Edgecombe lad — Morris spied the young man seated at the back of the hall, and was sure his backpack would contain more than a few cans of the offending spray paint, if anyone took the time to look.

Morris noticed that while they'd fidgeted during the early discussions about getting the local children's playground resurfaced, they had all sat up squarely in their seats at hearing the words '*direct action*' from Glenn Clifford. It made Morris nervous. That's all he needed — a rebellion on his hands.

The growth of direct action protests around the town was making everyone uneasy. There had been a few in recent months, and Morris was often unsure whether those involved truly did have the cause at heart. Whatever it was they were protesting about — whether it be the fight against climate change or the opening of a new animal research laboratory — sometimes it felt their main interest lay in causing as much disruption to ordinary working people as possible. In some ways, Morris preferred the Erins of this world when it came to protesting. Although she could grate on the nerves a little, harping on about her time as a CND activist and then later with Greenpeace, her heart was in the right place, and she would never lend herself to doing anything violent or unduly disruptive.

But with this new breed of protester — Morris let his eyes once again flicker towards Scott Edgecombe and his group of friends at the back of the hall — you could never be quite sure. He knew the group had been part of the protest in front of the planning offices late last year — chaining themselves to the railings or something — which might not have been particularly violent, but it had been a nuisance. And it might herald more to come.

"If we don't do something soon, he'll run roughshod over us all." Glenn Clifford was referring to Sir Cecil Pemberton, a local dignitary who lived in a huge mansion on the outskirts of the town. Owning a substantial amount of land around his vast stately home, he had submitted plans to the local authority to sell a sizeable chunk for residential development. *All for a huge profit, no doubt*, mused Morris, as he dutifully made his notes. The resulting furore had reached just about every corner of Bury St Edmunds — and beyond. The news had reverberated like shockwaves in the aftermath of an earthquake — and they were still feeling the aftershocks tonight.

Clifford continued. "He doesn't care about the local landscape or the local wildlife — or even the local residents. All he wants to do is make money. At the expense of us all."

"I agree. He can't be allowed to do it. He *has* to be stopped."

Morris looked up to see another man get to his feet. He groaned. His braised beef and red wine was looking more and more remote as the minutes passed by.

"Like I said — direct action," repeated Clifford, standing firm behind the plastic chair. "Hit him where it hurts. In his pocket. That's the only language these people understand."

"And what exactly does that mean, Glenn?" Morris didn't hide the weariness in his tone. The meeting was over-running. He took a furtive glance at his watch. The beef would be out of the oven by now, the wine poured.

"Anything. Burn him out if we have to."

Morris's eyebrows shot up, "You know you can't say things like that in here, Glenn. It's not helpful." His gaze slid towards the back of the room and the group of restless, impressionable youngsters still hanging onto every word. *You don't know who's listening,* he wanted to add. He wouldn't put it past any of the low-slung jeans and hoodie brigade to toss a match into Pemberton Hall.

But Clifford was on a roll. "Well, it's true. Kids these days have got the right idea. It's the only way anyone listens." He shot a scathing look at Erin. "Holding hands and singing kumbaya doesn't cut it anymore."

Erin bristled beneath her homemade cardigan, but kept her composure, "Direct action can take many forms, Glenn, but it doesn't need to be violent. I propose we canvass for more signatures to our petition — get some high-profile people on board through social media. There must be some local groups that can lend their support to us."

"Yada yada, it's all just words, woman. Words on a piece of useless paper. It's meaningless without physical action. No one cares anymore. That's the problem. No one cares until it hurts them." Clifford's eyes darkened. "And hurts them properly."

* * *

Nicki pulled the cardboard box out from under her bed. With her parents due to arrive on Sunday, she knew she needed to put some of Deano's photographs on display. They would be expecting to see him.

She felt guilty that she kept her brother hidden — stashed under her bed, away from prying eyes — but it was better this way. *Safer* this way. For reasons unbeknown even to herself, she hadn't got around to telling even her closest friends about Deano — and his disappearance. And neither had she admitted to anyone the role she had played in it.

It wasn't exactly lying, she would tell herself when the guilt prickled uncomfortably at her conscience. It just wasn't exactly being truthful. Only DCI Turner knew about Deano — having been one of her father's closest work colleagues at the time, and also a family friend, there was no way to have kept it from him. But everyone else? Nicki found it easier not to go there; not to have to relive the horrifying events of that day in November 1996. Not even Faye or Amy, two of her closest friends, knew about her little brother.

It was a convoluted web she had chosen to weave, and one she felt she had no choice but to maintain.

At least for now.

She pulled two framed photographs from the box and placed them on the bed. Her favourite photos of her brother — with his cheeky, impish grin and mop of unruly dark brown hair.

Also in the box were the only keepsakes she had of her childhood with Deano. It wasn't much. A couple of books she used to read to him at night, and a small teddy bear. She brought the bear to her face, inhaling the scent of it. Sometimes she could convince herself she could still smell her brother — still smell the coconut shampoo their mother would use on both of them. It was unlikely, after all this time, but she liked to feel close to him.

She picked up one of the books — a Ladybird book called *The Enormous Turnip* — and smiled. It had been Deano's favourite story for months, and he would insist she read it to him every night. As she looked at the worn and battered front cover, she could almost hear his delighted squeals as the story reached its climax.

After a few more moments spent reminiscing, she placed the books and teddy bear back inside the box, along with the photographs, tucked it under her arm and headed downstairs. Luna was waiting patiently at the bottom of the stairs, the look on her face telling Nicki that she was late in providing her dinner. While she had been away with Benedict, trying to find Deano, Jeremy had been on cat feeding duties and, by the looks of it, he had kept to the '*dinner at 6 p.m. sharp*' routine. Jeremy was a good friend — more than happy to help with looking after the house, and Luna, if Nicki was ever called away. Her friends wondered what their true relationship was — often reminding her what a catch the local reporter could be — but Nicki kept her cards close to her chest. Jeremy made no secret of the fact he would be interested in something more, which made her smile, but for now she was happy as they were: just friends.

Nicki placed the box on the sofa then followed the Russian Blue cat out into the kitchen. As well as getting Luna fed and watered, she needed to make sure she had everything ready for Sunday. She had come so close to cancelling it altogether — citing the strain of the new investigation — but she couldn't bear to hear the disappointment in her mother's voice, not when they had come so far.

She would make it work somehow; she had to.

Although it was getting late, Nicki still felt wired from the day's events — and in particular Gemma's feeling that Heather Shaw wasn't being completely honest with them. It might not mean anything, but it niggled just the same. However, she needed to bear in mind the horror the Shaws were going through. The grief they were experiencing would make them act differently; out of character perhaps. She needed to cut them a little slack.

A little . . . but not too much.

* * *

Morris Skinner locked up the community centre and trudged across the dimly lit car park towards his Saab. He pulled up the collar of his coat as the wind whipped around his face. His wife would have put his plate of braised beef back in the oven by now to keep it warm — but he could taste the smooth Merlot on his tongue already. As he relished the thought, he noticed Erin Fletcher just ahead of him, making her way towards the short path that led out onto the main road.

"Erin," he called, waiting while she turned back towards him. "You need a lift?" He nodded towards the Saab. "It's still a bit stormy out here."

Erin flashed an appreciative smile but shook her head. "I'm OK, Morris. I'm popping to the shops on the way back. But thanks anyway." With that, she disappeared behind a row of tall hedges that flanked the unlit path.

Morris nodded to himself and proceeded to unlock the car. As he pulled open the driver's door, he caught sight of the group of youths congregating on the far side of the car park, passing round a cigarette. Or maybe it was weed. Who knew. Scott Edgecombe was at the centre of things, as usual. Morris also noticed Glenn Clifford with them, talking animatedly if his hand gestures were anything to go by.

Morris had known Glenn for many a year — they had worked together at the British Sugar factory in the town; as far as Morris knew, Glenn was still there. A principled man, of that there was no doubt, Glenn Clifford had a keen edge to him — but it was a dangerous edge, too. Glenn had a quick temper that Morris knew had landed him in hot water on more than a few occasions in the past. But Morris also knew he couldn't hold himself personally responsible for everyone who lived in the neighbourhood — something his wife would remind him from time to time. *People are responsible for their own actions, Morris. It's not down to you to keep them in check.*

As chairman of the residents' association, he had very little clout anyway when it actually came down to it — he had barely been able to keep a lid on things as tonight's discussion about the proposed Pemberton Hall development had turned rapidly into a slanging match. He had tried to keep his usual detailed notes on who said what to whom, but even he couldn't quite catch it all. In the end he'd had to call a halt before things got even more out of hand.

He slipped behind the wheel, placing his briefcase on the passenger seat. Erin was now out of sight, but Glenn Clifford and his followers were still going strong. Morris decided to leave them to it and head home for his well-earned glass of wine.

CHAPTER NINE

College Lane, Bury St Edmunds

Nicki jumped, the knock at the door startling her. She had pulled various recipe books out of the kitchen cupboards — some having never even been opened before — and had spent the last hour poring through them in the vain hope of finding something suitable to cook on Sunday. She glanced at her watch. Nearly nine. She wasn't expecting company — she rarely had anyone call by unannounced these days, such was the state of her woeful social life. It wouldn't be Amy, as she and her younger sister Darcie were on a spa break in the Cotswolds. Amy was one of Nicki's closest friends, working as a nurse in the local hospital, while Darcie was one of Nicki's brightest detective constables; she couldn't wait for her to get back and re-join the team. It was also unlikely to be Faye; her crime scene manager friend would still be working, she was sure. If she wasn't still at the scene on the heath, she would be somewhere else. Sometimes her days were longer than Nicki's. And as for Caz — they were already due to catch up on Monday, so it was unlikely to be the pathologist calling by.

Nicki closed the recipe book and waited. Maybe whoever it was would go away.

Another rap on the door followed.

Rising from the sofa, she headed over to the front door. Cautiously, she pulled it open a crack, peering through the narrow slit around the side of the door frame. The pensive look on her face softened.

"Jeremy. What are you doing here? It's late." She pulled the door fully open, stepping back to let the reporter inside. "Or have I forgotten something?"

"No, nothing forgotten. I just thought I'd pop by — I was passing and saw your light was on." An impish grin crossed his face. "It's still a bit wild out there. Thought I might cadge a coffee before heading home. And return your key after my cat-sitting duties."

Nicki returned the smile as she closed the door. "Sure. Come on in, the kettle's just boiled actually. There might even be some biscuits somewhere." The pair wandered through to the galley-style kitchen. "Thanks for feeding Luna — I'm sure she appreciated it." She took hold of the front door key Jeremy produced from his pocket. "And while you're here, you can help me decide what to cook on Sunday."

"Sunday? Why, what's happening Sunday?"

As Nicki pulled two mugs from the draining board, she recounted to Jeremy the reunion that was happening at the weekend. Jeremy was aware that Nicki hadn't been in touch with her parents for some time — estranged, some may call it — but he, like everyone else, was unaware of the reason why.

"Wow, no pressure then!" He began leafing through a recipe book Nicki had left on the kitchen worktop. "If I were you, I'd keep it simple. There's not much that can go wrong with a Sunday roast."

Nicki splashed milk into the mugs and leaned over to give Jeremy a friendly peck on the cheek. "I knew I liked you for a reason," she smiled, handing him one of the mugs.

"I've been tying myself up in knots for days about this bloody Sunday lunch."

Jeremy gave another lop-sided grin. "It's true, you're not exactly Gordon Ramsay in the kitchen, are you?" Stepping to the side, he narrowly avoided a flick from Nicki's tea towel as she led them both through to the living room.

Seated on the sofa, Nicki eyed the reporter over the rim of her steaming mug. "So, what's the real reason you're out and about at this time of night? I know you, Jeremy Frost. You've got that look about you."

Jeremy swallowed a mouthful of his coffee, burning his tongue as he did so. "Rumbled," he eventually replied, giving Nicki a wink. "I've been doing some research for a new story — ended up hanging around outside a residents' meeting over on the other side of town, getting blown to bits in the wind. This stormy weather isn't going anywhere — might even get worse, so they reckon."

"What kind of story took you out to a residents' meeting on a night like this?"

Jeremy tapped the side of his nose. "Top secret, I'm afraid. My boss would have my balls on a skewer if I even hinted what it might be."

Nicki's eyebrows hitched. "Oh, *that* kind of top secret, eh?"

Jeremy gave a wink. "Anyway, what's happening with the body in the woods? You going to give your favourite reporter an exclusive?"

Nicki hesitated, masking her indecision by taking a sip from her mug. As much as Jeremy was her friend, and she trusted him implicitly, he was still a reporter. "We'll release further details as soon as we can. Until then . . ."

Jeremy gave her a knowing smile. "I know, I know. Can't blame me for trying, though."

"When I have something, you'll be the first to know. How's that?"

"Deal."

* * *

76

Glenn Clifford slammed the door to his ground floor flat behind him, not caring if he antagonised the batty old woman next door. She was always complaining about something or other. He pulled a cigarette from the packet he'd left on the windowsill of the front room and lit it. Smoking was banned in the flats — punishable by instant eviction, according to the landlord — but he didn't care; he had taken the batteries out of the smoke detector months ago. To make doubly sure he didn't set off any other hidden alarms, he pushed open the window to let the strengthening evening breeze waft in.

The residents' meetings were a joke. He didn't know why he bothered going sometimes. It was all wheelie bins, dog mess and lost cats. Although tonight there had also been mention of a body being discovered on the heath, but as there had been very little information to give, they soon moved on. They never discussed any of the real issues of the day; anything that really mattered. Take tonight, for example — just when they were getting down to the nitty gritty, actually starting to have a discussion about something with merit, that weak-willed long streak of piss they called the chairman closed it down. Why he'd ever been voted in as chairman, Clifford couldn't fathom — the bloke had no fight in him whatsoever.

After several more drags on the cigarette, he started to feel calmer. He wasn't really sure why Sir Cecil had got him so wound up. It wasn't as if he was really all that bothered if the bloke built several hundred houses on his land. It wasn't like he would be able to see them from this poky ground floor flat. But it was the principle of the thing — and Glenn Clifford was nothing if not a principled man.

He'd grown up in a small village just outside Rotherham, where back in the early eighties the whole area had been caught up in the miners' strike. His father had worked in the pit and had supported the strike from the very beginning. It had been a difficult and challenging time — Clifford had only been ten years old when it started, but he remembered it all too well. He may not have really understood the politics behind it all, but he certainly understood first-hand the effect it had on his family — and that of every other miner in the area. With no money coming in, times were tough. His dad would go out each day to man the picket lines, returning each night with fresh cuts and bruises. He heard the word 'scab' bandied about, but never really knew what it meant — other than it often caused a riot and his dad would end up down at the police station.

But one thing he did remember from those times was the passion; the camaraderie of the mining families all pulling together to support each other, to support the cause.

That was what was missing these days. People were too selfish, too caught up in their own little worlds to care about anyone else but themselves. Take Sir Cecil Pemberton, for example. He was so far out of touch with the society around him, it was as though he was living in another orbit entirely.

Clifford stubbed out the remains of his cigarette and lit another. Here was a golden opportunity to come together as a community, put pressure — *real* pressure, not some phony petition that no bugger would even look at — on the powers that be to backtrack on whatever planning consent may have already been granted. But instead they'd buggered about, bickering among each other as usual, and ended up doing nothing.

The kids had the right idea. In some ways they reminded him of his dad's workmates. Clifford could remember them congregating in their small kitchen back in Rotherham, planning their strategy for the next day's protests, while his mum tried to keep them all fed on the dwindling supplies given to them by kind-hearted strike supporters. Ten-year-old Glenn Clifford would listen at the doorway, not really understanding much of what they talked about, or what they were planning to do, but relishing the feeling that he was part of *something*.

He'd got the general idea of what was happening from the pictures that accompanied the newspaper headlines each morning. Black-and-white images of striking miners shouting and swearing, hurling bricks and bottles at the passing buses that were ferrying the 'scabs' across the picket lines and into the striking pits. Other pictures showed hundreds of miners surging towards the police lines, officers frantically trying to keep some kind of order; then the scuffles would break out, with policemen's helmets falling to the ground and getting kicked around in the dirt.

It looked loud; it certainly looked aggressive. And it was most often bloody, if the photographs were to be believed. But there was an unmistakable fire in every striking miner's eyes — a fire that bred an unwavering passion and commitment.

No one had anything even close to that these days.

Except maybe the kids.

Especially the ones that hung around the estate.

From what Clifford knew of them, which wasn't much, they didn't seem to be afraid of getting arrested by the local police, or of getting dragged away in police vans — much like his father hadn't been either.

They had *guts*.

They had *determination*.

And Clifford was convinced it was both guts and determination that would be needed to get rid of Sir Cecil Pemberton.

Abandoning his half-smoked cigarette, he crossed the small front room to where he kept his mini home gym. Sitting down on the weights bench, he grabbed a pair of dumbbells and began a series of bicep curls. Gritting his teeth, he increased the weight and performed more reps. He might be in his mid-forties now, but he was still proud of the shape he was in. He might like the odd cigarette or two — more so, recently — and the odd pint after work, but he ate reasonably well and looked after himself. He could easily bench press one and a half times his own body weight, and was in no doubt that he could look after himself in a tussle.

And a tussle was what they might well have to have.

Lying down on the bench, he swapped the exercise to one working his pectoral muscles. Gripping the weights, he grimaced through the pain and turned his thoughts once more to Sir Cecil. What he wouldn't give to smash a fist into that man's face and show him just what they all thought of him and his planning proposals. A tight smile curled on his lips as he felt the sweat start to collect in the small of his back.

As he continued to punch the weights higher, all he could see was the man's gloating expression. He had done a TV interview for the local news a few weeks ago, and shown such utter contempt and indifference towards the local residents of the town that it had made Clifford's blood boil. The man had called them all '*dim-witted country folk*'.

And nobody called Glenn Clifford dim-witted and got away with it.

Direct action.

That was what was called for here.

* * *

Baythorne Square, Bury St Edmunds

Erin Fletcher pulled the petition towards her. Two hundred and eleven names so far. It was a start, but it was way below the number they needed if anyone was going to take them seriously.

The meeting had gone as she had predicted — a lot of hot air and nothing concrete on how to actually move forward. It irritated her how lethargic some people were. They turned up on the pretext that they actually cared about where they lived, but they were mostly content to sit in silence and watch. More than happy, she also noticed, to drink the free tea and coffee, eat the free biscuits — but they would contribute not one jot to any of the discussions.

Discussions.

You couldn't really call them that. Morris did his best but his heart clearly wasn't in it. He hated confrontation and would do almost anything to ensure there were no raised voices or bad feelings. Which meant no one got the chance to say anything of any substance.

Erin would happily take over the stewardship of the meetings but she knew that was about as likely as snow in July. People laughed at her; saw her as some sort of joke. Something to poke fun at and mock. She didn't really mind — she had developed a thick skin over the years — but it annoyed her that nobody would actually *listen*.

They all made fun of her involvement in the CND protests back in the eighties — especially Glenn. But just because they were largely peaceful protests didn't mean they weren't effective. She had spent many months camped out at Greenham Common between 1981 and 1987, and still had fond memories of the times they had all joined hands and constructed human chains around the perimeter of the base. Glenn could laugh at her all he liked — they might not have firebombed anyone, or glued themselves to the pavement, but Erin was convinced that their actions had led to the eventual disarming of Greenham Common, the last cruise missile leaving the base in 1991. They'd stood by their cause and eventually won.

And it hadn't been all singing, dancing and chanting around campfires, as Glenn would have everyone believe. She could remember with startling clarity several occasions when she, along with some of the other women, had been arrested and removed from the base — only to be released without charge some time later, the police depositing them in the countryside many miles from the base, in the vain hope that they would then just find their way back to their real homes. Instead, each time it happened, they merely trudged the many miles back to the base to resume their protest.

Erin placed the petition to the side and turned her thoughts to their current predicament with Sir Cecil. He wasn't technically doing anything wrong — not legally, anyway. But morally? People like Sir Cecil irritated her. They came from such a privileged background, born into entitlement, that they couldn't see past their own butlers and bank accounts. She wasn't against 'direct action', as Glenn constantly droned on about — far from it. These days, it took something like that to get anything done, to make any kind of change, to get anyone to notice. She just felt you needed to be smarter about it.

And being smart was Erin's forte.

She pulled a notepad across the coffee table and started jotting down ideas on how to mastermind the downfall of Sir Cecil Pemberton.

CHAPTER TEN

Saturday 9 March 2019
Gainsborough Road Hotel

The breath caught in his throat as he sat bolt upright, T-shirt clinging to the cold sweat on his skin. It was the third time that week the same nightmare had dragged him from unconsciousness. He tried to catch his breath. Had he screamed? Shouted out loud? His throat felt scratchy and hoarse. Maybe mum and dad had heard him this time?

Trying to get his heart rate under control, Mason Browning reached for the glass of water on the bedside table and quenched his dry throat. He noted the time — just after six a.m. Lying back against the sweat-stained pillows, he drew in a deep breath.

And then he smelled it.

Again.

Hot dogs. Popcorn. That unmistakable aroma of freshly spun candyfloss that made your teeth ache.

Blinking rapidly, he glanced around the room — another bland northern hotel room in another bland northern town. He searched for any sign of a discarded burger to account for the aroma of fried onions still grazing his nostrils.

There was nothing.

He took another slug of water and let his gaze rest on the adjoining door that led to his parents' room next door. Something was up — he knew that much. Something more than usual, anyway. He had never seen his mother so strung out before — her nerves were run ragged. She was a nervous person at the best of times, but not like this. This was something different entirely.

And as for Dad — he just had a faraway look in his eyes, as if he were searching for the answer to an unspoken question.

Mason wasn't stupid. He had picked up on the signs back home, long before they had made yet another hasty exit and hit the road. He'd tried to talk to Dad about it, but all he'd got in response was a sad smile and a reassurance that everything would be OK.

Well everything clearly was *not* OK — for here they were, two months on, still lurching from one town to another, one anonymous hotel room to another. So much so that he didn't even know which town they were in right now. Sometimes he wondered why he went along with it. He was a fully grown man after all — he would be twenty-eight this year — and able to make his own informed decisions. Yet here he was, tagging along after his parents like a little boy lost. He should be out there, creating his own life and his own memories, carving out his own future — but instead he was here, doing whatever *this* was.

But he knew why he was still here. It was Mum. She had been fragile enough before they'd left home, but now she was even worse. The woman was literally shrinking before his very eyes — a mere shadow of the person he remembered. She had always *suffered with her nerves*, as his dad so eloquently put it, but recently things had changed. They both tried to hide it from him, but he could see it as plain as day. Mum retreated further and further into herself, and Dad — well, Dad looked like he might crack at any moment.

So here he was, feeling duty bound to do whatever he could to keep the family from disintegrating. For that was what it felt like at times; as though the cement the family was built upon was crumbling by the day. And it wasn't as if he could rely on his brother to help. Adrian was a waste of space, and that was putting it mildly.

Mason drained the water from the glass and set it back down on the bedside table. Again his eyes flickered to the door leading to his parents' room. Yesterday, when they had stopped at a set of traffic lights in whatever town this was, Mason had seen a police station out of the window. He'd also seen the look in his dad's eyes as they waited. It was only brief, a subtle glance at best, but he'd seen it all the same. And then, just for a moment, Mason thought he saw Dad's hand twitch on the steering wheel, as if he was about to pull over and stop outside.

Give themselves up.

The sickening disquiet he had felt when wrenched from his nightmare began to multiply, his mind racing out of control. What could they possibly be running away from? Because he was certain they were running away from *something*. Instinct told him he should bolt in the opposite direction, get the hell away from here, leave them to it.

But he knew he wouldn't.

He knew he couldn't.

Knowing sleep would be fruitless, Mason slipped out from beneath the hotel bedcovers and padded across to the window. Dawn would be breaking soon, sending swathes of pink and orange streaks across the sky. The overnight wind had blown away the rain clouds, bringing with it a bright yet blustery start to the new day.

But Mason felt anything but bright.

As he rubbed the sleep from his eyes, he noticed a figure bending down by the side of their van parked in the hotel car park. He knew it was his father, even from this distance — he didn't need to look too closely. It was the slope of the shoulders that gave it away, and the way he held his head to the side while concentrating. Mason peered through the glass, the disquiet deepening.

Dad was changing the plates on the van.

Again.

Who does that if they're not running away from something big?

Turning away from the window, Mason headed back to the bed and slipped beneath the covers.

If he closed his eyes, then he couldn't see it.

And if he couldn't see it, then it wasn't happening.

* * *

Carnaby Close, Bury St Edmunds

Scott knew he didn't have long. Despite the early hour, some nosy parker from the estate would no doubt be along soon to give him a piece of their mind — and he got enough of that at home. He gave the spray can another shake before adding to his artwork.

As he sprayed, he felt the mobile in his pocket vibrate. Ignoring it, he continued with the sweeping wide arc in a particularly bright shade of purple. He knew who it would be anyway — the same person who had messaged him five times already that morning.

After getting home from the meeting last night, Mum had had another go at him, berating him for hanging around with the 'wrong sort' again. But his mum didn't understand. His friends weren't all bad — sure, they got into scrapes on occasion, and probably smoked too much weed from time to time, but, as he'd pointed out to her yet again, it could be a lot worse.

That was an understatement, if ever there was one.

He wasn't really sure why they'd all trooped into the community centre for the meeting — but as they were handing out free biscuits on the door and the weather was still wet and windy, it had seemed like a good idea. His friends always moaned they didn't have much spare cash, looking at Scott to sub them when they went out. He didn't mind doing it on occasion, buying the odd round in the pub, forking out for chips on the way home — but he wasn't a pushover.

His nickname wasn't '*The Edge*' for nothing.

In the end they'd stayed for the whole meeting, even when the biscuits had dried up. The discussion about Pemberton Hall had got a bit out of control towards the end, and the bloke in charge had decided to close it down. Scott was glad and couldn't wait to get out; they had talked about getting a kebab on the way home — no doubt paid for by him. But when they all spilled out into the car park, someone lit a joint and they stayed huddled in the corner trying to keep out of the wind. Some were still talking about Sir Cecil bloody Pemberton. Scott was bored hearing about the man and wanted to get going; his stomach was rumbling and calling for the elusive kebab. But they all wanted to know how he'd got on targeting the 'big man' as they called him. So Scott had eventually told them all about it — embellishing a few bits here and there for effect, noticing how his friends grinned the more he dressed it up. He ended with how he'd tripped the man up in the street, giving him a smashed-up nose and a decent kicking.

And then Glenn Clifford had joined them, continuing the tirade he had begun inside. Before Scott knew what was happening, the conversation became more animated and then took a decidedly sinister turn. He assumed it was the weed talking — and maybe the cheap cans of lager one of them had produced from their backpack. But as the joint and the cans were passed around, the whole gang agreed on taking further 'direct action' against Pemberton Hall and the man who lived there.

What Scott had done so far was clearly not considered to be enough. Not by a long shot. They wanted more — and they wanted *him* to do it.

"*You're the man! You're The Edge!*"

Initially, Scott just stood there, mouth clamped firmly shut, avoiding the joint as it was passed in his direction. His mum had a nose like a sniffer dog — she would smell it on him a mile off.

But they kept on.

And on.

Eventually, he'd taken a quick drag and agreed to whatever it was they wanted him to do. It was the easiest way — the *only* way. And he was *The Edge*, after all.

When everybody went their separate ways, his mates all slapping him on the back as they left, he felt strangely elated. It made him feel good — made him feel like he belonged; that he was a part of something at last. Maybe it was just the effects of the joint, but he made his way back home with a lop-sided grin on his face.

Today, however, the smile had slipped a little. He'd headed out early, before his mum got up and could start having another go at him about the company he was keeping. Another day at the factory stretched out in front of him, which didn't exactly fill him with much joy. It wasn't like he didn't enjoy the job; he did — and the money wasn't bad, either. It just wasn't what he wanted to do with his life. What he really wanted to do was go to art college — something he'd thought about for as long as he could remember. But his grades — those that he'd managed to get, anyway — hadn't been good enough and he'd ended up slipping slowly through the cracks.

He stood back and admired his latest handiwork.

Not bad.

He stuffed the spray cans back into his rucksack and started jogging in the direction of the town. He would be late for work if he wasn't careful. As he jogged, his mobile vibrated once again. He knew the messages would keep coming if he didn't respond. Pulling the phone from his pocket, he glanced at the screen.

'*Remember what you have to do, Edge.*'

Scott sighed and hit reply.

'*Yes. Don't sweat it. It'll be done.*'

* * *

West Suffolk Mortuary

"I *want* to do it." Heather Shaw stared resolutely out of the car's windscreen. "I *need* to do it."

Mick switched off the engine, rubbing a hand over his bloodshot eyes. "I can't."

"It doesn't matter. You can stay here." With that, she released her seat belt and climbed out of the car. The ever-strengthening wind whipped around her coat tails as she hurried across the small car park towards the mortuary entrance.

Mick leaned back against the headrest and sighed. He just couldn't do it. Couldn't bring himself to see Cal like that. When the two police officers had called at the house yesterday, his heart had literally descended into his boots. That's what people always said when they received devastating news, wasn't it? That their heart went into free fall? But it was true — it was actually true. It was *exactly* what it felt like.

Heather had swayed by his side, grabbing hold of the door frame for support as the devastating words were delivered. But she was made of strong stuff, Heather. Hence, *she* was the one battling her way across the car park and into the cold, grey-looking mortuary. Not him.

He couldn't face seeing Cal lying there.

Cold.

Alone.

Dead.

* * *

Carnaby Close Post Office, Bury St Edmunds

Lana Edgecombe clutched the parcel close to her chest and inched forward in the queue. If she could have avoided going out today, she would have, but she needed to return an online purchase, and that meant a trip to the post office.

Ordinarily, she wouldn't have given it a second thought. She often popped in, had a chat with the staff behind the counter — it was a friendly place.

But that had been before the complaints had started.

Complaints about Scott.

She did her best with him, but he could be difficult to control sometimes. Always had been, if she was being brutally honest. A difficult baby; a difficult toddler; a difficult child. And now he seemed to be growing into a difficult man.

And then there had been the Trouble.

Lana was as sure as she could be that no one on the estate, and more specifically the post office queue, knew about that. No one in the town, even.

Instinctively, she glanced left and right, but no one seemed to be paying her even the slightest bit of attention. Those in the queue had their gaze either fixed to the floor or were looking elsewhere. Anywhere other than at her.

Or were they just avoiding looking at her because they *knew*?

Insecurity welled up once more — a feeling she was more than acquainted with — and she considered abandoning the queue and bolting for the sanctuary of home.

Home.

Was it really home? It was where she and Scott now lived, but that didn't necessarily mean it was their home. She had hoped the latest move would be their last. They had been here coming up for eighteen months now, and Scott seemed to be settling in well; as well as could be expected, anyway. He had got himself a job, an apprenticeship, and Lana had clung to the hope that he was at last straightening himself out.

But then he had started hanging around with the 'wrong crowd' again. She didn't know them personally, but everyone else on the estate seemed to — and they weren't backward in coming forward to voice their opinions. As far as she could tell, they were mostly younger than Scott, but that didn't seem to stop him getting drawn in. He always was '*easily led*', as various headteachers had informed her. The group made a nuisance of themselves across the estate — often an irritation rather than anything more sinister, she thought — but she could see the sideways glances she got when she filled her car up with petrol, or picked up her weekly shopping.

But what was she supposed to do?

She couldn't very well ground him; he was a grown man — age-wise, at least. And he was big. *Strong.* He towered above her in his socks. She knew he had taken steroids in the past, but thought — or hoped — he'd moved on from that. Maybe he hadn't. With his bedroom door locked, she had no way of knowing.

There was one more customer ahead of her in the queue. Lana bit her lip and moved forward. She was sure she wasn't the only one who struggled on their own — plenty of people were in the same position as her. Scott's father hadn't stuck around for long after the Trouble — he'd had it away on his toes at the first opportunity. He had tried to explain himself, giving the feeble excuse of everything being too stressful. The *police*. The *recriminations*. The *hatred* that inevitably followed. So he'd had to get away.

Lana hadn't had that luxury. She couldn't run away like her spineless husband, waste of space that he was. She couldn't abandon her son and leave it to someone else to pick up the pieces. Scott had needed her then, more than ever. So she had stood by him and endured the increasingly painful taunts, and the inevitable mudslinging that came soon after.

They moved away not long after the Trouble. A new start. A new place. A new life. And, for the most part, it had worked. Scott hadn't got on very well at school — but that was to be expected, given what had happened. But she had persevered and got them through the tough times.

Sometimes when she looked at him she saw hope. Hope for the future. Hope that he had finally put the Trouble behind him and they could both move on.

But then she'd see the all-too-familiar look in his eyes when he went out to meet his new group of friends. The defiance was back. The coldness was back. She feared that all the good she had managed to achieve over the last twelve years was steadily being unravelled. And then she questioned whether he had really changed at all.

"Mrs Edgecombe?" The voice startled Lana out of her thoughts. She was now at the front of the queue. "What can I do for you today?"

Lana tried a smile and placed her parcel on the counter. Although she was probably imagining it, she thought she felt several pairs of eyes boring into her back. It made her skin prickle. She needed to get home.

CHAPTER ELEVEN

Bury St Edmunds Police Station

"What road did he say it happened on?"

Roy clicked the mouse to bring up the CCTV images. "Guildhall Street — just outside the Westgate pub."

Nicki grabbed a vacant chair and dragged it across the incident room. "And it was yesterday? Around midday?"

Roy nodded. "Yeah, just before." He gave the mouse a few more clicks before finding the correct time frame. "Here we go. Guildhall Street." Fast forwarding the reel, he paused it at 11.57 a.m. "And there he is, top corner."

Although in black and white and somewhat grainy, Sir Cecil was clearly visible walking briskly along the road towards the camera. Moments later, he was struck from behind.

"Not particularly clear," commented Nicki, watching as Roy rewound the images and played them again. "We can't really make out who's behind him." Whoever had struck Sir Cecil was dressed in nondescript dark clothing, a coat with the hood up, face barely visible. They had stepped out from a recessed doorway as the man passed by, disappearing out of sight just as quickly. "Let it play on."

Roy let the images play once more, and several seconds later they saw the second blow to Sir Cecil's head — again from behind, and again the assailant stepping out from nowhere at the last minute. Moments later they saw the third assault, as Sir Cecil sprawled head first into the gutter. After several swift kicks to the side and then the back of the man's body, the assailant ran off, face still obscured.

"See what you can do with the images," sighed Nicki, getting to her feet. "I don't expect much. We certainly can't see the guy's face. Maybe take a look at any other cameras nearby and see if you can trace him either before or after the assault. He must have come from somewhere. But don't waste too much time on it. We've got enough on at the moment." She didn't hold out much hope of getting anything useful from the images, but DCI Turner had said they at least needed to *look* like they were doing something, even if it came to nothing. Sir Cecil could be persistent and wasn't averse to making complaints to higher authorities if needed. With a murder on her hands, Nicki could well do without the added distraction of trying to round up some yob that had taken a dislike to Sir Cecil. There were plenty of people who would have gladly tripped him up, and would be even more keen to give him a good kicking into the bargain. Left to her, it wouldn't be top of her list of priorities.

"Will do," replied Roy, already reaching for the keyboard. "I'll be in my office if you need me."

* * *

West Suffolk Mortuary

Heather Shaw made her way along the corridor, following the mortuary receptionist. The whole place was deathly quiet — apt, really, in a place that housed the dead. They took a sharp turn to the left, passing through a set of double doors into yet another corridor. Soft, muted lighting illuminated their way, and a faint aroma of something flowery was in the air.

"Dr Mitchell is just through here." The receptionist came to a halt outside the final door in the corridor, '*Viewing Room*' on the name plate in its centre.

Heather swallowed past the lump in her throat. With her heart beating so fast it made her feel faint, she wished she had Mick by her side, had his hand to grasp hold of. Instead, she put a hand on the cool wall to steady herself.

The receptionist pushed open the door and Heather stepped inside. The room was bright, the walls a soft cream. There was a small sofa against one wall, with a low-rise coffee table in front that housed a simple vase of carnations and a box of tissues. A woman was standing in the centre of the room.

"Mrs Shaw? I'm Carolyn Mitchell, the lead pathologist here." The woman held out her hand.

Heather hesitated briefly, still trying to steady herself, before taking the proffered hand. It felt soft and warm, and she was instantly grateful for the human touch.

"The process is just as I explained over the telephone. Please take things at your own pace. We're not in any rush."

Heather nodded, already feeling her red raw eyes prickling with more tears. She didn't think there could be any left to shed. Once again, she wished Mick was by her side — but she didn't blame him for not wanting to come; for wanting to remember Cal as he had been. It was something that had crossed her own mind, too. Did she really want her last memory of her son to be here — laid out cold on a mortuary slab?

But as she had explained to Mick, she *had* to do it. There was even a small part of her — admittedly a *very* small part — that wanted to make sure it *was* him. That this wasn't all some huge and terrifying mistake. That they had got the wrong person. The police had told her that identification wasn't strictly necessary — the fingerprints and his photograph had been enough to prove it was Cal. But there was still a part of her that wanted to be sure.

Although Mick had brought Cal up as his own, he didn't have that unbreakable, unshakable bond that a mother had for their child. Cal was her own flesh and blood. She had brought him into this world, and now she owed it to him to be there as he left it.

"Ready?" Dr Mitchell gave a sad smile and gestured towards another door.

"Ready," Heather confirmed.

* * *

Bury St Edmunds Police Station

Nicki felt she had barely sat down at her desk and lifted the first file that needed her attention when Roy's head appeared around the door frame. She quickly followed him back to the incident room.

"Can you zoom in any closer?" Nicki edged her chair towards Roy's desk.

Roy enlarged the image. "It loses the clarity a little."

It did — but the people in the frame were still immediately recognisable. Nicki glanced at the clock in the bottom right-hand corner of the screen. "So, this is two-fifteen in the afternoon on Saturday the second?"

"Yes. I couldn't find our assailant on any of the other street cameras for yesterday's assault on Sir Cecil, so I started going backwards, looking at the previous days. And then I found this — from seven days ago."

Calvin Shaw and his stepfather were frozen in the middle of the screen.

"When do we first see them?"

Roy rewound the images. "About forty seconds before — just a little further along the street towards the cathedral. They both come into the frame around the same time, Calvin slightly ahead of his stepfather." He let the images play through, showing the pair making their way along Churchgate Street.

"What does their body language tell you, Roy?"

"Looks to me like they've had an argument of some sort, boss. Calvin looks like he's trying to get away."

Nicki nodded. "Play it again."

Roy dutifully started the images from the beginning, showing Calvin striding ahead of Mick Shaw but eventually being caught. Mick could then be seen grabbing his stepson by the arm and spinning him around. Even though grainy, it was clear the two came face to face, mere inches between them.

"Calvin starts to back away," added Roy. "Then . . ."

The images needed no further commentary. As Calvin turned away, his stepfather made another grab for him, this time pulling him into a headlock. The pair seemed to tussle for a few seconds, Mick swinging a punch at Calvin, which missed its connection. Momentarily wrong-footed, Mick loosened his grip and Calvin appeared to wrench himself free.

"See how he squares up to his stepfather?" Roy tapped the screen. "But then seems to think better of it." The reel played out, Calvin turning on his heel and heading out of shot of the camera. "And this is just five days before he dies."

Nicki got to her feet. "I think we need to go and have another chat with Mick Shaw, Roy. Get your coat."

CHAPTER TWELVE

Seymour Street, Bury St Edmunds

Nicki closed the door to the living room, leaving her alone with Mick Shaw. "How are you both holding up?" When Calvin's mother had answered the front door, Nicki had detected more than a little tension in the air. The woman wore a particularly pained look on her face.

Mick Shaw grimaced. "We're not long back from the mortuary. Heather wanted to go and see Cal." He broke off, muscles tensing along his jawline. "I think I let her down. I couldn't face it. I couldn't face *him*."

Nicki's cheeks flushed as she sat down on the edge of the sofa. "Of course — I'm sorry. I should have checked with you before we called round."

Mick shook his head, lowering himself into an armchair. "It's fine. What can I help you with?"

On their arrival, Nicki had explained that she had a couple of questions to ask Mick, so DS Carter had discreetly ushered Heather into the kitchen on the pretext of making a fresh round of tea. Gemma Huntley joined them, leaving Nicki and Mick Shaw alone.

"It's just a couple of questions really — mostly about your relationship with Calvin." Nicki eyed the man cautiously. What they had witnessed on the CCTV footage had looked like a full-blown argument in the street — and if Calvin hadn't turned away, managed to get away, who knew how it would have ended.

"I'm not sure I follow." A guardedness entered Mick Shaw's tone. "I brought him up as my own, like I told you. As far as I was concerned, he was my son. Cal saw it that way, too."

Nicki nodded. "I'm sure he did. I'm just wondering — what with most modern families being as they are — did you ever have any fallings-out with Calvin? Any arguments? Particularly recent ones?" She continued to train her gaze on Calvin's stepfather, watching for any subtle reaction.

There was nothing except for another tightening of the man's jawline, followed by another brief shake of the head. "Nothing that I recall."

"Nothing at all? What, ever? It would be quite unusual, wouldn't it, for there to be nothing at all — no arguments, no differences of opinion?" Nicki only had to look at her own family to know how fractious things could get. "Even the closest of families fall out at some point."

The head shaking continued. "Cal was a good lad. We had a good relationship. I considered him to be the son I never had. I would do anything for him, anything at all — and for Heather."

Nicki plastered a smile on her face. "Well, that's good then." She knew right there and then that the man was lying.

The only question was why?

* * *

A6 Services

Annette stared through the passenger side window. They had left the hotel earlier that morning, stopping at a service station to stretch their legs and stock up on supplies. She hadn't been able to summon the strength to go far. With every step she took, her whole body shuddered, so she quickly returned to the relative safety of the van. With the engine off and heaters stilled, it soon felt cold, so she pulled her cardigan more closely around her shoulders. The weather outside was deteriorating fast — the storm didn't look like weakening anytime soon.

She could see Mason sheltering from the wind beneath a clump of trees. Her heart gave an involuntary lurch. She felt such overwhelming love for the boy — just pure, unadulterated love. And although Mason was now almost twenty-eight, heading for his thirties, he would always be her 'boy'. *Her Mason.* A solitary tear trickled down her cheek. She couldn't help it.

How had they managed to get themselves into this mess?

Immediately, a pained chuckle lodged in the back of her throat. She knew perfectly well how they had managed it — and it was all down to her.

Everything was her fault.

* * *

Tuesday 22 October 1996
Warcester, Southern England

"Mason?" Annette Browning swayed by the side of her son's bed.

She had woken up in a daze, disoriented and shaking. A wave of nausea engulfed her as soon as she summoned the strength to swing her legs off the sofa and get to her feet. She spied the empty bottle of wine on the coffee table and the packets of sleeping tablets and antidepressants by its side. She knew mixing them wasn't a good idea — she wasn't stupid. But sometimes it was the only way to beckon the oblivion she so desperately craved.

Once she had stirred from her blurred slumber, she stumbled unsteadily towards the stairs. The house was quiet.

Too quiet.

She squinted at the clock on the mantelpiece as she stumbled past to see that it was already eleven o'clock. Where was Mason? Why wasn't he tearing around the house like a mini tornado as he usually would be by this time? She could hear Adrian was awake, wailing in his cot bed. At this time of the morning he would be hungry. And need changing.

But instead of attending to Adrian's cries, she felt compelled to head towards Mason's room.

And now here she was, standing by Mason's bedside, frozen in time.

It didn't make any sense. None of it did. She swayed some more, grabbing hold of the bookcase at the end of the small single bed to steel herself. Mason swam in and out of focus; one minute he was there, the next minute he wasn't. Annette closed her eyes and dipped her head down, waiting for the fogginess to clear.

Mason.

When she opened her eyes again, she saw the boy was lying half in and half out of the covers, his duvet slipping towards the floor. One pale leg was visible. It didn't move.

"Mason?" she repeated.

Annette staggered towards the head of the bed, reaching out towards her son's forehead. He'd been so feverish the last couple of days — complaining of a blistering headache and feeling sick — and she'd been regularly dosing him up with liquid paracetamol. She remembered consulting her Children's Health Handbook and reading that that was what she was meant to do. It was what she had always done in the past when either of the boys had been under the weather with any variety of sniffles, coughs and teething problems. Paracetamol and plenty of fluids.

It was what you were meant to do.
It was what would make him better.

But Mason didn't look better.

His hair clung in sweaty clumps to his head, his pyjamas saturated. Dried vomit decorated the front of his Mickey Mouse top. The acrid smell made Annette want to gag.

"Mason?"

Her fingers brushed his forehead and then she recoiled, pulling her hand back as if she'd been scalded by something hot. But Mason didn't feel hot.

He felt stone cold.

* * *

Saturday 9 March 2019
A6 Services

Annette was torn from her memories by the sound of the van door slamming shut. Larry handed her a takeaway coffee cup, which she took in her trembling hand.

"I got us some sandwiches for later, too." Larry Browning swung the plastic carrier bag into the back seat. "In case we're too late to get something at the hotel. Where's Mason?"

Annette brushed the tear away from her cheek and nodded through the passenger side window. "He wanted to check in on something for work."

Larry gazed across the service station forecourt to where his son leaned up against a tree, phone clamped to one ear. "Good job I changed the SIM cards in our phones." He took a gulp of his coffee, grimacing at the taste. "Sorry," he muttered, gesturing towards Annette's as-yet untouched cup. "It's not the greatest."

Annette gave a tired smile, her heart heaving. "He knows something's up, Larry — Mason does. He has done for a while now, I'm sure. We can't keep expecting him to change his plans for us — to keep uprooting him like this. It doesn't feel right. He's not stupid."

"I know he's not stupid, Annie."

Annette gripped the cardboard coffee cup in her hand and shuddered once again. It was time. "I think we should tell him. About everything. We have to stop lying to him — and to ourselves. Before it's too late. He needs to know what happened. And he needs to hear it from us."

Larry swallowed another mouthful of the foul-tasting coffee. Eventually he nodded. "I know. But let's just get somewhere safe first." He paused and half-turned his head towards the rear of the van. "We need to get settled again before we do anything drastic." He returned his gaze to his wife and tried a reassuring smile. "We'll deal with Mason — when the time is right."

* * *

Seymour Street, Bury St Edmunds

"Anything further from Mrs Shaw?" Nicki kept her voice low. Although the kitchen door was closed and Mick and Heather were together in the living room being entertained by Roy, Nicki knew they couldn't be too careful. "She still not giving anything away about who Cal's biological father might be?"

Gemma shook her head. "No. Either she *really* doesn't know, or she's convinced herself over the years that she doesn't know. Maybe she's blocked it out and told herself that it doesn't matter anymore. She's quite convincing though."

"It's probably nothing, but keep an ear out in case either of them mention something. Whoever he is, he has a right to know about Calvin's passing." Nicki paused, listening out for any telltale footsteps in the hallway outside. There was nothing. "What about her relationship with Mick? Any tensions?"

"Nothing unusual, given the circumstances. I told you how they met, didn't I?"

Nicki nodded. "In the supermarket — over a carton of broken eggs?"

"He seems devoted to her. He'll do pretty much anything for her. But I think today has been hard on them both — with the visit to the mortuary. Makes it all real somehow, doesn't it? He was a little distant when they got back — Mick."

"Distant? How so?"

"Just quiet. My guess is that it might be because he didn't go in to view the body with Heather. I heard them talking about it — well, Heather was talking about it, he was just . . . quiet. Maybe this all brought it home for him — how he's not actually Calvin's real father. I wouldn't say they fell out about it, but . . ." Gemma left the rest of the sentence unsaid.

"And nothing to suggest what Mick and Calvin might have been arguing about in the street last Saturday? It was only five days before he died." Nicki had already forwarded Gemma the CCTV footage. "From what we can see, it looked quite heated. Yet Mick has just told me, bold as brass, that they have a good relationship, no fallings out — recent or otherwise. I don't want to confront him with what we know just now. I feel that might be better done under caution at a later date, if we're still thinking that he's being less than honest with us."

Gemma could only shrug. "He's not mentioned anything to Heather while I've been here. And I don't get the vibe that anything was festering — about an argument, that is. Maybe she just didn't know?"

"Keep a close eye on them both. I want to know the minute anything seems off." Nicki headed for the door.

"Are we thinking Mick had something to do with Calvin's death?"

Nicki had asked herself the very same question before they left the station.

Was that what they were thinking?

"I'm not sure," she eventually replied, before pulling the kitchen door open. "But let's keep it in mind."

* * *

A6 Services

Larry knew his wife was right. They couldn't carry on the way they were — that was becoming more and more obvious as time went on. He had changed the plates on the van three times now, but it wasn't something he could do long term. And they couldn't keep moving from hotel to hotel like this. It made them look guilty — which they obviously were.

But it made them look guilty in a *bad way.*

Yet he and Annette were not bad people. If anything, they were the opposite — they were trying to do good.

Trying and clearly failing.

There had been many occasions on their route north when he had felt the urge to turn himself in; to drive to the nearest police station and end the nightmare they had found themselves living through day after day. Yesterday, they had pulled up at a set of traffic lights in some town or other — driving through so many, they all seemed to blur into one after a while — and the familiar 'POLICE' sign had caught his attention. It would have taken a matter of seconds to pull over and go in and tell their story, accept their fate. Face up to what they had done.

But instead he'd stepped on the accelerator as soon as the lights turned green, and the opportunity was lost.

"Dad?" Mason slipped into the passenger side of the van. "I'm worried about Mum."

Larry shook the thought of the police from his mind and cast a hesitant glance at his son.

His son.

He had regarded the young man sitting by his side as his son for the last twenty-two years. It felt so natural that sometimes he forgot that he wasn't actually Mason. Not the *real* Mason, anyway; not the boy they had lost that fateful night back in October 1996.

Taking another child had been wrong — so very, *very* wrong — and Annette knew that now. In fact, she always had. Snatching another child the way she had, it was so far from right that it was on a completely different planet. But Annette had been so fragile back then, even more so than she was right now. Losing Mason that night had been tragic beyond all comprehension. Neither of them had known what to do, such had been the shock of it all. After coming home

105

from his work trip to discover Mason lying stone cold in his bed. Larry hadn't had the heart to make his wife's life any worse than it was already.

In the days that followed, Annette plunged into the depths of depression, and had been on the verge of taking her own life on several occasions. Larry couldn't bear watching her suffer. And then she had snatched the boy. He'd immediately seen a new light in her eyes that night — the boy had reawakened a new lease of life in her, a new passion. Depression and despair were replaced with joy.

How could he destroy that?

So Larry had taken the path of least resistance and accepted the new Mason into his life, *their lives*, as if the old one had never even left.

It sounded so crass now. What had he been thinking? How could they possibly have made it work? But make it work they had — sort of. For the last twenty-two years anyway. But Benedict Thatcher from next door, poking his nose in where it wasn't wanted, had forced their hand; forced them to take to the road and try and outrun the past.

But it hadn't worked. Everything was crumbling around them now; the perfect world they had built was slowly disintegrating in front of their very eyes. And if they weren't careful, they would all be taken down with it. Mason included.

"I know," he eventually replied. "I'm worried too. You've always been . . ." Larry could feel his throat starting to constrict. "You've always been such a tower of strength for her. For both of us. There's not many that would stick by us like you have. I want you to know that, whatever happens, it doesn't go unappreciated."

"I don't think all this is helping." Mason gestured out of the window at yet another service station forecourt. "Moving on all the time." He returned his gaze to his father. "We need to stop running — from whatever it is we're running from."

Larry felt himself nod and his chest heave, just as he spied Annette returning from the toilet block. "I know, son. And we will. Soon."

CHAPTER THIRTEEN

Bury St Edmunds Police Station

"It's fine, Graham. Go." Nicki waved her hand towards the door of her office.

"But we're right in the middle of things here."

Nicki waved her hand again. "We can spare you for one afternoon, Graham. It's the weekend. Go and see your kids. There's nothing that can't be done tomorrow. We're waiting on lots of results to come in, so . . . shoo! Before I change my mind!"

DS Fox gave her an appreciative smile. "Thanks. Before I go, though, I've just unearthed an interesting thing about our victim's stepfather, Michael Shaw."

"Oh?" Nicki's eyebrows hitched. "Interesting how?"

"Put his name through the system — came up with a hit for a violent offence back in 1999. He was part of a group that attacked a man waiting at a bus stop. The man died later in hospital. Shaw was lucky to get away with a conviction for affray. It seems like he was present when the initial confrontation took place, but wasn't on the scene when the victim received his injuries shortly afterwards." Fox gave a shrug and moved towards the door. "Shows a propensity for violence, if nothing else. I've put the details up on the board."

"Thanks, Graham. You get yourself off now."

After Fox had disappeared, Nicki considered the new information on Mick Shaw. The man was lying about his relationship with Calvin, and now it turned out he had a violent past. Was that enough to make him a real suspect?

Nicki rubbed her tired eyes. As well as the case weighing heavily on her mind, she could feel the shopping list for tomorrow burning a hole in her pocket. She pulled the offending article out and sighed. A supermarket wasn't her favourite place to be any day of the week — but especially not on a Saturday afternoon. The very thought made her heart sink. But she knew the sense of dread she felt wasn't wholly due to the impending crush in the vegetable aisle, or the inevitable queue at the checkouts — it wasn't even down to the dinner looming with her parents tomorrow.

Much of the unease she felt was due to the case.

Gemma was keeping her eyes and ears open at the Shaws' home — there was definitely something off that they needed to get to the bottom of. Mick claiming that he and Calvin had a near-perfect relationship and never quarrelled wasn't borne out by the images they had all seen on the CCTV recording. People didn't usually lie without a reason, not in Nicki's experience anyway. If any more evidence pointed towards Calvin's stepfather, then she would have no hesitation in bringing him in for questioning.

After checking in with the rest of the team, she finally left the station for the arduous trip to the supermarket.

* * *

2 Old Railway Cottages, Dullingham, Nr Newmarket

Benedict watched Adrian Browning reverse his van off the drive next door and roar out of sight. Their paths hadn't crossed all that often since Larry and Annette had departed, leaving their youngest son home alone to fend for himself. Benedict had no reason to believe that Adrian wasn't coping on his own — but he shuddered to think what state the house would be in by now. He occasionally heard loud music coming from within, the odd whiff of smoke from the back patio that didn't smell like tobacco — but, other than that, Benedict barely saw his young neighbour.

He turned away from the window and resumed his seat on the sofa, laptop open.

Back to the email.

No further details had come through yet, but the initial message had given a decent enough outline of what was involved — and what was expected of him.

He knew he would have to tell Nicki — not the exact details of the job, but the fact that he would be going away for a while. She was starting to rely on him being around. He wouldn't mention it yet, though. From what he could tell, she had enough on her plate with the current investigation. And with their hunt for Deano.

And now there was tomorrow, too.

Worried that she might blurt something out about their search for Deano, Nicki had asked Benedict to come along to lunch with her parents. He'd readily agreed; he needed to keep an eye on Nicki as now definitely wasn't the time for divulging what they knew about Deano's disappearance.

But as he thought about tomorrow's lunch, his nerves began to jangle. Although he mixed relatively well socially — he could meet and greet most people without it being an issue — being introduced to retired Detective Superintendent Hugh Webster bothered him. It made him nervous, and Benedict Thatcher prided himself in having nerves of steel. No one got under his skin.

Ever.

He was sure Hugh Webster would be amiable, and had no reason to doubt the two of them would get along just fine.

It wasn't necessarily the *man* that made him nervous.

It was the email.

Benedict closed the laptop. Looking at it wouldn't make what he had to do any easier.

* * *

Pemberton Hall

Sir Cecil poured himself another brandy. His head didn't hurt so much anymore, but his nose still throbbed. He'd been lucky not to break it, landing face down on the pavement like that. He was only grateful there hadn't been anybody else about to witness yesterday's fall from grace — other than the swine who'd tripped him up. His back and sides ached, telling him he would no doubt be getting some lovely bruises soon.

He could just imagine if there *had* been someone else there — whipping out their blasted mobile phone to record him scrambling to his feet, nose bloodied. There was no question that it would have been all over social media in a matter of seconds. He could have gone viral.

He slugged back the brandy and poured another. If he ever managed to get his hands on whoever did it, he would make them pay. He hated this little town even more now. He couldn't wait to push ahead with his planned development — he'd soon see who had the last laugh then, wouldn't he? Maybe he would allow the developer to buy up more land — build even more houses. That would teach them.

One of the local rags had interviewed him not so long ago, and he knew he hadn't won over many fans with what he'd said, but he had always been brought up to be truthful. Even if that meant trashing someone else's feelings.

His father had taught him that much.

Father.

Sir Cecil almost choked on the word. The man had been no father to him, not in the true sense. Fathers loved and nurtured their offspring; taught them about life; celebrated their achievements and helped guide them through childhood into adulthood.

Sir Alfred Pemberton had done none of that with Cecil. At least, not that he could recall. He'd always been made to feel like he was in the way, a problem to be dealt with, an annoyance to be subdued. If that was fatherhood, Sir Cecil was glad he had never had the misfortune to marry.

But at least he'd got his revenge in the end.

When he'd got the call to say that his father was terminally ill, he had almost clapped his hands with joy. Instead, he'd dutifully shown up on the doorstep of Pemberton Hall to offer his heartfelt condolences. It was expected of him to be in the house while his father passed — to be ready to take over the reins of running the place. But there were only pound signs in Sir Cecil's eyes at that point, not tears.

And when the old man lingered on a little too long, what did it matter that he might have helped him on his way? Some people might look upon that as an act of kindness.

Good old Sir Cecil — always the loving son.

He gave a throaty chuckle and poured another brandy.

* * *

Seymour Street, Bury St Edmunds

Mick poured the hot milk into the mug, stirring vigorously. The rich cocoa aroma lifted to his nostrils. Heather had agreed to take the sleeping tablets prescribed by the doctor later, her body wracked with exhaustion.

The afternoon had been tense, and not just because of the earlier trip to the mortuary to view Cal's body. He wondered if he had made the right decision, choosing not to see Cal. It felt right, but it also felt very wrong at the same time. Heather had been distraught when she had eventually returned to the car, and he hadn't pressured her for any details. He hadn't really said anything at all. What could he say anyway? Nothing was going to make any of this better.

He was tempted to put a couple of the tablets into Heather's mug right now, rather than wait until later. He could see how much she was struggling with everything. It might give her a few hours of peace — and it would also give him time to think. To think about Cal; about what had happened.

The packet of tablets sat by the side of the kettle. It would be so easy.

But he knew he couldn't do it.

Mick had done plenty of things wrong in his life already — he didn't need to add drugging his wife to the list.

Being quizzed about his relationship with Cal by the detective earlier had served to unnerve him a little. It was as if they knew something that he didn't. But then the questioning had stopped and the detectives went on their way. Maybe he was worrying over nothing. *Maybe*.

Just then the door opened and Gemma Huntley popped her head round. "I'm going to be on my way now. Can I get either of you anything before I leave?"

Mick shook his head and raised the mug of hot chocolate. "Just about to take this through to Heather. We'll be fine, thank you."

Mick waited until he heard the front door opening and closing before stepping out into the hallway. They would be fine, he could feel it. Him and Heather. They had to be fine — for Cal's sake.

* * *

Bury St Edmunds Police Station

Nicki pushed open the door to the incident room.

"Calvin's phone is still switched off, or else it's dead. No movement there. And I've found the post that Scott Edgecombe commented on." Matt gestured towards his computer screen. "Last May. He said some pretty hateful stuff."

Nicki peered over the detective's shoulder. "Any indication as to why he had such a grievance?"

Matt shrugged. "Not really. Just seemed to take a dislike to Calvin and his business for some reason. I took a look at Edgecombe's social media accounts, too. He does tend to antagonise people — says things purely to spark an argument, from what I can make out. Maybe he just gets some sort of perverse kick out of upsetting others."

Nicki nodded. "Keep digging in case there's something else. Roy, any updates?" She turned towards DS Carter seated at the back of the room.

"I've contacted a lot of local retailers who stock the same polypropylene rope, asking for details of any purchases in the last three months. Is that a good enough time span?"

Nicki nodded again. "Let's start with that. Let me know what you get. Ask for details of the transactions, CCTV if there is any. The usual."

Roy swung his chair back round to face his computer monitor. "Will do."

Glancing at her watch, Nicki saw the time was just after four thirty. "Don't work too late," she announced, heading for the door. "Get yourselves off home at a reasonable hour. We'll catch up first thing Monday."

* * *

Seymour Street, Bury St Edmunds

The hot chocolate had gone down well — so much so that Mick had made them both a second cup. He'd toyed again with the idea of the sleeping tablets, but Heather seemed to have calmed down now and had promised she would take some before bed.

After Gemma left, they'd both sat down in the living room and looked through the family photograph albums. Mick wasn't sure whose idea it had been — one minute they were sitting in relatively comfortable silence, the next the coffee table was covered in albums. Mick went along with it as Heather seemed to take some form of comfort from the exercise, even though he noticed her lips trembling and fresh tears staining her cheeks as each album revealed more and more pictures of their beloved Cal. Mick hadn't been in their lives for Cal's first birthday, or his first Christmas, but he could see just how happy and devoted Heather was to her baby son.

Then there was his first day at school, his first nativity play, his first school sports day.

As Heather turned the pages, Mick noted just how much like his mother Cal had been. The shape of his face, the colour of his hair, even the way he smiled. When she turned the final page, Mick felt Heather shudder by his side, as if closing the door on Cal's life. They sat in silence for a while, each submerged in their own memories — some good, some bad.

Then he felt Heather reach for his hand. "We need to talk," she murmured simply, giving Mick's hand a squeeze. "About Cal." She looked up into his steel-grey eyes. "It's time."

* * *

College Lane, Bury St Edmunds

The supermarket had been every bit as hellish as Nicki expected, but she'd managed to grit her teeth and grab everything from the shopping list before escaping. Now, standing in her galley-style kitchen, surveying her purchases, she wondered if she could really pull this off.

Jeremy had been right when he'd said she was no Gordon Ramsay — she very rarely cooked from scratch, usually citing her busy caseload at work. In reality, it was probably more down to laziness on her part. She couldn't remember the last time she'd cooked a roast dinner — and suddenly the enormity of the weekend hit her square in the face. She was meeting her parents for the first time in goodness knows how long — what if it all went spectacularly wrong? What if they couldn't get past what had happened to Deano? What if they couldn't broach the enormous crevice that had divided them since his disappearance?

Nicki turned away from the shopping bags and reached for the bottle of Pinot Grigio she'd just removed from the fridge. A glass would help settle her nerves before embarking on some of the preparations for tomorrow's meal.

Luna jumped up onto the worktop, starting to sniff around the bags, her little nose twitching. Nicki smiled and ruffled the fur behind the cat's ears.

"Nothing in there for you, sweetie."

Luna continued to bury her head inside the bag that contained the joint of beef, and Nicki scooped her up into her arms and set her back down on the floor.

"Your food bowl is down here, madam." Nicki nudged the cat towards her dinner. "You need to let me get on in peace and quiet. We've got important visitors tomorrow."

For the next forty-five minutes Nicki put the shopping away and made a start on some of the vegetable preparation. As she did so, her phone beeped twice with incoming messages. Both were from Jeremy, wishing her luck for the meal tomorrow. She thought about replying but, as she had her hands full with peeling a mound of potatoes, she decided to leave it. Part of her wished Jeremy was coming tomorrow — but he didn't know anything about Deano, and that was one can of worms she wasn't intending to rip open any time soon.

As she methodically peeled and sliced the potatoes, her thoughts turned back to the current investigation. She'd left Roy making contact with local retailers regarding the type of rope used to hang Calvin's body from the tree — maybe something would come from that. The thought buoyed her. They needed a breakthrough soon if they were going to make any headway.

Mick Shaw still unnerved her. The man was hiding something about his relationship with Calvin, but Nicki couldn't be sure what that something was. On the outside, the Shaws looked to be the archetypal, perfect family unit.

But when you prodded deeper into any family, cracks would always start to show if you looked hard enough.

And Nicki knew just how easily they could fall apart when exposed to trauma.

Pushing Calvin and Mick Shaw from her mind, she reached for the bag of carrots. Tomorrow would be here before she knew it. She needed to be ready.

CHAPTER FOURTEEN

"Caz, what have you got for us?" Nicki slipped behind her desk, shifting the ever increasing pile of paperwork to one side. The message had pinged through to her phone two minutes before, the pathologist clearly getting an early start to her Sunday. "You mentioned DNA?"

"I did. If you remember, your young lad from Hardwick Heath suffered a sizeable open wound to his left cheek."

Nicki pulled a copy of Calvin Shaw's post-mortem report towards her and flicked over to the observations. "I do remember — but it didn't kill him, right? The punch to the face?"

"No, not even close. Broke the skin though, which has allowed some transference of forensic material from the assailant into the wound. From that, they've managed to isolate a DNA profile that doesn't belong to your victim."

"The killer?" Nicki's eyebrows arched.

"No idea — but it was the person who punched him. Logic, I guess, would tell you it should be your killer, but that's out of my remit. No doubt you'll be notified in due course if and when a match is made on the database."

Nicki thanked Caz and ended the call. Her thoughts began to free fall — if the national database threw up a match, then the case could be closed more quickly than anticipated. But she wouldn't hold her breath. She knew the chances of their killer already being on the system was remote at best. But it didn't stop her feeling a small buzz of anticipation.

Her eyes trawled the chaos that currently represented her desk. As tempting as it was to get stuck in on this quiet Sunday morning, she knew she couldn't. She shouldn't even be here now. That morning she'd left Luna eating her breakfast, promising her that she would only be half an hour; an hour at best.

In reality, it had been nearly two.

She'd woken up early, her brain whirling and worrying about the impending meal, so she'd decided a quick visit to the station might settle her nerves. Now she was here, hiding away in her familiar cocoon, she didn't want to leave. But with her mother due to arrive any time after nine — her father heading straight for the golf course with DCI Turner — the clock was ticking. It was far too late to bail out now — that ship had sailed a long time ago.

DS Fox was on leave, but the rest of the team were planning to come in and carry on in her absence. She had popped various post-it notes on desks in the incident room with reminders of what actions needed following up, urging them to call her if needed.

Knowing she couldn't delay any longer, she switched off the computer monitor and grabbed her keys.

* * *

Bury St Edmunds Golf Club

"How is she?" Hugh Webster chipped the ball, watching it land close to the hole. "And I mean *really*."

DCI Malcolm Turner hung back a little, close to where his own ball had come to rest just inside the green at the sixth hole, and pulled a putter from his golf bag. He knew this particular question had been coming — had known it the moment Hugh called him to suggest the long overdue round of golf. If he was being honest, he was surprised it had taken six holes before the words had escaped Webster's mouth. But even though he'd been expecting the question, he wasn't much closer to knowing how to answer it.

Not entirely truthfully, anyway.

The Webster family had so many secrets, it was hard to keep up.

Hugh Webster turned his tall, six-foot frame towards the DCI, and Turner knew he wouldn't be able to fob him off with 'she's fine'.

Nicki *was* fine, as far as he knew — although the word 'fine' could cover a lot of ground and a lot of emotions. Whenever he himself enquired how his detective inspector was coping — which admittedly he felt he didn't do often enough — that was usually the word she plucked out from all the other options available.

Fine.

"I think the investigation last year took it out of her, if I'm honest," he eventually offered. "As it did most of her team."

It wasn't a lie.

The hunt for six-year-old Lucas Jackson had reawakened many a nightmare for Nicki — the case closely resembling that of the disappearance of her own brother some twenty or so years ago. He knew it was something that had haunted her every day since.

DCI Turner knew he was the only person outside of Nicki's family that was aware of her past. Her closest friends, her colleagues at the station — none of them knew of the trauma she'd been through. More specifically, no one knew about Deano, or the part she'd played in his disappearance.

On more than one occasion he'd pleaded with her to confide in someone — confide in those closest to her — for keeping that part of her life hidden couldn't be healthy for anyone. It was something she politely acknowledged but had yet to do anything about.

Typical Nicki.

"I can imagine," replied Webster, stepping out of the way so the DCI could line up his shot. "It affected me and Anne, too, when we saw it in the news. Something like that — it brings it all back."

Turner had known Hugh Webster for many a year; they had worked together when Nicki's father was a detective superintendent, and the DCI remembered the man well. They had remained friends long after Webster had taken his retirement — meeting up for the odd round of golf, or even the odd fishing trip. Detective Superintendent Webster had been a towering force when he was in his prime, but now — here on the putting green at the sixth hole at the Bury St Edmunds Golf Club — the man looked a shadow of his former self. It was as though someone had let all the air out of him, deflating him like a tyre with a slow puncture.

"How have you and Anne coped over the years?" Turner took the opportunity to steer the conversation away from Nicki. "It must be hard for you, the more time that passes." He took the shot, overhitting it a little and sending the golf ball a few feet past the hole.

"It is hard, I won't lie. Sometimes we feel like we're getting there, you know? Managing, I think is probably the correct term to use. Managing life without him, but . . ." Webster paused. Turner thought he heard the man's voice hitch. "It never quite leaves you. The pain. The horror. Even after all this time. It doesn't take much to bring it all back to the surface. It's always just waiting there, ready to pounce."

The DCI headed across the green to where his ball had come to rest, watching Webster complete his easy tap-in to win the hole. Once he had despatched his own ball, successfully sinking it into the hole this time, they picked up their bags and headed towards the seventh tee. They were lucky that the wind had died down overnight. A game of golf in a force ten gale wasn't fun.

"She still thinks we blame her." Webster set his golf bag down at the top of the fairway, his face taut. "Nicki. She still thinks we blame her for Dean."

Turner pulled a driver from his bag. "I know. I've tried to get her to talk to you both. I can see how it eats her up sometimes, but . . . you know Nicki. And what's she's like."

Webster smiled. "Stubborn. Just like her father." He, too, selected a driver from his bag and stepped towards the tee. "But we don't — blame her, that is. We never did. It was just . . ." The words caught in his throat as he placed the golf ball down, ready for the tee shot. "It was just the way it was. It happened. It was no one's fault — there was no one to blame. Only those that took Dean."

"I guess the hardest person to forgive is yourself," added the DCI, stepping back to watch Webster swipe the ball clean off the tee. "And I'm not sure Nicki ever will."

* * *

College Lane, Bury St Edmunds

Nicki was glad she'd already placed the photos of Deano on the mantelpiece. After getting back from the station, she'd immediately launched herself into the kitchen and was just finishing the meal preparations as her mother knocked at the door. After the initial greeting, the obligatory hugs and kisses on cheeks, her mother gravitated towards the fireplace, a sad smile on her face as she gazed at little Deano's impish grin.

It made Nicki feel guilty, once again, at how she had hidden him away. She wasn't quite sure what that level of deceit really said about her. And it wasn't as if the deceit ended there, either. Why hadn't she wanted to tell her parents the good news about Deano? Surely the most logical thing to do — the most *humane* thing to do — would be to tell them?

But, in true Nicki style, she had kept it to herself. What was one more lie on top of all the others?

She kept telling herself that she was protecting them; that she didn't want to get their hopes up, only to dash them soon afterwards. Because sometimes even Nicki didn't believe it was true — especially as they'd failed to find him last week — telling herself that Benedict had somehow got it all wrong, that Deano wasn't alive and well, as he'd told her. It wasn't as though she'd actually seen him for herself, was it? Maybe it had all been a terrible misunderstanding.

Then there was the alternative: Deano was alive and well but they never found him. Or he didn't want to come home.

Which would be worse? Knowing he was alive but never seeing him again, or knowing he was dead and being allowed the time and space to grieve?

So she'd kept quiet. If she mentioned it now, then potentially all she would achieve would be to make everything a hundred times worse — if that were even possible. She'd brought enough heartache into the family already — she didn't need to actively create more.

"Penny for them?"

Nicki whirled around at the sound of her mother's voice.

"I think that might be ready now." Anne Webster nodded towards the pan where Nicki had been stirring the gravy, staring vacantly at the hob.

"Sorry, miles away." She put the wooden spoon down and turned off the heat.

"They should be back soon, but we can always put it in the microwave if they're delayed."

Nicki turned towards her mother and, at that precise moment, standing in her steam-filled kitchen, she saw things through her parent's eyes for the first time in a long while, maybe even ever. She saw behind the hurt, behind the grief, behind the sadness — and what she saw was something entirely different than she'd believed.

The coolness she'd always thought she'd seen had actually just been sorrow — deep, heart-breaking sorrow and pain.

And what had Nicki done? She'd used it as a reason to blame her parents for pushing her away, for pushing her out of the family. But, if anything, it had been Nicki herself who'd pushed *them* away. In that split second, standing side-by-side amid the aroma of the roasting beef in the oven, Nicki saw things as they really were.

She saw Nicki the defiant and rebellious teen; the one who thought the whole world was against her. She saw the Nicki who then withdrew into herself, closed herself off from those around her, keeping everyone at arm's length. She then saw the Nicki who'd upped sticks and moved away at the first opportunity — changing her name to cut herself off from her family even more. Nicki had always dressed the name change up as being necessary for her to move on and put the past behind her; put the Webster name behind her. But had that really been the case? Hadn't it all just been her running away from the very people who loved her and wanted to protect her?

"I'm sorry," she replied. "For everything."

"I know you are, dear. I know." Anne Webster patted her daughter's hand and pulled her into an embrace. As far as hugs went, it wasn't as cool as Nicki had been expecting. If anything, it was warm and loving. "It's good to see you, Nicki. We've missed you."

"I've missed you, too," Nicki heard herself saying, not realising she was speaking out loud. "I've missed this so much."

Before her mother could respond, the front door opened and closed.

"We found this young man loitering on the doorstep so we thought we'd best bring him in." Hugh Webster entered the living room, closely followed by DCI Turner. Benedict Thatcher brought up the rear, clutching a bottle of red wine.

CHAPTER FIFTEEN

College Lane, Bury St Edmunds

"You didn't fancy joining us for a round, then?" Hugh Webster handed Benedict a glass of wine.

"Not really a golfer, I'm afraid." Benedict gave what he hoped was a humorous smile, accepting the drink.

"Well, the way I managed to play this morning, you wouldn't think I was either!" DCI Malcolm Turner poured his own glass of wine and joined the others standing by the fireplace.

"Oh, you weren't that bad, Malcolm. I've seen worse."

"You lie so eloquently, my friend." Turner edged closer to the wood burner that was kicking out some welcome heat. "But there's no getting past the fact that I'm more than a little rusty these days. When was the last time we got together for a game?"

Webster shrugged and sipped his wine. "I've no idea, but it's been too long."

"You know each other well, then?" Benedict took a mouthful of his red wine.

"We used to work together, back in the day." Turner placed a hand on Hugh Webster's shoulder. "We worked out of the same station and this man here was the best detective superintendent we'd had in a long time — but don't let him get too big-headed about it."

"So — a bit of a family tradition then?" Benedict let his gaze stray towards the galley-style kitchen where Nicki and her mother were putting the finishing touches to the roast dinner. "The police?"

Nicki's father glanced over his shoulder. "I guess you could call it that, yes. Although it's all changed since my day."

"And what do you do, young man?" DCI Turner turned his attention to Benedict. "And how do you know our Nicki here?"

Benedict had been expecting the question, but he could still feel the colour threatening to flood his cheeks as he prepped his answer. He'd discussed it with Nicki beforehand, neither of them feeling that divulging Benedict's true line of work would be something for the dinner table. Not with three police officers in the house — even if one was now retired.

"Shipping," he replied, hiding his face behind his wine glass. "I sell space for shipping containers on freight lines throughout the UK. All very boring stuff."

"Shipping?" The DCI's eyebrows rose. "Unusual. How did you manage to get into that? Are you a nautical person, Benedict?"

Benedict smiled, genuinely this time. "I can't even swim." Taking another sip of wine, he was grateful to see Nicki heading towards them, her face glowing from the heat of the kitchen.

"It's ready, folks. Sorry, it's going to have to be on your laps — as you can see, I don't have a dining room."

"Well, I think it's lovely — such a quaint little town-house." Anne Webster followed her daughter into the living room carrying a huge bowl of roast potatoes, which she placed on the coffee table. "I certainly don't mind eating on the sofa."

Everyone took their places, Nicki and her mother going back and forth to the kitchen to bring out the plates and cutlery. Everyone's plate was piled high with freshly carved roast beef and an assortment of vegetables.

"Help yourselves to the potatoes," announced Nicki as she collapsed onto the sofa next to Benedict, blowing a strand of hair from her face. "I won't gloat but they're my best yet."

"Shall I get you a glass of wine?" Benedict was already getting to his feet. "You look like you could do with one."

"A large one, please!"

While Benedict busied himself topping up everyone's glass, fetching a fresh bottle from the kitchen, Nicki allowed herself to lean back against the cushions and relax. She couldn't remember the last time she'd cooked a roast dinner — there wasn't usually much point with just her and Luna in the house; although Luna would happily wolf down a roast any day of the week. But it had been nice — reminding her how things used to be.

Before Deano.

"So, how did you two meet?" Nicki's father reached for the bowl of roast potatoes. "Have you been seeing each other long?"

Nicki drew her gaze away from the mantelpiece and away from Deano, grateful for the wine glass in her hand to hide behind. It was another question they had been expecting. She felt Benedict stiffen slightly as he resumed his seat next to her, grabbing his plate and spearing his fork into the roasted vegetables.

She took a swig of wine before replying, "We're not together — not like that." She flashed a glance at Benedict beside her. "We're just friends. He's helped me out with a few things — things around the house, you know?"

Hugh Webster handed the bowl of roast potatoes to his wife and picked up the gravy jug. "And how did your paths manage to cross? I can't see a lot of shipping going on in this part of the world."

Nicki took another mouthful of wine. Her head felt fuzzy from the heat of the kitchen, and the wine wasn't helping. Although they'd practised the answers to most of the questions they thought would be asked, her mind was suddenly blank. She couldn't remember what she was meant to say. How had they met? She couldn't very well tell them the truth. "Um . . ." She began blinking rapidly, as if that might somehow help. It didn't.

"I helped jump-start her car — end of last year when we had that cold snap." Benedict came to the rescue. "I was passing, had some jump leads in my car, we got talking — simple as that really." Benedict popped a carrot into his mouth. "Then we found out we had something in common — running."

Nicki almost choked on her wine.

Running.

She was certainly good at that.

She slid another sideways glance at Benedict, seeing the small smile hiding behind his fork.

He's enjoying this.

"Well, it's always good to have a man about the place, isn't it, Hugh?" Anne Webster passed the potatoes to DCI Turner. "Help yourself, Malcolm. Before they go cold."

"How has work been for you both lately?" Hugh Webster directed the question to the DCI. "I don't suppose the job gets any easier."

Malcolm Turner tipped some roast potatoes onto his plate and grimaced. "It certainly doesn't. You got out at just the right time, Hugh, I can tell you that much. Resources are stretched to their limit, and beyond. There's only so much we can do before the whole house of cards comes tumbling down around our ears."

"We saw that case you were handling at the end of last year, Nicki." Hugh Webster gave his daughter a sad smile, his eyes straying to the photograph of Deano on the mantelpiece. "It must have been hard for you. Brought back a lot of memories."

Nicki felt a piece of roast beef stick in her throat. "It was fine," she eventually managed, coughing to dislodge the meat. "We got a good result in the end."

"Nicki and her whole team did us proud." DCI Turner poured gravy onto his plate. "She wouldn't let it go, though — worked tirelessly night and day. She's definitely a Webster."

Nicki busied herself by cutting up more slices of beef on her plate. "I was just doing my job."

"You went above and beyond what was expected, Nicki. Above and beyond." Turner's voice was soft. "Which is why you're such an outstanding police officer. You clearly take after your father. Your honesty and integrity are clear for all to see."

Nicki's face darkened. She didn't feel at all honest right now. In fact, she felt the exact opposite. She was spinning such a web of lies she was sure she would trip herself up before too long. It would be so simple just to tell them — get everything off her chest and come clean. Why couldn't she tell them that Deano was alive — whereabouts currently unknown, *but alive*.

Instead, she took another swig of wine. She'd spoken to her parents more times in the last three months than she had in the last three years. If not longer. The thaw she thought she'd detected during their customary Christmas phone call had continued well into the New Year. She'd always assumed her parents held her responsible for Deano's disappearance — that they blamed her for what had happened. But in the last few weeks, and sharing a kitchen with her mother today, she'd seen a completely different side to them. They didn't blame *her*, they blamed themselves.

Spending time with them both today, she could see that they had learned to cope — with their loss and with their grief. None of it had gone away. They had just learned to live their lives without Deano.

How could she possibly burst that bubble now? It would drag everything up again in the cruellest way possible.

The Webster family had been through enough pain — they didn't deserve any more.

Eventually it was her father who saved the day. "Who's for more beef? I'll carve."

* * *

Jeremy Frost reached for the whisky he'd poured himself an hour ago but which had sat untouched on his desk as he worked. He'd been so engrossed in digging into Scott Edgecombe's past life that time had sped past in a blur. He'd needed to call in a few favours, but it hadn't been as onerous as he'd thought it would be once he got started — and even less so once he'd discovered that the family lived here in the town.

The Edgecombes had lived in Carnaby Close for the last eighteen months or so. But they didn't seem to settle in one place for too long before moving on. Not that that meant anything necessarily — though people didn't usually leave behind a life without there being a good reason for it, and usually the reason was that they had something they wanted to hide.

And once Jeremy started delving into the Edgecombes' past, all manner of secrets began to unravel.

He took a mouthful of the whisky. It burned his throat but he didn't care. He already had a fire raging in his belly with the new story — the alcohol merely gave it extra fuel.

It would be front page — had to be. Something like this was too explosive to be buried on page nine. And it might even be career-changing if he played his cards right. Maybe some of the nationals would pick it up, and then . . . who knows? Although he liked writing for the local *Gazette*, he didn't want to stay there forever. He had ambition that went far beyond reporting on potholes, local church fetes and the petty crime that inevitably popped up in a town of this size. He wanted to be at the very heart of things — *exciting* things, *newsworthy* things. Things that made people sit up and listen.

He downed the rest of the whisky and scanned the notes he'd managed to collate so far. It was a start, but it was nowhere near enough. All he had right now were the building blocks — next he needed to go on and create the story.

Glancing at his watch, he knew there was little more he could achieve tonight. He was waiting on a few call-backs, but not everyone worked Sundays like he did; he would need to wait until the morning for anything meaningful. He briefly wondered how Nicki was getting on with her parents. Picking up his phone, he considered dropping her a text, but quickly decided she probably had enough to deal with today. Instead, he reached for the whisky bottle once more and re-read his notes on Scott Edgecombe.

* * *

College Lane, Bury St Edmunds

Nicki sighed with relief and sank down into the softness of the sofa cushions.

"That went well, I think." Benedict placed two mugs of strong coffee on the low-rise table before seating himself beside her. "They're nice, your parents."

"I guess so." Nicki gave a tired smile. "That it went well, I mean — not that my parents aren't nice. They are." She rubbed her eyes, feeling the grit beneath her fingers. The tension she had felt in the build-up to today was finally leaving her body. "I feel shattered now."

"Drink this. It'll help clear your head." Benedict gestured towards the mug. "Then you can go and run yourself a bath."

Nicki reached for the coffee. "Nice thought, but I need to tackle that lot back there." She waved towards the kitchen. "I can't wake up to that kind of carnage — I need to be in work early tomorrow." Taking a mouthful of the strong, black coffee, she instantly felt guilty about taking the day off — especially as the new investigation was only a couple of days old. Part of her — a large part — felt she should have been at her desk, working. But seeing her parents for the first time in a long while wasn't something she had wanted to miss.

The lunch had gone well, and they had then spent the rest of the afternoon and evening catching up on what had been happening in each other's lives. The time had gone by surprisingly quickly, everyone feeling at ease in each other's presence. It was as if the last twenty-two years hadn't happened at all.

Nicki hugged the warm mug to her chest and closed her eyes. Her thoughts inevitably returned to the station. She couldn't very well go there now — not only was it far too late, she'd drunk too much wine and her head was spinning.

"You go have your bath — that's an order. I can sort out the kitchen."

Nicki smiled gratefully over the top of her mug. "Thanks, you're a star." After another mouthful of coffee, she added, "Do you think we did the right thing? About Deano, I mean. Not telling them what we know?"

Benedict shrugged. "That's your call, but . . . I'm not sure we really have that much to tell them. We don't know where he is yet."

Nicki shivered despite the hot mug in her hands. "I'm covering up a crime, Ben. Well — at least not reporting one when I should. The Brownings are guilty of abduction if nothing else. I should have called it in as soon as you told me about it, but . . ."

"But you couldn't quite bring yourself to believe it," finished Benedict, rising from the sofa. "It's understandable. Being cautious like that, I mean. It is a pretty 'out there' kind of story."

"One call and we could have every police force out there looking for them. Why am I not doing that?" Nicki felt herself shrug at her own question.

Benedict placed a hand under Nicki's arm and pulled her to her feet. "Now is not the time to question the wisdom of that particular decision. Go on — get upstairs and start running that bath. I'll deal with the battle scene that's masquerading as your kitchen." He gave a smile. "We can talk about Deano another time."

Nicki sighed and made her way towards the stairs. "Thanks, Ben. I'm not sure what I'd do without you here right now."

Benedict lingered in the doorway to the kitchen. He needed to tell her. And now was as good a time as any. "I've been meaning to tell you — I've had a job come through. I'll need to go away for a while — not right now, but soon. I'm not sure how long I'll be gone." He paused, sensing Nicki's disappointment. "But we'll deal with your brother first. Decide what to do next."

He watched Nicki disappear up the stairs and listened for the telltale sound of the taps being turned on in the bathroom. He'd been right to tell her about him going away. He didn't want to just disappear like he had the last time. She didn't deserve that. But the reason for his disappearance he would have to keep to himself.

It wasn't a job he particularly wanted to accept — but it was one he couldn't refuse. Jobs weren't negotiable, not at this level. The orders came in, you carried them out. That was just the way it was. And it had been that way for such a long time now, he didn't know any other kind of life.

He started to fill the sink with hot, soapy water.

So long as Nicki never found out what he was about to do, then all would be fine.

CHAPTER SIXTEEN

Pemberton Hall

He knew the man was dead — but still gave him a prod with the poker to make sure.

Dead.

He wasn't quite sure how that made him feel.

He should feel relieved. Pleased, even.

Maybe he did.

He remained where he was, hovering by the still body of Sir Cecil. Other than his own ragged breathing, there was complete silence in the room, the only sound the gentle tick-ticking of the mantelpiece clock. He glanced down at his hands.

At least he'd had the foresight to wear gloves.

But he didn't need the clock to tell him that he needed to act quickly. That he needed to get out of there.

With another glance at the dead body by his feet, he made his way over to the window that looked out onto the landscaped gardens beyond. He knew no one could possibly see inside — there was no one around for miles. But it still made him shiver. He glanced back at Sir Cecil's body and a form of clarity and order started to return.

He needed to get rid of the body.

His mind started to race.

Although he knew the house to be empty, he didn't want to stay a second longer than he needed to. It didn't look like there had been too much disruption to the drawing room itself — the chairs were still upright, the man's brandy glass still sitting on the fireside table.

But he needed to get rid of the body.

Dead bodies began to smell after a while — and who knew what visitors made it up to Pemberton Hall these days. He couldn't guarantee they wouldn't get disturbed and he couldn't risk the man being found too soon. He'd watched enough of those true crime TV shows to know that clues were always left behind, no matter how careful you think you might have been. *Every contact leaves a trace*, wasn't that what they said?

Pulling a tartan rug from one of the high-backed armchairs near to the fire, he laid it on the floor next to Sir Cecil and began to roll up the body like a stick of rock. The cast-iron poker, with what looked like blood on its tip, still lay by Sir Cecil's side. He picked it up with a gloved hand and tucked it inside the blanket.

Sweeping the room through squinted eyes, he saw nothing else out of place. Nothing to suggest what had happened.

As he bent down to grab hold of the rug, his eyes caught the graffiti on the wall above the sideboard. A smile teased his lips — it was good work. Maybe some of it would look good on his headstone — if anyone ever found him.

Grabbing the end of the rug, he began to pull the body towards the door.

* * *

Monday 11 March 2019
Carnaby Close, Bury St Edmunds

Lana found herself looking out of the upstairs bedroom window for the umpteenth time that night. Scott still wasn't home, and it was now past 1 a.m. Not that that in itself was all that unusual, not these days, but it was starting to worry her.

Scott would always worry her, she knew that much. She would never be able to relax, not really. Never be able to sit back and say her job was done, no matter how old he was. She'd come to terms with that a long time ago. She'd had to.

There were certain sides to his character that would always have the potential to lead him down dark paths; *the wrong paths.*

You're mixing with the wrong people — she could hear herself saying it as she stared out of the window. *They're a bad influence.*

But she knew that Scott was no longer her little boy. He was a grown man in charge of his own mind, his own decisions, his own actions. *Which was exactly what worried her.*

There was no mistaking the fact he was being even more distant than usual, spending every moment of his free time with the gang from the estate. And then there were the steroids. His demeanour had changed in recent weeks, just like it had when he got sucked into it the last time. He was sullen and argumentative, more secretive as the days went by.

She cast another look out of the window. She knew it was pointless. Scott would come home when he was good and ready. But she just needed to know he was safe — and not doing anything stupid.

Which inevitably led her to thinking once more about the Trouble.

It was like night following day, sunshine following rain. She always ended up thinking about the Trouble.

Although it was some twelve years ago now, it felt like yesterday. She'd always told herself that she hadn't seen it coming — that she'd never once thought her precious son could be capable of doing something like that. But had that really been the truth? Had she really been all that surprised? She'd had fifteen long years to think about it.

Lana shuddered. If she had thought him capable, then surely that meant she was to blame too?

But she *couldn't* have known, could she? Not about something like that.

Shuddering once again, she resumed looking out of the window and willed Scott to return home.

* * *

The Moreton Hall Pub, Bury St Edmunds

Water.

That was the best way to dispose of a body, wasn't it?

Shallow graves were always dug up by some yapping, over-excited dog; bodies in ditches inevitably disturbed by inquisitive ramblers. And he certainly didn't have the stomach for cutting the man into pieces — he wasn't a butcher, for Christ's sake. Burning wasn't a particularly attractive option, either. He had no idea what a burning human body would smell like, but he was sure it wouldn't be pleasant. Or very discreet.

So, that just left water.

But the town wasn't blessed with too many waterways.

He could travel further afield, but that would involve driving for miles with a dead body in the boot. He would be outside his comfort zone, heading into the unknown, which was when you made mistakes.

And he'd made enough of those already.

He knew the cameras in the vicinity of the pub weren't working — there had been something about it in the local paper. Back at Pemberton Hall, a plan of sorts had flickered into his head, quickly multiplying as he'd loaded Sir Cecil's body into the back of the car. The man was of average height, his body still warm and malleable. It didn't take much effort to get him loaded into the boot and out of sight.

He'd then waited until the early hours of the morning so he wouldn't be seen, Sir Cecil's body trussed up in the boot of the car.

When he'd eventually set off, the journey to the pub didn't take long, the streets deserted as most people were safely tucked up in their beds at that time of night. Arriving at the pub, he'd pulled the car up as close as he could and stepped out into the chill. It was more awkward getting the body out of the boot than it had been getting it in — but he eventually heaved the man onto his shoulders and staggered towards the pond. The surface looked quiet and calm, inviting almost.

Negotiating the wooden fence that surrounded the pond had been easy enough, and he dropped Sir Cecil's body into the water. It made little or no sound as it slipped in, barely causing a ripple.

CHAPTER SEVENTEEN

Monday 11 March 2019
The Moreton Hall Pub, Bury St Edmunds

Nicki pulled the Toyota into the car park and killed the engine. Through the windscreen, she could easily see the activity on the other side of the pond. Exiting the car, she trudged towards the crime scene tape that already cordoned off the area, nodding at the lone PC with the logging clipboard. Ahead of her, she saw DS Fox. He made his way towards her.

"Morning, boss."

Nicki tried to smile but could barely manage a grimace. The early morning wake-up call hadn't been welcome. She'd had a fitful night's sleep at best; the relaxing bath hadn't done its job, and once in bed she'd tossed and turned until well after four a.m. when her body finally decided to succumb.

"Morning, Graham," she managed. "What do we know so far?"

"Call came in around six-fifty from a member of staff turning up for work." Fox flipped over a page in his notebook. "Young woman by the name of Ella Webb was walking past the pond, heading for the main entrance, when she saw something floating in the water. Initially she thought it might just be some rubbish blown in by the wind, or maybe some fly tipping — there's been a spate of that in the area lately. But when she got closer, she saw the plastic bag floating, and then the body beneath."

"And we're sure?" Nicki gestured over the detective sergeant's shoulder towards the pond. "Who it is, I mean? We're sure it's him?"

Fox gave a slow nod. "I don't think there's any doubt about that. He's a pretty recognisable face around here — even if said face has been underwater for however long."

"Well, we need to keep that little gem away from the media for the moment. I don't want all hell breaking loose before we've started to piece together what might have happened to him."

Nicki headed towards the white forensic tent that had been erected next to the pond, masking what lay inside from prying eyes. Not that there were many of those around at this hour — the pub wasn't due to open for another three hours. Fox followed.

"This here is Ella," he said, as they passed the entrance. A young woman hovered by the open door, ashen-faced.

Nicki nodded a greeting as she passed. "Morning, Ella. Sorry you had to deal with this today."

Ella gave a shudder. "Can I make a coffee for anyone?"

Fox's eyes lit up. "That would be brilliant, thanks. Two sugars for me."

Nicki smiled. "Sure. If Charlie is around, can you let him know I'll pop in for a word in a bit?" Nicki knew Charlie Dorner, landlord of the pub, very well, and she was sure that this morning's discovery would be a headache he could do without.

Ella nodded and scuttled back inside, probably glad to have something constructive to do rather than watching the macabre performance currently being played out before her.

Nicki continued towards the tent, just as a familiar figure backed out of it.

"Hey." Caz pulled her elasticated hood down and headed in Nicki's direction. "You heard the news, then?"

Nicki's eyes trailed over the pathologist's shoulder "We're sure it's him?" It was the second time she'd asked that question in as many minutes. "A hundred per cent?"

Caz stepped to the side as two crime scene investigators passed by, the flaps of the forensic tent pulled back. She gestured towards the gap. "See for yourself."

Nicki didn't have to step any closer. Even from this distance the man's identity was unmistakable.

Sir Cecil Pemberton.

Dead.

* * *

Carnaby Close, Bury St Edmunds

Erin pulled her chunky knitted cardigan around her as she hurried across the road. There was a chill in the air accompanying the strengthening breeze. She clutched the handful of leaflets tightly in her hand, not wanting a sudden gust to wrench them from her clutches and scatter them to the four corners of the town. She had wondered if coming out this early was such a good idea, but she'd been up half the night printing the damned things, so she might as well see it through.

She posted a leaflet through each door along Carnaby Close but, when she got to the flats, the door to number twelve opened before she could reach the letterbox.

"Well, well, well, what do we have here?" Glenn Clifford plucked the leaflet from Erin's outstretched fingers. "My, my — a leaflet! That'll put the fear of god into the man!"

Erin gave him a withering look. "At least I'm trying to do something," she replied, curtly.

"Oh, I'm not knockin' it, darlin' — I'm just not sure Sir Cecil gives a flying monkey's how many leaflets you litter the streets with. Anyhow . . ." He gave a grin and gestured towards the bundle of papers in her hand and the bulging bag over her shoulder, "I thought you were an environmentalist? How many trees did you chop down for this lot?"

Erin's eyes narrowed. "They're made from recycled paper, I'll have you know."

"Of course they are." Clifford grinned some more. "I believe you."

Just then, the sound of a car disturbed the morning quiet. Both turned their heads to see a Skoda estate car speeding towards them, coming to a sudden halt outside the houses opposite. At that moment, the door next to number twelve swung open.

"Not that wretched car again." Clifford's neighbour Eileen's face bristled. "He comes and goes at all hours of the day and night in that thing." She nodded across the street towards the mud-splattered car. "It's an eyesore. I pity his mother, I really do."

Scott Edgecombe exited the car, his gym bag on his shoulder. "What's your problem?" he shouted, glaring towards the welcoming party. "Want a picture?" Head down, he charged towards his front door.

"He's up and about early," muttered the old woman. "Up to no good, no doubt."

Erin handed Eileen one of the leaflets and hurried on by. She had no desire to get caught up in another row with Glenn Clifford, and Eileen Harris's constant moaning would only grate on her nerves.

* * *

The Moreton Hall Pub, Bury St Edmunds

Caz and Nicki nursed their coffees at the bar.

"You'll need to remain shut while the crime scene investigators are here." Nicki sipped her cappuccino and afforded the landlord of the pub a sympathetic smile. "I can't say how long it'll be, but I'm sure they'll be as quick as they can."

Charlie nodded from behind the bar. "It's fine. I don't think any of us feel like opening up today anyway. I've already sent Ella home."

"Good idea. We'll let you know when you can re-open." Nicki watched Charlie head back towards the kitchen. Once out of earshot, she turned to Caz. "Anything more you can tell me about the body so far? Other than his identity?"

Caz made a face. "I won't know if he drowned until I examine him back at the mortuary, but I did note a couple of sizeable head wounds. I can't say if they were caused by him falling in, or if they were present beforehand. There were some additional facial injuries, too. I'll do the usual toxicology and bloods."

"He reported an assault in the street on Friday." Nicki wiped cappuccino froth from her upper lip. "I'll check the report to see exactly what injuries were sustained. From memory I think it was a suspected broken nose, or at least a bloody one. Maybe some other scrapes. Not sure if there was any mention of a head injury, though."

"I should be able to tell you pretty quickly if the injuries had anything to do with his death. I'll schedule the post-mortem for later today. You want to send someone down?"

"Probably. Give us a call when you know what time it'll be." The thought of attending a post-mortem didn't fill Nicki with much joy. After such a disrupted night's sleep, it was the last thing she fancied. "I'll send one of the team along."

"Far be it for me to speculate, but if this turns out to be a suspicious death, I dare say there'll be plenty of people in the frame for it." Caz's eyes sparkled over the rim of her coffee mug. "It's no great secret that he wasn't exactly the most popular guy on the planet."

Nicki had already thought as much herself once she'd heard, and then seen, who the victim was. Usually, with a suspicious death, you would dig into the victim's background — find out who their enemies were, who they might have rubbed up the wrong way immediately before their death. For Sir Cecil, that list was likely to be a long one.

"Can't say I'm looking forward to wading through the possibilities," she agreed, draining her mug. "I'd better get going — rouse the troops."

Caz joined her in heading for the door. "How did yesterday go, anyway?"

Yesterday.

With the early morning call from the station, yesterday now seemed like weeks ago. "It was . . ." Nicki hesitated, hand on the door. "It was actually very good. Fun, even."

Caz raised her eyebrows as they stepped outside. "Well, you can update me tonight. Catch you later." With that, the pathologist headed towards the rear car park, leaving Nicki to head over to where she had left the Toyota.

Pulling out her phone, she started to let the team know the news.

They had another one.

CHAPTER EIGHTEEN

Bury St Edmunds Police Station

"What do we know about him? Other than what's appeared in the media, obviously." Nicki looked pensively towards her team.

DS Fox slid a piece of paper out from the pile on his desk. "The family have owned Pemberton Hall for generations — Sir Cecil lived there as a child, but was sent away to boarding school, and then on to university. Multi-millionaire, by all accounts — mostly inherited money, but he is known for his land and property investments. I won't go into the obvious unrest his recent planning proposals have caused in the town — it's well documented in the local press. But I did stumble across something interesting."

"Go on."

"Well — and I stress this is just supposition — a rumour was circulating a while back, not long after Sir Cecil moved permanently back to Pemberton Hall after his father's death." Fox paused. "It seems that some people were hinting that maybe not all was as it seemed with the demise of the previous occupant. Some even dared to suggest that Sir Cecil himself had had a hand in it — hurried it along, so to speak."

"Killed him, you mean?"

Fox shrugged. "Like I said, it was just a rumour that appeared in one of those online chat forums. I don't think it was pursued any further. They probably didn't fancy being on the wrong end of a libel case. But, reading between the lines, that was what was being suggested. Seems like there were more than a few people who considered Sir Cecil might have wanted his father out of the way sooner rather than later — to help shore up some of his rumoured financial worries."

"Do we know if there's any credence in that? Was he definitely having money troubles?"

Another shrug. "No idea. It was just something mentioned in one of the forums — as far as I know, it never progressed further than just online chatter. We can delve into his financial affairs if you think it's worth it? It was no secret that the old man was ill, and not expected to live much longer in any case. Reports say he'd seen a doctor just the day before he died — so I don't think his death was totally unexpected. Sooner, maybe, but not unexpected."

Nicki frowned. "Make a note about the financials — we might need to take a look. But if he did help his father on his way, then do we think this could be a motive for Sir Cecil's own murder? An aggrieved family member maybe?"

Fox consulted his paperwork again. "According to preliminary checks, there don't appear to be any family members to speak of. Sir Cecil was an only child, and he didn't have any offspring. Never been married. I think there may be some distant cousins somewhere, but it's not a big family."

"Dig around just the same. Find the next of kin, or at least the closest living relatives he has. Someone might know something. All families have secrets." Nicki went up to a fresh whiteboard and began writing details of what they knew so far — which wasn't much. "While we're waiting for the post-mortem to be scheduled later today — and, Graham, I'd like you to pop along to that one — let's get the preliminaries underway. CCTV from the roads around the pub is a priority — although I'm told those in immediate proximity were out of order." After she'd finished writing, she turned back to face the team "And take another look at the assault complaint from Friday — just in case they're connected in some way. Oh, and let me know what injuries Sir Cecil reported at the time, so we know which ones pre-dated his death."

"What about the Calvin Shaw case?" DS Carter looked up from his computer screen. "Do you want us to focus on Sir Cecil today?"

Nicki shook her head. "No — we need to press ahead with Calvin, too. What else is new on that front?"

"I spent most of yesterday going through some of the CCTV and other reports coming in from the local DIY retailers that have sold similar coils of rope in recent weeks." Roy tapped his computer monitor. "Some were more agreeable than others to divulge the information. I've already discounted quite a few."

"Good. Keep on that today. We mustn't lose sight of the fact that the rope might lead us somewhere in relation to Calvin's death. We need to make sure we don't get sidetracked with this new investigation." Nicki heard her phone chirp with an incoming message. She glanced at the screen, then frowned. "Hold that thought, though, Roy. Faye is up at Pemberton Hall. Initial visit raised some questions, so she's pulling in a full team. Let's head up there and see what's what."

* * *

Stainsby Hotel, Rochdale

Mason's heart stilled.

Dad had taken the van out not long after breakfast, heading to the services nearby to fill up with petrol — a sure sign that they were moving on again. They'd only been here two nights, and hadn't even unpacked properly this time. The van was now back in the hotel car park, but Dad had gone out in search of newspapers and an up-to-date road atlas, saying something about not trusting the sat nav.

After breakfast, Mum had taken a sleeping tablet and gone back to bed for a lie down. She was doing a lot of that lately. Mason had been asked to keep an eye on her, so he'd settled himself down at the cheap hotel room desk, watching the reassuring rise and fall of the thin duvet that covered her slight frame.

He'd flicked on the TV for something to do, keeping the sound turned down so as not to disturb her, but there was nothing worth watching on the bunch of free channels that came with the room. Then he'd tried to find something to read, but all he could find in the hotel drawers were a tourist's guide to Lancashire and a copy of a Gideons Bible.

His head thumping from a restless night's sleep, he'd decided to try and find a packet of painkillers. It was then that he'd rummaged through Dad's bag — the one he kept by the side of the bed.

And found the folder.

He leafed through the bundle of newspaper articles, and with each fresh cutting his hand trembled a little bit more. One after the other slipped through his fingers — tabloids, broadsheets, local newspapers, even magazines. *There were so many.*

But they all had one thing in common.

Mason pulled out one of the cuttings, looking at the face staring back at him from the newsprint. He was under no illusion who the face belonged to.

It was him.

It was him as a five-year-old boy.

Mason skimmed the rest of the article, the words swirling in front of his eyes.

Missing.

Abducted.

Presumed dead.

Mason's heart hammered, his stomach clenching. Presumed dead? He pulled more cuttings from the folder, his hands shaking harder with the touch of each one. Headlines jumped off the pages — '*snatched*', '*missing*', '*paedophile ring*' — quickly followed by '*murdered*', '*killer*', '*sex offenders*'.

Blinking rapidly, Mason turned his wide-eyed gaze towards his mother's still form beneath the duvet. He'd always known Annette and Larry weren't his real parents, his own mum and dad having died in an accident when he was a child, along with his sister. He didn't remember much from those days — his first real childhood memory was Annette's warm hand enveloping his own, drawing him in close and telling him that *everything was going to be all right*.

He could distinctly remember that day; it was cold and he could see his breath billowing out in front of him like a fluffy white cloud as he cried. Then he heard Annette's voice, soft and kind, telling him that he needed to be a big, brave boy and come and live with them.

They would take care of him now.

They would love him like their own.

Mason read the articles again, feeling his blood turning to ice in his veins.

Snatched.

Murdered.

He picked out another cutting. This one had several other images lined up next to his own cheeky five-year-old grin.

It was them — his real parents. It had to be.

Mason felt his whole world shift.

Maybe his parents weren't dead.

They certainly hadn't had an accident like he'd been led to believe all those years ago.

That meant they could still be alive.

* * *

Pemberton Hall

Nicki and DS Carter stood in front of the antique sideboard in Sir Cecil's drawing room, their white protective suits rustling as they moved.

148

"Quite to the point," commented Roy, nodding towards the spray paint adorning the wall.

'*Die, you fucker.*'

'*Burn in hell.*'

Nicki agreed. "So it would seem."

The graffiti was in a variety of colours — red, blue, yellow and green — the letters stretching some twelve inches high or more, covering just about the whole wall.

"Looks like they missed one." Roy pointed towards a stray can that had rolled beneath the sideboard, a small plastic forensic marker by its side. "Maybe they were in a hurry or were disturbed."

With the scene of crime investigators doing their thing, Nicki and Roy edged out of the drawing room, keeping to the metal stepping plates provided. Faye was taking a video of the scene which the team would view later, an important element in trying to piece together what may have happened in Sir Cecil's drawing room. As they walked, Nicki noted the plush carpet underfoot. There appeared to be muddied footprints at regular intervals, but Nicki knew the surface was unlikely to give them much usable evidence.

As she made her way to the door, Nicki took a final sweep of the room. Faye had informed her that there looked to have been an altercation of some sort — she'd found some darkened stains that could possibly be blood visible on the hearth, and a discarded, half-smoked cigar had burned a hole into the rug. It was possible this was the room in which Sir Cecil had met his end — assuming he didn't drown, of course.

Two crime scene investigators were busy taking swabs — they would know soon enough if they were looking at blood. Nicki saw the open box of Cuban cigars on a small nest of tables by the side of a large wing-backed armchair. The half-smoked one lying on the rug would most likely belong to Sir Cecil rather than any assailant — dropped in haste when confronted by his attacker? It was possible.

Leaving Faye and her team to continue processing the room, Nicki and Roy found their way back out into the passageway that led away from the drawing room. Nicki had never been one for stately homes, but her parents had been fully paid up members of the National Trust, and as a child she could remember being dragged around many an old and dusty house. As she walked, old memories began to stir — of Deano running along stone passages and ducking beneath the carefully roped off areas, an impish grin on his face.

Nicki shook them away. Now was not the time to be thinking about Deano.

The drawing room hadn't been particularly warm, but at least there was some evidence that the fire in the grate had been recently lit. The rest of the house had an icy chill to it, together with a musty, unloved smell that clung to the heavy drape curtains as they passed. They poked their heads into various rooms on the ground floor, but most looked like they were uninhabited by Sir Cecil — some even had a succession of white sheets covering the furniture beneath.

When they had arrived at Pemberton Hall, two possible points of entry had already been identified. One was a window that had been forced open at the rear of the house, and the other was a wooden door that was unlocked. Both areas were dusted for fingerprints and footprints, and closely examined for any other fibres or signs of who might have entered the house uninvited.

After walking around much of the ground floor, Nicki and Roy headed back to the drawing room. As soon as they stepped back inside, Faye made a beeline for them. "Nicki? This might be something of interest." She held out a plastic evidence bag. "Found behind the armchair next to the fireplace, tucked under the corner of the rug."

Nicki took the evidence bag, immediately recognising the contents.

"Well, I'll be damned," breathed Roy, peering over her shoulder.

* * *

Alive.

Mason gripped the cutting tighter. It made no sense — yet at the same time it made perfect sense.

Placing the bag back down by the bed, he turned to face the person he'd called his mother for the last twenty-two years. She was fast asleep, though Mason was convinced she must be able to hear his fast-beating heart from beneath her duvet.

This was why she'd been looking so frail recently, he thought, edging around the bed. Why she'd been a bag of nerves, jumping at the slightest noise like a nervous kitten. *This* was the secret they'd both been keeping from him all this time.

The reason they were running.

Running.

Mason reached the window and nudged the curtains aside. The van was still there, but there was no sign of Dad anywhere.

Dad.

Even the word felt wrong now.

His real dad could very well be alive, out there somewhere, wondering where he was.

Alive.

Mason ran for the door.

CHAPTER NINETEEN

West Suffolk Mortuary

Caz pulled the overhead light down, focusing the intense beam onto the man's face. Unlike a good proportion of the bodies that ended up on her mortuary slab, there was no mystery as to this one's identity. There may well be mystery surrounding how they came to end up here, but not who they were.

Sir Cecil Pemberton.

One of the most recognised faces in the town — maybe even beyond. You would've had to have lived under a rock for the last few months not to be aware of who he was.

Was.

For Sir Cecil Pemberton was no more.

DS Graham Fox stood silently by the side of the exam-ination table. Caz had remarked how well he looked now, having mostly recovered from his injuries and dispensed with the use of his walking cane. She'd received a polite nod in response, the man's face taut with concentration. Sometimes she forgot what post-mortems were like for others — and from the look on Fox's face, she guessed he would rather be anywhere else than standing here right now. She smiled. "Ready, detective?"

After receiving another wordless nod, she activated her recording device and began. "A Caucasian male, known to be aged fifty-six. Height one hundred and seventy-nine centimetres. Weight seventy-five kilos. External examination shows the body to be in reasonable health. BMI within normal parameters. Noticeable external injuries are limited to the upper limbs, torso and head. Taking the upper limbs first . . ." Caz paused, taking Sir Cecil's right arm in her gloved hands. "On the right side we have a series of contusions on the forearm. Each looks consistent with blunt force trauma. Not forceful enough to break the skin — it may well have been that the victim's clothing prevented skin breakage." Caz placed the right arm down and picked up the left. "Similar contusions to the left forearm plus noticeable lacerations to the dorsal side of the left hand." She gestured towards the mortuary technician to bring over a sample tube. "Swabs taken for analysis."

Caz then stood back to allow the technician to take a series of photographs of each set of contusions. "The injuries on both forearms could be consistent with defensive wounds." Photographs complete, she resumed her place by the side of the examination table. "The torso shows heavy bruising around both flanks and the lower back. Looks more consistent with a kicking, this time, but the contusions look slightly older. Possibly forty-eight hours or more."

Caz's gaze then travelled to Sir Cecil's face. "Most of the more serious external injuries are located on the victim's head." Leaning in, she used a gloved hand to tilt the man's head to the side. "There is a clearly visible wound to the temporal region on the left side. Deep contusion and a possible fracture beneath — this will be confirmed in due course." Keeping hold of Sir Cecil's head in one hand, she gestured to the technician to assist her in rotating the body onto its side. "The occipital area also shows an extensive open wound, again with a suspected fracture beneath, to be confirmed in due course."

Caz and the technician returned Sir Cecil's body back to the examination table. "We then have a less extensive wound to the left maxilla area, plus superficial abrasions to the central forehead and external nose. Nasal swelling and a healing laceration suggests a possible fracture. There is some skin loss over the maxilla injury — samples and swabs will be taken for routine analysis." The technician brought more sample tubes over.

Caz knew Sir Cecil's head had been encased in a plastic bag when they dragged his body from the pond, the significance of which was still unclear. Just from the external examination alone, she didn't believe asphyxiation was the likely cause of death for this one.

The bag had been removed at the scene to aid identification and had already been spirited away to the forensic lab in a secure evidence bag. DNA evidence would degrade if it was submerged in water for long enough, and Caz wondered if the killer might have inadvertently done them a favour in using the bag. Placing it over the victim's head like that may well have gone some way to preserving forensic detail.

Time would tell.

External examination complete, she glanced towards DS Fox, his face still concentrating on the body. She picked up her scalpel. "Let's see what we can find on the inside, shall we?"

* * *

Bury St Edmunds Police Station

Nicki tacked a photograph of a small section of coiled rope to the whiteboard. "This rope was found beneath a rug in the drawing room at Pemberton Hall. Tests are being carried out but I think it far too much of a coincidence for this not to be the same rope that was used to string up Calvin Shaw."

"So we're looking at the same killer?" voiced Matt, chewing the end of his pen. "For both Calvin and Sir Cecil?"

"As far as I know, there's no suggestion Sir Cecil had any rope on his body when he was pulled from the pond, but

I'm having the divers go in later today to see if they can find anything." Nicki tapped her biro against her chin. "But why would there be a similar type of rope at the two locations if they weren't connected in some way? Faye and her team seem increasingly convinced that the drawing room was where Sir Cecil met his attacker. The stains on the fireplace are certainly blood. But we need to be cautious. We'll treat them as separate cases for now. If we get firm evidence to the contrary, then we'll reassess." Nicki let her voice trail off. Were they looking at two completely independent cases here? Until they knew the cause of death for Sir Cecil, anything was possible.

But the rope changed things.

Nicki glanced back at the whiteboard, sighing. "And as much as it pains me to say it, we need to draw up a list of Sir Cecil's enemies. People who didn't like him." She flashed what she hoped was a humorous grin at the team. "I know it's going to be a rather long list, judging by what's been in the media in recent weeks, but the answer might just be in there somewhere. And then we cross reference those with anyone who might have any type of connection with Calvin Shaw. If there is anything to link the two, however tenuous, we need to find it.

"Matt, keep looking at cameras in the immediate vicinity of the pub. Whoever took Sir Cecil there had to have used some kind of vehicle. We know the cameras closest to the scene weren't working, so check neighbouring streets." Nicki received a nod in response. "Roy, you carry on looking into the rope, but also check out the cameras close to Calvin's flat."

"I've discounted a few more DIY stores. Those customers that paid by card were easy to identify, and I've spoken to a few already — they all have alibis and I don't feel fit the criteria of who we're looking for." Roy pulled out his notebook. "I've only got a few more left to check, plus some more CCTV, for the time scale we've used."

Nicki nodded then glanced at the wall clock. "Good. Keep at it — the answer could very well be there somewhere.

Graham should be back from the mortuary soon. We'll have another briefing later when hopefully we might have some more news."

* * *

Caz reached for the packet of chocolate digestives and ripped off the wrapping. She needed a sugar hit, fast, and her love for this particular brand of biscuit was well known throughout the mortuary. Some found it odd that she could eat so soon after completing a post-mortem; only minutes before, her hands had been inside the body of a dead human being, removing their organs, slicing open their stomach to reveal its acidic contents.

But Caz was able to compartmentalise. She had to. The minute she shed the plastic apron, the rubber boots, the elasticated cap, she was Caz again. Not pathologist Caz. Just ordinary Caz — the thirty-something slightly-mad woman with a craving for chocolate.

And right now, that particular Caz was hungry.

The sugar soon hit the spot and, suitably refreshed, she reached for her phone and called Nicki's number.

"He didn't drown," she said, once the call was connected. "Your man from the pond. He didn't drown."

"You're sure?"

"Hundred per cent. No classic signs of drowning were evident — no frothing in the airways, no water in his lungs, no water damage to any of the air spaces. I could go on, but I won't bore you with the technicalities. All you need to know is that he was dead before he hit the water." Before Nicki could comment, Caz continued, "But what I did find were two skull fractures — one on the side, one on the back of the head."

"And which one killed him?"

"Either one could have, but my money would be on the occipital fracture — the one at the back. The blow to the side could have knocked him off his feet, stunned him maybe, but

I don't think it was fatal. The blow to the back of the head would definitely have got him. Cause of death — fractured skull with massive associated brain haemorrhage." Caz bit into a fresh biscuit. "There were other more superficial injuries to his face — a fractured nose with a healing laceration, and also an open wound on his cheek. Although I think the nasal fracture is probably older."

Nicki had looked at the report into the assault on Sir Cecil and noted the injuries he'd sustained — possible fractured nose, abrasions to forehead and nose. It fitted. Apart from the wound to the cheek. "Time of death?"

"I would estimate somewhere between 6 p.m. on the Sunday night, and when he was found early this morning."

"Anything else?"

"Some defensive wounds on both forearms, but I can't accurately date them. They may have been older."

"And the plastic bag?" added Nicki. "He definitely wasn't suffocated with it?"

"No signs of asphyxiation at all. The bag was put on post-mortem — after he died. I'm not really sure of the relevance of it but it could very possibly have helped preserve the head from the effects of the water. You might get some results from the lab if you're lucky."

"Thanks, Caz. Any idea how long he might have been in the water?"

Caz crunched her way through the digestive. "Not long. My guess would be only a few hours at the very most. You're lucky the body didn't sink — it may have got caught on something as it went in. I've sent the usual samples away — skin and tissue scrapings, bloods and swabs. I've done a toxicology screen, too. DNA will degrade in water, but you might get lucky."

Nicki sighed as she ended the call. She felt luck was something they would need in shed loads if they were going to crack this one anytime soon.

CHAPTER TWENTY

Rochdale Town Centre

Mason ran blindly through the torrential rain. His shirt was drenched through, clinging to his skin, his hair plastered to his scalp. He had no idea where he was going and he didn't much care. Nothing mattered, not anymore. Not since he'd found the cuttings.

Dean Webster.

As soon as he'd seen the name written in newsprint, he'd known. It was as if someone had turned on a tap — memories started to freefall out of control, in their most painful and raw form. As traumatised as he must have been, it wasn't surprising that he'd managed to push Dean Webster to the back of his young, developing mind. After Annette and Larry had come into his life, he'd slowly closed his mind to the past, packing it up and hiding it away so it could no longer hurt him.

Then he had simply grown up as Mason Browning, allowing himself to be nurtured by his captors and shaped into the little boy they so desperately wanted him to be.

And, just like that, Dean Webster was no more.

The avalanche of memories continued to tumble as Mason ran along the pavement. Tears streaked his cheeks, mixing with the rainwater pelting from the skies above, but still he blundered on.

He had no clue where he was heading — only that he needed to get away from whatever tangled web Annette and Larry had woven. As he ran, more and more of the thoughts cluttering his mind started to make some form of sense.

The constant moving; the constant tension; the constant feeling that something wasn't quite right. Then there was the changing of the van's registration plates; the nondescript hotels; the inescapable conclusion that they were running away from *something*.

And now he knew just what that something was.

The past.

His past.

His past as Dean Webster.

He'd left the newspaper cuttings in the folder in Dad's bag, exactly as he'd found them — although he couldn't resist taking just a couple with him. Ducking into the doorway of a betting shop, out of the driving rain, he worked to steady his laboured breathing. Pulling his wallet from the back pocket of his soaked jeans, he slid out one of the two articles he'd salvaged.

'*FAIRGROUND HORROR — BOY SNATCHED.*'

Fairground.

Even with the rainwater dripping from the end of his nose, Mason felt he could once again smell the now-familiar aroma of fried onions and hot dogs, popcorn and candyfloss. Was *this* why they were such deep-seated memories, haunting him in his dreams? Aromas that he'd last smelled just before his five-year-old world had imploded and changed forever? There must be some psychological study somewhere on how, at the very moment of a sudden and traumatic event, certain memories were frozen in time and preserved in the deep subconscious.

He could even hear it now. The tinkling of the bells on the roundabouts; the delighted screams of the children as they thundered down the helter-skelter. Even the 'roll-up, roll-up' from the fairground workers as they tried to entice you onto that one last ride.

Mason clutched the sides of his pounding head, suddenly assaulted by everything he'd experienced that fateful day back in November 1996.

* * *

Thursday 7 November 1996
Little Wynham Fair

The smell of fried onions was making him feel sick now. His tummy hurt.

Dean Webster let himself be led away from the caterpillar ride, his bobble hat pulled firmly down over his head. "Mummy?" he cried, chin wobbling. "Where's Mummy?"

The hand was warm — he could feel that even through his woollen mittens. The woman pulled him through the crowd, away from the caterpillar ride, away from everything.

"Mummy?" he repeated, his voice shaking as he stumbled after her. "Where's Mummy?"

As they reached a quieter part of the fairground, the woman stopped and turned towards him, kneeling down so she could look him straight in the eyes. Her face was kind, her cheeks pink from the cold, and she had a nice smile.

"Do you understand what I've just told you?" She gave his mittened hand another soft squeeze. "About Mummy and Daddy?"

Dean started to shake his head, his bottom lip trembling. "N . . . no . . . no. Where's Mummy? I want Mummy."

The woman enveloped him in another hug, pulling his chilled face towards her woollen scarf. Dean sniffed, breathing in the scent of perfume mixed with sweet caramel.

"You poor, poor little thing. Come here." The hug tightened. "But everything will be all right now. You're safe. I've got you. Nothing bad will happen to you now."

Tears blurred Dean's vision. The woman had said something about Mummy and Daddy, and his sister, but he couldn't remember what it was now. None of the words made any sense to his five-year-old brain. "I want my mummy," he sobbed. "I want my mummy."

"I know you do, poppet." The woman wiped away his tears with a gloved finger, shushing him all the time. "But Mummy and Daddy aren't here anymore, my sweet. They've had an accident and gone to heaven. Your sister, too. But you don't need to worry — you poor little thing. You're going to be just fine. I've got you now. *Everything* is going to be just fine."

And that was the day the whole world shifted for little Dean Webster.

* * *

Monday 11 March 2019
Rochdale Town Centre

Mason pulled out the second article he'd taken from the folder. This one was dated 1 November last year and it was about the investigation into the disappearance of a little boy called Lucas Jackson.

Another fairground.

Another missing child.

But that wasn't what had drawn Mason's attention to the cutting.

It was the picture of the detective inspector leading the investigation — her photo front and centre of the article. He'd known it was her the minute he saw it. He couldn't explain how. But it was definitely her.

Detective Inspector Nicki Hardcastle.

His sister.

* * *

Roy settled down behind his computer monitor and let the images play through once more. He'd spent the last two and a half hours trawling through reel after reel of the remaining camera footage from the DIY stores in a thirty-mile radius of the town. It was slow going but he'd almost got to the end of the list now. The likelihood of finding what they were looking for was relatively slim — painfully slim, if the truth be told — but it had to be done. If only just to cross it off the list.

The rope used to string up Calvin's dead body was a multi-purpose polypropylene variety sold by hundreds of stores. The only slight chink of light was that it looked relatively new, so it was possible it had been recently purchased. But purchased where, nobody really knew. *Most likely online*, mused Roy, as he took another mouthful of coffee in a vain attempt to keep his eyes open and glued to the screen. Which made this whole pantomime a spectacular waste of time.

He dunked the end of a KitKat biscuit into his coffee and watched the minutes roll by. He had one more reel to look at. Most of the DIY stores had been amenable to providing details of anyone purchasing a similar coil of rope, and those that had paid by card transactions were easy to eliminate with a quick phone call. Which left just one more store to go.

The images Roy was currently concentrating on came from a security camera located at an independent DIY store situated several miles out of town. The store had grudgingly confirmed that a coil of rope was purchased two weeks ago and that the customer had paid by cash, which instantly put Roy on the back foot.

The camera was centred on aisle seven, which, from the grainy images, appeared to house any number of random household and DIY items, ranging from ironing boards to stepladders. But Roy wasn't interested in those — his eye had been caught by the small section that displayed cable ties, metal chains and rope.

Rope.

The shop had opened at eight o'clock that morning and Roy fast forwarded to the correct time frame for the rope purchase. As he did so, he yawned and reached for another KitKat. Then, as the grainy footage played on, he saw it.

Hand hovering over the mouse, he clicked to freeze the image. A lone figure dressed in a dark hoodie had initially wandered along the aisle without breaking his stride, quickly disappearing out of camera shot.

But then he was back.

And he stopped directly in front of the rope section.

One of the ropes on sale looked to be very similar to the blue polypropylene variety that had ended up wound around Calvin Shaw's neck, and also tucked under Sir Cecil's drawing room rug. But it was impossible to say for sure.

Hairs on the back of Roy's neck began to spike as he watched the figure hesitate, looking left and right, up and down the aisle, before extending an arm to unhook a coil of rope from the display. Dropping the KitKat back onto the desk, he tapped the mouse to allow the images to play on at half speed, and watched the figure slip away.

CHAPTER TWENTY-ONE

Bury St Edmunds Police Station

DS Carter got up from his seat and approached the white-boards. "This is an image of a person seen to be buying an identical coil of rope to the one seen at both the crime scene in the woods and in Sir Cecil's drawing room." He tacked a blown-up copy of a still taken from the CCTV in aisle seven of the DIY store. "As we've already identified, the rope is blue polypropylene, used for a variety of purposes. It's sold just about anywhere — but this one was bought just two weeks ago."

"And you say the payment was cash?" Nicki frowned towards the board.

"Yes. And the store doesn't have cameras at the check-outs, unfortunately."

"So this is the best image we have?" Nicki wasn't hopeful the grainy shot of the back of the person's head was going to be much use to them. Then she saw the smile on Roy's face, and a gleam she recognised enter his eyes. "Spit it out, Roy."

Roy turned to pin another series of images to the white-board. "I picked him up again in the car park." He tapped the first image. "This is him leaving the shop. And these two here . . ." He tapped the last two images in the sequence. "These show him making his way towards the car in the corner. Unfortunately, the car itself is just out of camera shot, and all we can see is him approaching the passenger side door."

Nicki trained her gaze on the final image. Roy was right — all they could see was the passenger door of a dark-coloured vehicle. But what was unmistakable was the image of the person with a coil of rope slung over his shoulder.

"At present, this is all we have."

"Any idea of the make of car from that angle?" Nicki frowned at the image again.

"Difficult to tell," replied Roy. "What I planned to do next was see if any of the surrounding street cameras picked it up as it left."

Nicki nodded. "Do it. We might get lucky. It could all still be innocent — buying a coil of rope doesn't necessarily make him our killer — but the time frame fits. Put all the details up on the board and do some more digging. See if we can at least trace the car when it leaves the car park. And, although I hate to say it, Roy, keep looking at other stores. Those that haven't responded yet." She turned towards DS Fox.

"What did you manage to glean from the post-mortem, Graham?" Nicki went over to the window and pulled the blinds shut, the sound of the wind outside battering against the glass.

Fox pulled out his notebook. "The report should be with you first thing tomorrow, but in essence, two big hits to the head, skull fractures at both sites with massive brain haemorrhages. Either one could have killed him, but Caz Mitchell favours the occipital." Fox tapped the back of his head as he turned the page. "Usual swabs, scrapings and blood work sent off to the lab. For his age, he was otherwise in good health. And although found in water, he definitely didn't drown. But the relevance of the plastic bag on the head isn't known. As for the time of death, any time after 6 p.m. last night."

Nicki nodded. "That's pretty much what Caz told me over the phone. We'll just have to wait for the lab results to come in and cross our fingers they give us something to go on."

"If Sir Cecil's cause of death was a brain haemorrhage from being whacked around the head, but Calvin Shaw's was asphyxiation, what are we now thinking about them being linked?" asked Matt. "There's quite a big difference between the two."

Nicki had thought of nothing else since speaking to Caz earlier. Three days in, she was conscious that the investigation into Calvin's murder was stalling. And now they had another. Were they linked, despite the different kill methods? They desperately needed a breakthrough somewhere — that one chink of light to lead them in the right direction. Otherwise they were just stumbling about in the dark, blindfolded.

"Still no further forward with that, Matt," she eventually replied. "We need to find whatever it is that links them — if they *are* linked. Keep going with the rope angle — see if we can't find that car somewhere."

* * *

Stainsby Hotel, Rochdale

"He'll be back." Larry Browning wasn't even convincing himself with his words. "It's not that late."

Annette's eyes flashed towards the window and the rapidly fading light outside. The sky had darkened with yet more storm clouds, and the rain had started up once again, beating against the glass. "He's been gone hours. It's nearly five."

"He's a grown man, Annie." Larry didn't know what else to say, so decided silence was probably best. He gathered up the mugs and headed back towards the complimentary tea and coffee tray, snapping on the tiny plastic kettle for yet another unwanted hot drink. They had already eaten that day's packet of shortbread biscuits and his stomach was rumbling. He picked up the laminated menu for the bar downstairs and waved it in Annette's direction, but she shook her head.

Ordering some food would give him something else to focus on. Something other than Annette. He knew just by looking at her that she was struggling — the world as she knew it was disintegrating before her eyes and there was precious little he could do to stop it. It was a scenario he'd played out in his own head on many an occasion in the past — often deep in the middle of the night when sleep was only a passing whim — but the same questions would invariably surface. What would they do when the truth came out? When Mason finally learned what had happened to him?

When he'd got back from filling the van up with petrol earlier that day, he could see that his bag had been opened. Annette had still been asleep, tucked beneath the covers, and Mason was nowhere to be seen. He hadn't told Annette about the bag when she eventually woke; instead, he told her that Mason had gone out to stretch his legs. He wasn't really sure what else he could say.

It had been wrong to bring the cuttings with him, he knew that. He wasn't even sure why he had when he thought about it now. It just felt the right thing to do, keeping them close — and he couldn't very well leave them at home in case Adrian found them. But he should have locked them away somewhere safe — safer than his overnight bag anyway. Maybe somewhere in the van instead. But there was no point worrying about that now.

He had known the risks in bringing them with him, yet he'd still done so, and then chosen to leave them virtually out on display. It was almost as if he *wanted* Mason to find them.

Wanted them all to get caught.

A distinct chill descended, making him shiver. *Was* that how he felt?

Watching Annette by the window, he wondered whether he'd been wrong to help her the way he had all those years ago — help her to create *this*, whatever *this* was. This *existence*.

For that was all it was really, an existence based on lies. And everyone knew that a house built on lies would eventually crumble.

But the past was immaterial right now — decisions made then couldn't be changed. If Mason had indeed seen the cuttings, which seemed more than likely the more Larry thought about it, then he would have surely recognised his own face in the photographs. And it wouldn't have taken him long to connect the dots; he wasn't stupid.

Now the lad had disappeared.

"I'm going to pop downstairs and order some crispy chicken wings. Are you sure you don't want anything?" Larry swiped his wallet from the bed and headed for the door. He needed to get some fresh air, clear his mind. "Maybe something for later?" He was dismissed with another shake of the head, and gratefully stepped outside.

Once the bedroom door closed behind him, Annette inched her chair closer to the window and watched the rain thrumming against the pane. The lights in the car park had flickered on as soon as the storm clouds snuffed out the late afternoon light, faint beacons of muted yellow peering through the gloom. Their van was parked on the other side of the car park, beneath a bank of trees. Far enough away, yet close enough to keep an eye on. She never wanted to be too far away from Mason.

Her own Mason.

Annette's bottom lip began to quiver. *My poor, poor Mason* — the beloved son she had let down so catastrophically twenty-two years ago. Not a day went by when she didn't think of him, yearning to see his smiling face once again.

And then the guilt would come crashing back down.

It pained her that Mason was out there in the cold — all alone in the back of the van. It wasn't what she wanted for him. No mother wanted that for their child. And they certainly couldn't live like this for much longer, that was becoming abundantly clear, lurching from one hotel room to another, carrying all their worldly goods with them in a couple of suitcases thrown in the back of a battered old van. Sooner or later, the lies would catch up with them, trip them up and pin them down — and then she would lose him all over again.

The more she thought about it, the more she wondered if she deserved it.

CHAPTER TWENTY-TWO

Seymour Street, Bury St Edmunds

Mick Shaw scraped yet another meal into the bin. Neither he nor Heather had felt hungry enough for the spaghetti bolognese he'd made. It was normally something he enjoyed cooking — the only dish he could really manage without burning — and he'd wanted to try and do something normal. But things weren't normal, were they? Things were very far from normal — about as far as they could possibly get.

DC Gemma Huntley was sticking to them like glue, too. He didn't mind all that much, most of the time; it was good for Heather to have someone else to talk to. With everything that had happened, he just didn't know what to say to her right now. Sometimes the words just stuck in his throat. He'd cancelled all his jobs for the foreseeable future — there was no way he could focus on work — but they just seemed to be getting under each other's feet. Often it was like walking on eggshells, trying not to say or do the wrong thing; it was exhausting. And most of the time, Heather merely sat by the window and stared into space.

"Can I get you anything before I head off?" The family liaison officer made him jump. He whirled around, almost dropping the plate he still held in his hands. "Sorry, I didn't mean to scare you," she added, smiling. "More tea, maybe?"

Mick shook his head. *God, not more tea.* "No." He tried his best to return the smile. "We're fine. Heather will probably head up to bed soon. She's shattered."

It was a lie — he knew that, and Gemma probably did too. Heather would sit up through the night, staring at the walls. Sometimes she would leaf through old photo albums, reminding herself of happier times, much like they had the other evening. They'd left the albums out on the coffee table and Mick had noticed one or two had made their way up to the bedroom. But mostly she just stared at the walls. She didn't want to take the sleeping tablets again, complaining that they left her too groggy the next morning.

"And how are you?"

Mick hesitated by the sink. He could see his hands starting to shake, so he turned around to slip the plate into the soapy water.

"I know the visit to the mortuary must have been traumatic for both of you."

The mortuary.

Mick started to clean the plate. The visit to the mortuary seemed such a long time ago now. He wondered how many people knew that he hadn't been able to face looking at Cal. How many people knew that he couldn't even do that one simple thing. *For Cal.* For the boy he called his son. It looked bad — he was well aware of that. What kind of father left his wife to do something like that alone?

"It can't have been easy," persisted Gemma, taking a step towards him.

It can't have been easy for Heather; he was sure that was what the liaison officer really wanted to say. *It can't have been easy for Heather to do it alone.*

He felt his cheeks start to redden. "I'm OK. We're OK. Thank you." He flashed a look over his shoulder and could tell by the woman's expression that she didn't necessarily believe him, but seemed to be giving him the benefit of the doubt.

Gemma turned to head for the door. "I'll be getting on my way then. I'll see you both in the morning. If you need anything in the meantime, my mobile will be on all night."

Mick grunted a response he hoped didn't sound too disrespectful, and waited to hear the front door open then close behind her. Satisfied he was now alone, he made his way out into the utility room.

Soundlessly, he pulled open the door to the tumble dryer and retrieved the cloth bag he'd put in there earlier. It had been the safest place he could think of at such short notice, but he knew it wasn't suitable long term. He would have to find somewhere else. They didn't use the tumble dryer — it needed a replacement part and Mick hadn't quite got around to it — but with a police officer in the house, it made him nervous.

Placing the cloth bag on the worktop, he slipped a hand inside and pulled out Cal's laptop and mobile phone.

* * *

College Lane, Bury St Edmunds

"So how was it really?"

Nicki didn't need to ask what Caz was referring to. She handed the pathologist a wine glass. "It was OK, actually. Better than OK." She seated herself next to her friend on the sofa. "Actually, it was really good."

"See, I told you. You were worrying about nothing."

Nicki gave a tired smile and took a sip of the Pinot Grigio. "I know. It's just, after all this time, I wasn't quite sure how things would go." Nicki had told Caz about the split in the Webster family — how she had become estranged from her parents, and how she'd then changed her name to seek a new beginning — she just hadn't told her the reason why.

"Well, your new friend Ben has left your kitchen spick and span — he looks like a keeper to me." Caz grinned and sunk her first mouthful of wine. "Watch out, though — Jeremy will be getting jealous!"

Nicki narrowed her tired gaze across the top of her glass. "We're just friends, nothing more exciting than that."

Caz continued to grin and nudged the plate of spicy samosas towards Nicki. "Eat. You look done in."

Nicki knew she looked like death — she could see the dark circles beneath her eyes when she looked in the mirror, the puffiness of her eyelids. But it was always the same when she was knee-deep in a new investigation — it consumed her every waking moment. And it had been a particularly long day, what with the early morning call out to the pond, followed by the visit to Pemberton Hall. Gemma had checked in after leaving the Shaw family home — updating Nicki on her day spent with Calvin's parents. The feeling that the man could be involved in his own stepson's death had left a bad taste in everyone's mouth.

And then there was Deano.

"I'm fine," she managed, picking up a samosa. "I'm sure I look a lot worse than I feel. It's just the case, that's all. Well, both of them, actually." The lie was swallowed whole with the Indian delicacy.

Caz gave her an '*I don't believe that for a second*' look before scooping some red onion chutney up onto a poppadum. "Talking of which, after the PM on Sir Cecil today, are you any closer to knowing if the two cases are connected? Tell me to mind my own business . . ."

Nicki waved the comment away. "It's no secret. We're struggling to find a connection between the two victims, to be honest. They moved in completely different circles."

"I can imagine."

"But with the rope found in the drawing room at Pemberton Hall the same as that used to string Calvin Shaw up in the woods — how can they not be connected?"

"Oh?" Caz's eyes widened. "I hadn't realised. That puts a different spin on things, I guess. Definitely the same rope?"

Nicki shook her head. "We're not sure. It's the same *type* — but not necessarily the same rope. We're having it tested as far as we can. We're also trying to find local retailers who might have sold some recently. It's a long shot, but we've got a potential lead — although it's nothing more than that, really. A lead."

"But it's certainly suspicious, right? I mean, I'm no detective, but what are the odds that the same type of rope is found at both scenes, but they aren't connected?"

Nicki knew Caz was right. The odds were certainly small. She nibbled at the corner of her samosa. "But the causes of death are different — which is making us think twice about looking for the same perpetrator."

Caz swallowed her poppadum and took a glug of wine to wash it down. "Maybe your killer is just diversifying." She broke up another poppadum. "They do that sometimes — the clever ones, anyway."

Nicki groaned. That's all they needed — a diversifying killer. And a clever one, too.

"Anyway, how's Jeremy?" Caz looked coyly over the top of her wine glass. "A little birdie tells me he's been in touch a few times lately."

"And I'm guessing that little birdie must be our friendly crime scene manager?" Nicki couldn't help a smile forming on her lips. Faye was nothing if not indiscreet.

"I couldn't possibly comment on my source," giggled Caz. "Anyhow, spill."

"There's nothing to spill, as you well know. Jeremy and I are friends, that's it. You know I'm far too busy for anything else. *With anyone.*"

Just then, Nicki's mobile chirped with an incoming message. She considered ignoring it, but glancing at the screen, she saw it was from Roy.

"Shit," she breathed, once she'd read the short text. "Shit, shit, shit."

CHAPTER TWENTY-THREE

Tuesday 12 March 2019
Seymour Street, Bury St Edmunds

Heather tipped her half-drunk coffee down the sink and started to put last night's plates and cutlery away. Mick had made an effort to cook her favourite dinner, but neither of them had had much of an appetite. Spaghetti bolognese had been Cal's favourite, too — maybe that was why it had stuck in her throat.

The food now languished in the rubbish bin, the dishes and plates stacked up on the draining board ready to be put back in the cupboards. She reached for the open packet of paracetamol. She'd barely slept last night and now had the mother of all headaches wreaking havoc between her temples. She poured herself some water and swallowed a couple of the tablets.

The *Daily Express* had landed on the doormat at 6.30 a.m. — just like it always did. She had initially left it lying there, not wanting to see Cal's name splashed across its pages once again. The story had made most of the national newspapers now — not necessarily front page, but as good as. For the local papers it was an even bigger story, the most newsworthy some of them had had in weeks. They'd all descended on it like a pack of wild dogs.

With the newspaper staring back at her from the mat, it wasn't long before she felt compelled to take a quick look. The urge was just too strong.

The headlines were of some political scandal or other, for which she was grateful. At least it wasn't Cal. But she knew she wouldn't have to turn many pages to see his smiling face staring out.

The thought turned her stomach.

Today he was on page five. Seeing her son's name and picture in print made her legs turn to rubber and she had to grab hold of the kitchen worktop to stop herself from falling. She wished she hadn't looked — if she didn't see the words then she could pretend none of it had happened, that none of it was real, that Cal would walk through the door at any moment, popping in to borrow something or cadge some food.

She found herself smiling through her sadness. Cal had always had a knack of turning up on the doorstep just as she was dishing up dinner — so much so that she often set out another plate for him, ready and waiting.

Heather rubbed her eyes to stop fresh tears from falling. There would be no need for the extra plate anymore. That thought alone caused her physical pain.

With the newspaper now folded up on the kitchen table, she reached for more crockery from the draining board. She could hear Mick moving around upstairs, the floorboards creaking as he crossed the bedroom. Soon, she heard his tell-tale footsteps on the stairs. Light on his feet he was not.

"Morning," he greeted, voice still thick with sleep. "What time did you get up?" He glanced into the adjoining utility room where freshly laundered clothes were piled high and another wash churned in the machine.

"I couldn't sleep," replied Heather, taking a handful of cutlery and slotting them into place in one of the kitchen drawers. "I had to keep busy."

Mick stepped up behind her, circling his arms around her waist. "You should have woken me up."

Heather tried to relax her muscles, knowing he could probably feel the tension raging within her, but it was impossible. Instead, she extricated herself from his grip and handed him a casserole dish. "You can make yourself useful by putting the rest of the washing-up away." She tried a smile.

Mick took the dish and, as he turned, spied the folded newspaper on the kitchen table. "Anything in the news?"

Heather turned away. "A little."

Out of the corner of her eye she watched Mick abandon the casserole dish and scoop up the newspaper. As she flicked on the kettle, she saw him scour the headlines then flick through page by page, stopping at page five.

She felt her heart squeeze, knowing he would be reading about Cal. None of this felt real to her — even viewing Cal's body on Saturday hadn't felt real. This was all happening to someone else — some other family, some other son.

Not her Cal.

"I'll make some fresh coffee." With her hand hovering over the kettle, Heather heard her husband resume flicking through the pages. She silently cursed herself for not tossing the paper into the bin along with last night's dinner, but he would only go and buy another one. They couldn't run away from what had happened, no matter how much they wanted to.

Mick cleared his throat. "How's that coffee coming along?"

Heather felt her shoulders tense but she didn't turn around. "Won't be a minute." She tried to inject some element of normality into her tone. "How about you go through to the living room and I'll bring it in with some toast?"

Mick squeezed her waist once again and she tried a weak smile in response. It was hard for her, but it was also hard for him — though in a totally different way. She didn't blame him for not wanting to view Cal with her at the mortuary — she could have done with his reassuring grip on her hand, but she didn't blame him. How could she? The emotions he felt at losing Cal were bound to be different to her own.

Once he had disappeared, she popped two slices of white bread into the toaster then picked up the newspaper again. Mick had left it open at page seven. Halfway down the page, an article caught her eye.

'*BODY FOUND IN SUFFOLK PUB POND —*
MAN NAMED.'

* * *

Bury St Edmunds Police Station

Nicki threw the morning edition of the *Daily Express* onto her desk, narrowly missing the mug of coffee Roy had brought in with him. "This is all we need."

Roy swiftly moved the mug to a safer distance. "Thought you'd want to see it as soon as, boss. It's appeared in most of the other nationals, too. And it's all over the internet."

Nicki grunted and tried a tired smile. "Thanks — for the coffee, too."

Roy gestured towards the newspaper. "How do you think they got the name?"

Nicki could only shake her head. "No idea. Sir Cecil's name was specifically kept out of the press release for a reason. He's so high profile I didn't want to ignite the inevitable bonfire that would follow if his name was made public before we even had an inkling of what happened to him." She sighed. "The DCI wants to see me — I'm guessing he's seen the good news for himself. I've a feeling he'll want a full-on press conference pronto to try and patch up this leaky ship."

Roy made a face and started to head towards the door. "I can't see it being anyone on the team that tipped the press off."

Neither could Nicki. "I'm sure it wasn't one of us, Roy. There were plenty of other sources that knew of his identity — you've got everyone who attended the crime scene, anyone connected with the mortuary, the pub. It's quite a wide net." She rubbed her temples; they were starting to ache already. "Tell the rest of the team I'll be through shortly. I just need to make a phone call or two."

Roy departed and Nicki grabbed her phone, quickly dialling the only person she could think of who might be able to help.

"Jeremy," she said, as soon as the call was connected. "I need a favour."

* * *

Seymour Street, Bury St Edmunds

Heather left her own coffee and toast untouched on the table by the side of the sofa. Mick had got dressed and gone out, for which she was quietly thankful — she didn't think to question where he'd gone. Right now she needed time to herself; *she needed time to think*. She felt as though she were on some sort of rollercoaster, hurtling out of control, direction unknown. She glanced at the clock. It wouldn't be long before the family liaison officer turned up and, as appreciative as she was of the detective's company, this morning she really needed to be alone.

Heather picked up the newspaper again.

It was bad enough seeing Cal's name plastered across the inside pages, but when she saw Sir Cecil's it made her catch her breath. Seeing the man's name in print like that . . .

Her eyes flickered to the photograph the journalist had used alongside the article. It wasn't a particularly flattering one. The man was standing in front of a pair of wrought iron gates with an irate look on his face, as if in the middle of some tirade or other. The article was short, and Heather could already sense the lack of outpouring of grief at the man's demise.

With another wave of nausea looming, her thoughts were interrupted by the doorbell. Knowing it would no doubt be Gemma, she rose to her feet and tried to plaster a suitably welcoming smile on her face.

* * *

"It's obviously not ideal. We wanted to keep Sir Cecil's identity out of the papers while the investigation was in its early stages." Nicki's displeasure was evident in her tone, but she knew the leak wouldn't have come from within her team. "But now it's out there, we need to be on high alert."

"Time wasters?" volunteered Matt, biting into a breakfast sausage roll.

"Exactly. Every Tom, Dick and Harriet will be calling to give us the benefit of their wisdom, naming anyone from Lord Lucan to Santa Claus for who put him in the pond. I can't think many people will be shedding a lot of tears over the man's demise. Calls are being screened as they come in."

"Have we decided if we're linking the cases yet, boss?" Duncan moved to take a seat by the whiteboards, a greaseproof paper bag in his hand. "The press hasn't latched onto the idea yet, but it might not take them long."

Nicki thought back to her discussions with Caz last night. Two murders. Three days apart. It wasn't something that landed on their doorstep all that often as a rule, which would usually be sufficient to suggest they were linked. The rope was a strong connection, too — but why had the killer, if there *was* just the one, murdered them in completely different ways? Was it — as Caz had suggested — that they were diversifying? The thought made her shudder. That might mean the killer hadn't finished . . .

"We keep an open mind, Duncan. Treat them separately for now, but look for any common denominators — anything that can connect them, however tenuous. Have we traced Sir Cecil's next of kin yet?"

Duncan unwrapped his cheese toastie. "Like we said before — father dead, mother died while he was an infant. No siblings. There is a distant cousin I located yesterday — aged eighty-one, lives in the Outer Hebrides."

Nicki gave a tired smile. "I think we can probably discount them. Let's get that list of anyone with a grudge against

Sir Cecil finalised. Matt, Duncan? Can you both take that?" They nodded their agreement. "Anything from forensics yet?"

Roy raised a hand. "Tests are showing the rope at Pemberton Hall is identical to the one found on Calvin's body."

"Which also ties in with a report we've just had uploaded regarding the dive team who searched the pond yesterday." Nicki waved a piece of paper in the air. "A small section of rope was found, which matches that found in the drawing room at Pemberton Hall. They also located a tartan rug, which the lab will analyse and see if it's connected to our body, and a cast-iron poker."

"CCTV isn't giving us many leads," added Roy. "Do you want us to carry on with that this morning?"

Nicki grimaced. "Maybe take another look at the house-to-house statements instead — the ones around Calvin's flat. See if any mention doorbell camera footage." The detective gave a nod.

"The finalised post-mortem report on Sir Cecil is now with us as well. No surprises. It's as we said yesterday." Nicki waved another piece of paper in the air. "Cause of death — massive brain haemorrhage after being whacked a couple of times around the head. Fractures found at the base of the skull and at the temple. It's possible the poker found in the pond could be our murder weapon. Some evidence of other injuries, suggesting he'd had a bit of a beating or kicking at some point, but he did report the street assault on Friday, so it's possible those injuries could be from that. Some defensive wounds on both arms."

"What's the significance of the plastic bag on his head?" asked Matt, stuffing the last of the sausage roll into his mouth. "If he didn't die of asphyxiation?"

Nicki shrugged. "Of that, I'm not too sure at this stage."

"Maybe the killer didn't want to see Sir Cecil's face — after, you know, he or she had done the deed?" Duncan made short work of his toastie. "Might mean they knew him?"

"I think everybody knew him, Duncan. I'm not sure it takes us that much further forward." Nicki flicked through the report. "A few other findings, none of which present any great surprises. Evidence of moderate to heavy alcohol consumption, some cirrhosis of the liver. And although he seemed to be in fairly good shape for his age, more evidence of a less than healthy lifestyle. Fatty liver, gallstones, some tobacco damage to the lungs. I think we are all aware he liked the odd cigar. Other than that, pretty unremarkable."

"Perils of the privileged, eh?" commented DS Fox. "Too much booze, rich food and cigars. At least none of us here can afford that kind of lifestyle . . ."

"I've seen you put away a fair few pints on occasion, Gray," laughed Matt, crunching up his sausage roll wrapper and tossing it in Fox's direction.

"That may well be true, but I'm still in the prime of life, me." Graham patted his stomach to a smattering of laughter.

"When you've all finished," smiled Nicki, heading for the door, "let's crack on."

* * *

Rochdale Town Centre

He hadn't had the best night. He was neither built nor prepared for sleeping on the streets. The weather had been atrocious — torrential rain for much of the time, and a wind that cut through you like a dagger. But he hadn't really been expecting to sleep much anyway.

He'd spent most of the night riding the night buses, keeping warm while on a circular tour of the town. To begin with he stared out of the window, taking in the buildings as they passed — but after a while it all became a blur. Then, when the rain eventually stopped, he spent some time walking.

Walking and thinking.

He'd switched his phone off as soon as he'd left the hotel, not wanting Mum or Dad to be calling him every five minutes. He knew they would be worrying about him — Mum especially — but he needed peace and solitude. He needed time to *think*.

Dean Webster.

The more he said it, the more sense it made. That feeling of never quite belonging. Now he realised why. He'd always known he was adopted — it had been no secret as he was growing up —but he'd still felt like an outsider in the family, despite them both loving him like he was truly their own. There was always a feeling that there was something more to it; something he couldn't quite put his finger on. As if there was this one, massive secret that only his parents knew about.

And now it all made sense.

There *was* a massive secret — he'd just never contemplated that it would be this.

Dean Webster.

He felt the strangest emotion ripple through him, and he wasn't quite sure what it was. Excitement? Nervousness? Fear? Maybe it was all three. Or maybe it was just familiarity. The name Dean Webster, when he said it out loud, made him feel comfortable. Like it *fitted*.

But what was he meant to do now? It wasn't like he could just pitch up back in his old life and claim to be Dean Webster again. People would think he was mad. He had documents — official documents — in the name of Mason Browning. A driving licence. A bank card. A passport. *That* was who he was — as far as everyone else was concerned, anyway.

Changing his name hadn't felt so strange at the time. As a frightened and bewildered five-year-old, he'd gone along with whatever the adults told him to do. Because adults were always right, weren't they? You could trust them. And, although it had taken a while, he'd eventually forgotten all about Dean Webster, and become Mason Browning.

He pulled his jacket more firmly around himself. He was just about drying off, having spent the last half an hour sheltering in the bus stop. Several buses had come and gone in that time, but he'd boarded none of them. He didn't know where he was intending to go. He'd run out of the hotel in just the clothes on his back, with his wallet and phone. Nothing else. What was he meant to do now?

If he went back to the house in Suffolk, Adrian would be there — but he suspected his brother knew nothing about Dean Webster and would most likely be as shocked as he was when he learned the truth. But it wasn't really Adrian he was worried about.

If he left and went back to his old life, what would happen to Larry and Annette? He would basically be throwing them to the wolves, forcing them to own up and admit what they'd done all those years ago. That they'd snatched a five-year-old boy and brought him up as their own.

But Larry and Annette were good people — as mad as everything was, he didn't hate them. Not yet, anyway. He'd had a good life with them; a good childhood. They had brought him up with love and kindness. He'd wanted for nothing — he couldn't fault them there. So how could he repay them by turning them in?

He knew it sounded mad, but he didn't want anything bad to happen to them. He'd had a lot of time to think about it while riding the night bus, and had decided he didn't want them punished for what they'd done.

Stockholm Syndrome seemed to be closing in fast.

But what other choice did he have? He could either get on the next bus going south and go and find his old life — his *real* life as Dean Webster — or he could turn his back on the truth and walk away, back to Larry and Annette.

And what they had in the back of the van.

The van.

The thought made him shudder.

When he'd run from the hotel yesterday, he'd fleetingly thought of taking the van — just jumping in and driving off. Dad had given him a spare key, in case of emergency. And, for a moment, Mason considered that this was exactly that — an emergency.

He'd sat in the driver's seat for a while, his mind whirring with what he'd discovered, keys swinging in the ignition. He wasn't quite sure what made him look in the back. He'd been in the van plenty of times on their travels north, squashed in among the rest of their possessions, but in that moment something had made him look further.

Which was when he saw it, hidden beneath the old tarpaulin.

> *Precious son and brother — taken too soon*
> *Five years old — RIP*
> *Mason Douglas Browning*

Seeing the inscription on the headstone caused his heart to almost stop in its tracks. As had the small coffin-like box buried with it.

Mason Browning.

Suddenly more pieces started slotting into place, and the real reason Larry and Annette had taken him became clear.

The *real* Mason Browning was lying in the back of the van.

* * *

Bury St Edmunds Police Station

Roy settled down once more behind his computer screen. All the house-to-house statements were in and logged onto the system — and after forty-five minutes of scanning each and every one, he'd determined no one had seen anything untoward in or around Melrose Avenue. Everyone described Calvin as a pleasant young man, never any trouble, who didn't seem to have many, if any, visitors to his flat. *Kept himself to himself* was mentioned more than once.

Several people along Melrose Avenue had doorbell cameras fitted, and Roy saw that three video files had been uploaded to the system. Settling further back in his seat, he began to watch.

The first two files showed recordings from cameras located on houses on the same side of the road as Calvin's flat, all in the twenty-four hours prior to his estimated time of death on Thursday evening. Neither showed much to pique Roy's interest. The cameras were motion-activated, so only showed images when something moved to trigger them into action, and the road was a quiet one with very little through-traffic. During Thursday morning, there was a postman doing his rounds, several schoolchildren passing by on their way to the local school, and various parcel delivery vans. Nothing out of the ordinary; everything completely normal. As evening fell, Roy saw nothing more exciting than a cat strolling by, followed some time later by what looked like a fox.

Sighing, he loaded the third file. This camera gave a slightly different perspective of the street, housed on a door immediately opposite Calvin's flat. Roy soon saw the familiar comings and goings of the street on that same Thursday: the postman delivering his letters; groups of schoolchildren making their way to school; parcel delivery vans dropping off Amazon purchases.

Roy gave a yawn as the recording turned to the evening. Again, very little movement activated the doorbell camera. There was something of note, however. At seven p.m. Calvin left his flat, dressed in the dark hoodie and jeans he was later found in on Hardwick Heath. Roy made a note of the timing. He then saw the same black cat sauntering across the road, the same fox sniffing in the gutter.

Just when he thought the recording was coming to an end, about to reach forward and click the 'stop' button, Roy's hand froze. The camera was activated once again, capturing more movement in front of Calvin's front door. Roy inched closer to the screen.

The man had walked quickly up to the entrance to Calvin's flat, pausing only briefly before disappearing inside. Roy checked the time stamp: 8.45 p.m. Five minutes later, the camera activated once more to show Calvin's door opening and the same man emerging. Without seeming to hesitate, the man pulled the door shut behind him and disappeared back into the darkness.

Roy rewound the images until the man's face was clearly visible.

"Gotcha."

CHAPTER TWENTY-FOUR

Bury St Edmunds Police Station

"It's him, without a doubt."

Nicki peered over Roy's shoulder. The image frozen in the centre of the computer screen couldn't be any clearer. "What the hell is he doing at Calvin's flat at—" She checked the time stamp in the corner of the monitor. "Eight forty-five? By that time, the poor lad could very well have been dead and strung up on the heath. Our secretive lovebirds stumbled across him approximately two hours later."

"Looks like he had a key, boss. Just lets himself in." Roy nodded towards the screen. "And he didn't have that bag with him when he went in."

Nicki peered more closely at the image of Mick Shaw, noting the light-coloured bag clutched in his left hand as he exited Calvin's flat. "What *are* you doing?" she muttered beneath her breath.

"What do we do now, boss?"

"Well, I think we need to go back and have yet another chat with our Mr Shaw, don't you?" Nicki straightened up. "But first, I want to know what was in that bag."

* * *

Jeremy Frost ended yet another fruitless call. He had just about exhausted all his usual contacts. Whoever had leaked the story confirming Sir Cecil as the body in the Moreton Hall Pub pond, nobody was prepared to admit it. Nicki wouldn't be best pleased, but there was precious little else he could try. Sometimes stories leaked out and there was no way of tracing them back to the source.

He rubbed his eyes and reached for his notepad. Although he'd been more than happy to try and help, he really did have more pressing things to be getting on with. And Scott Edgecombe came very high on that list. The story was taking shape at an alarming rate, gathering speed the more he dug into it. After twelve years, people were now prepared to talk, previous loyalties forgotten.

He looked at the rough draft on his notepad. It needed work — some corroboration here and there, maybe a few more quotes from those in the know — but it would definitely be explosive when it hit. That went without saying. What he didn't know yet was what Nicki's reaction might be. He'd had to dig deep into his own police contacts for a lot of the information — maybe too deep at times — and that might get Nicki's back up a little.

But he wasn't prepared to stop. Not on this one.

* * *

Seymour Street, Bury St Edmunds

Gemma Huntley closed the door to the kitchen behind her. Nicki had forwarded her the still images from the doorbell camera showing Mick Shaw leaving his stepson's flat on Thursday evening, carrying a bag in his left hand. The image wasn't too clear but the bag looked to be light in colour; that was just about all she could glean from it. It wasn't much to go on.

She knew she couldn't search the house properly, not without raising suspicion, but while she was inside the Shaws' home, Nicki had asked her to keep an eye out for a bag matching that description. If she managed to find one, Nicki would then take the necessary steps to make the search more formal. As a plan, it wasn't much, but it was all they had.

There were various items hanging on the back of the kitchen door — an apron, an umbrella, and several bags — but Gemma could see that none of the bags matched the description from the doorbell camera. Her eyes scanned the rest of the kitchen. She'd already opened most of the cupboards over the last few days, getting used to the layout while supplying the Shaws with tea and other sustenance. She was quite sure she hadn't seen a bag. The same went for the utility room. There was very little out there except for a washing machine and tumble dryer.

A few moments earlier, she'd also had a discreet look around the hallway when passing through to the living room. There was a coat stand by the front door with several jackets and scarves hung up, and another umbrella. But no bags that she could see.

Then there was upstairs.

Although tempting, Gemma didn't really have much of an excuse to go rooting around upstairs. The bathroom was up there, but there were only so many times she could feign the excuse of needing to use the toilet — and even then, she couldn't afford to be caught rummaging around in the bedrooms, nosing in wardrobes and under beds.

Sighing, she swept the kitchen once more. As far as she could tell, there was nowhere obvious the bag could be lurking. It wouldn't be the news Nicki wanted to hear.

Just then, the kitchen door opened and Heather came in with a washing basket full of clothes. Gemma noticed how tired she looked, the circles beneath her eyes becoming darker with each day that passed.

"Here, let me take that." Gemma went to take the basket from Heather's hands. "You look shattered."

Heather gave a weak smile. "It helps — keeping busy."

"That's as may be, but how about you put the kettle on and make us a fresh cuppa — I'll pop the washing on."

Heather allowed Gemma to take the basket, the detective feeling how cold the woman's hands were. "Maybe something to eat, too."

Another weak smile, accompanied by a nod. "OK. Thank you."

Gemma took the basket through to the utility room and was just pushing the last of the clothes into the washing machine when something caught her eye. Frowning, she closed the machine door and selected the cool wash before stepping closer to the tumble dryer. The door looked to be closed, but was still open a fraction — a piece of cloth or clothing stopping it from shutting completely. Kneeling down, Gemma peered through the transparent door and saw a light-coloured item sitting in the drum.

The detective's heart quickened. Checking back over her shoulder, she heard Heather clattering around in the kitchen getting mugs and plates out of the cupboards while the kettle was boiling. She knew she had to be quick — Heather could walk in at any minute, and Gemma wasn't sure what excuse she would have for rummaging around in the tumble dryer.

Without hesitating any longer, she gently teased the drier door open and looked inside. At which point, she saw it quite clearly.

It was definitely the bag from the doorbell camera footage. It had to be.

Resisting the urge to pull it out and find out what was inside, Gemma instead pulled out her phone.

* * *

Rochdale Police Station

Clara Eastwood looked down at the handwritten notes she'd managed to scribble down and frowned. The story was an incredible one — unbelievable, even. She'd been one of the front desk clerks here for several years now, and she could categorically say she'd never heard anything quite like it.

The man hadn't wanted to give his name but Clara had logged his appearance on her notepad. He'd looked to be in his late twenties, soaked from the pounding rain outside, a little out of breath. There was no smell of alcohol about his person, and he looked well cared for — certainly not dishevelled. Maybe a little unshaven, and his eyes looked as though he'd gone without sleep for a while.

But *normal*.

Clara frowned again as she re-read her notes. Although the man looked normal, what he'd told her certainly wasn't. When she'd asked for his name, he'd said that it would *take some explaining* and refused to comment further.

But he'd had kind eyes and a kind voice. He certainly didn't look like he was a time waster.

After entering the details onto the system, she turned to her colleague behind her. "John? Do you know anything about a child abduction from 1996?"

* * *

Seymour Street, Bury St Edmunds

As much as it pained her, Nicki knew they didn't have a lot of choice. Pulling up outside the Shaws' property on Seymour Street, she glanced across at DS Fox seated beside her. "Ready?" Fox nodded. "Once we're inside, I want you to go with Gemma to where she's located the bag. Secure it while I'm dealing with the stepfather."

Nicki and Fox exited the Toyota, two uniformed officers joining them from a patrol car parked behind. Gemma had texted Nicki five minutes ago to say both Mr and Mrs Shaw were seated together in the living room. She confirmed she had discreetly locked the back door and taken the key — just in case.

Nobody expected Mick Shaw to be difficult and make a run for it, but Nicki knew from experience that you could never be too sure. And the sheer size of the man would make it difficult to stop him if he decided to chance his luck — hence the presence of the two uniformed officers. It may be overkill, but Nicki needed this to go like clockwork.

The knock at the door was answered after only the briefest of waits. With a knowing look, Gemma stood back to allow Nicki and Fox to enter first, followed by the officers. Silently, they all made their way into the living room.

Mr and Mrs Shaw looked up from where they were seated on the sofa, both sporting a mixture of worried, wary and confused expressions on their faces as the extra bodies filled the room.

"Mrs Shaw. Mr Shaw. I'm sorry to have to do this." Nicki stepped forward, focusing her attention on Calvin's stepfather. "Michael Shaw. I'm arresting you on suspicion of the murder of Calvin Shaw. You do not have to say anything but it may harm your defence if you do not mention when questioned something that you later rely on in court. Anything you do say may be given in evidence."

Both uniformed officers moved across to the sofa, helping Mick Shaw to his feet.

"You're arresting him?" Heather's face was ashen, her eyes wide with shock. "For murder? Mick? What's happening?"

Mick Shaw stood rooted to the spot, avoiding his wife's gaze, one uniformed officer on each side of him.

Heather's already trembling hand flew to her mouth. "No, no, no — you've got this all wrong." Whatever colour had been in her cheeks had drained clean away. "No — this isn't right, not Cal!" She began howling like an injured animal. "Not my Cal!"

Mick remained silent, his gaze focused on Nicki.

"Mr Shaw. You've been arrested on suspicion of murder and your rights have been read to you. Is there anything you don't understand?" Out of the corner of her eye, Nicki saw Heather Shaw's legs buckle beneath her and the woman collapse backwards onto the sofa. Gemma had just re-entered the room and was quickly by her side, offering a supportive hand.

Mick Shaw's eyes flickered towards DS Fox who was standing in the doorway, his gaze lowering to the plastic evidence bag the detective was holding. And the beige-coloured cloth bag that could be clearly seen within. Realisation and a sad acceptance seemed to cross the man's face, and he nodded.

"I understand."

One of the uniformed officers proceeded to handcuff him, the noise of the metal clicking into place sounding altogether too loud in the heavy silence of the couple's living room.

Heather Shaw was sobbing now. "You can't think . . . Tell them, Mick." The words caught in the back of her throat. "Tell them they've got it wrong!"

Mick Shaw started to walk towards the door, led by the two officers. He cast a look back over his shoulder as they reached the doorway. "I'm sorry, Heather," he said, his voice low and steady. "I'm sorry."

"I must remind you that you are under caution, Mr Shaw," Nicki warned as she followed them out into the hallway. "Anything you say can be taken down in evidence."

Before leaving, Nicki flashed a look of gratitude towards Gemma, knowing that at least Calvin's mother would have some degree of support while they took her husband in for questioning. It didn't sit right with Nicki — none of it did. How on earth could someone kill their own flesh and blood and then string them up like that? But then again, Calvin wasn't Mick Shaw's true flesh and blood, was he? So maybe that was the difference.

"We'll be taking your husband down to the Police Investigation Centre for questioning, Mrs Shaw. DC Huntley here will stay with you and keep you updated." Nicki hoped the sad smile she directed at Calvin's mother looked genuine. "Try not to worry."

CHAPTER TWENTY-FIVE

Bury St Edmunds Police Station

"Let me know as soon as you have anything on either the laptop or the phone." Nicki's voice sounded faint on the other end of the line.

"Will do." Roy seated himself back in the incident room, swapping the phone to his other ear. "I've just dropped them both off with the tech guys — they've promised to put a rush on it for us."

"Good. Graham and I are staying here to do the initial basic interview with Mick Shaw. It'll buy us some time. But the minute you hear anything, let me know."

The call ended and Roy turned his attention to his desk. While he waited for any news on the analysis of Calvin's laptop and phone, he decided to take a look at the other items that had been recovered from the young man's flat.

Calvin Shaw's life sat bagged up in front of him in a series of polythene evidence bags. Not much for twenty-two years on the planet. As he reached for the first evidence bag, Roy couldn't help thinking about Ellis. His friend had been younger than Calvin, but not by much. He could distinctly remember the police investigation that followed — the whys and the why nots; the shock; the terror; the disbelief. Then the inevitable recriminations and guilt that came soon after. Why hadn't anyone seen anything? Why hadn't anyone realised how he was feeling? Why hadn't anyone stopped him? *Why, why, why?*

Roy was no closer to the answer now than he had been back then. All he did know was that on that day — standing in Ellis's bedroom while they cut him down — he'd made a solemn promise to be a better person. *To be a better friend.*

None of that helped Calvin Shaw much, though.

Roy looked down at the first bag. The log told him it contained the contents of a bedside table. There were a couple of paperback books that didn't look like they had been opened, a charging bank for an iPhone, a packet of paracetamol and a cigarette lighter. All very innocuous. All very ordinary.

Now they'd managed to find Calvin's phone and laptop, Roy's investigative nose was twitching. The fact they were taken from the flat around the time of his death suggested there might be something incriminating on either or both of the two devices. Otherwise why take them? Roy mentally crossed his fingers that the tech team would come up with something fast.

The second and third bags were just as uninspiring as the first. The contents of random drawers; more detritus of modern life. Calvin's clothes had been bagged up separately, ready to be shipped back to the Shaws when they were ready, or onto the nearest charity shop if they weren't.

But it was the final bag that piqued Roy's interest.

It contained yet more odds and ends, labelled as the loose contents of the living room — specifically the windowsill area. Roy recalled seeing on the crime scene photos and video taken from inside the flat that there was a pile of junk mail stacked up beneath the window. He emptied it onto his desk.

A collection of pizza takeaway flyers; several charity bags asking for bric-a-brac and good-quality clothing; an advertisement for tree cutting services; three leaflets offering funeral plans; and even an advert for a Christmas Savings

Club, though it was only March. There was also a water bill showing Calvin was in credit to the tune of £12.67, a copy of the new council tax charges for the coming tax year, plus a confirmation letter for his booking of festival tickets later that summer. Beneath all this lay three unopened envelopes.

Roy stacked everything to one side, leaving out the three envelopes.

The handwriting on each of the envelopes was neat, written in black ballpoint pen and block capital letters, and all three bore a first class stamp. Still sealed, each one had '*RETURN TO SENDER*' printed across the front in large red letters.

* * *

Police Investigation Centre, Bury St Edmunds

With the preliminaries out of the way, Nicki decided to get down to business. The recording equipment was running, both audio and visual, which would capture everything that was said within the walls of the interview room. At least, Nicki hoped the man would talk. After his '*I'm sorry*' in the living room at the Shaws' home, he'd said nothing on the short journey to the Police Investigation Centre, and had only confirmed his name when the custody sergeant booked him in and authorised his detention. Nicki hadn't a clue what might be racing through the man's mind right now — or what words might escape his mouth — but she hoped she was about to find out. He declined the offer of legal representation, which had advantages and disadvantages for both sides, but Nicki just prayed that the next words she heard weren't going to be '*no comment*'.

She straightened out the paperwork on the table in front of her and exchanged a discreet nod with DS Fox seated by her side.

They were ready.

"Tell me about the evening of Thursday seventh of March — that's Thursday last week. Take me through where you were and what you were doing." Nicki tried to keep her voice light and steady. She was itching to ask him why he had gone to Calvin's flat at a time when the poor lad could already have been dead, but she wanted Mick Shaw to explain himself first. She would lay the trap and see if he duly tripped himself up — because, right now, Calvin's stepfather had no idea they were in possession of the doorbell footage.

He's wondering why we're asking. Nicki saw a slight frown cross Mick Shaw's brow. The man hesitated before eventually replying.

"I was working during the day. Came home about four o'clock. Then spent the evening at home with my wife."

Nicki gave a slow nod. This was exactly what Shaw had told officers when they'd attended to give the couple the devastating news about Calvin. "You're sure you didn't go out that evening — not even just to put the bins out?" She held the man in a steely gaze. "Nothing at all?"

Another brief hesitation. Then a shake of the head. "No."

Nicki cast her eyes down to the paperwork in front of her. "And what can you tell me about the bag found in your tumble dryer?"

This time there was silence from the other side of the table.

"Are you aware, Mr Shaw, of what we found inside that bag?" Nicki could see the muscles in Mick Shaw's jawline tensing, his eyes starting to blink rapidly. The man was feeling distinctly uncomfortable, so Nicki decided to press on. "I believe you know exactly what we found inside that bag, Mr Shaw. And I also believe that you were the one to put them there. Isn't that right?"

The seconds ticked by, but eventually the man's head dropped, his eyes lowered to the table. "I can explain."

"Good," replied Nicki, curtly. "You're going to need to."

* * *

Roy placed his mobile back down on the desk. He'd had to leave another message — the boss must still be interviewing the stepfather. The three letters from Calvin's flat lay stretched out before him. He'd taken the opportunity to photocopy each one, plus both sides of the envelopes they'd come in, leaving the originals tucked away in their protective plastic evidence bags.

He'd read each one several times now, dissecting every word. The letters were all from Calvin, his handwriting neat and uniform.

A voice from the dead.

Roy had felt his detective instinct prickle when he'd first seen the address written on the front of each envelope. The letters had seemed unimportant initially, subsequent events rapidly taking over — but it was just those subsequent events that now planted a seed of curiosity in Roy's mind.

And if the address on the front of each envelope had piqued his interest, that was nothing in comparison to what he'd felt when he read the contents.

He read each one again.

And reached for his phone.

* * *

Police Investigation Centre, Bury St Edmunds

"I took them from his flat."

"Took them from whose flat, Mr Shaw?"

Mick Shaw closed his eyes and sighed, his voice barely audible. "Cal's flat. I took them from Cal's flat."

"You took the laptop and mobile phone from your stepson's flat. When was this, Mr Shaw?" Nicki kept her eyes trained on the man across the table, willing him to start telling her the truth. All of it. She had the camera footage loaded on the laptop, ready to go, but she needed to hear the words from his own mouth first. Eventually, she heard them.

"On the evening of seventh March. Last Thursday. I'm not sure what time. It was late."

"Last Thursday. That would be the same evening that Calvin's body was found, would it not?"

Calvin's stepfather nodded, pain searing his eyes. "Yes."

"Did you not expect him to be home at that time of night? You said it was late?"

Mick Shaw shook his head. "No. I knew he wouldn't be there."

Nicki's heart began to beat faster. She was sure that Fox's was doing the same next to her. "You *knew* he wouldn't be there? Why is that, Mr Shaw? By your own admission, it was late at night — where did you expect him to be?"

The question hung in the air. More seconds ticked by, more tensing of muscles in Mick Shaw's jawline, but nothing further was said. Nicki decided to go for the jugular.

"Maybe you knew Calvin wouldn't be at home, Mr Shaw, because you already knew he was hanging from a tree on the heath? And you put him there."

"No!" Shaw's head shot up, eyes blazing.

"No? But you've just said you didn't expect him to be home. I repeat the question — where did you think he was, Mr Shaw? Because, according to the pathologist, Calvin may already have been dead by that time."

Fear mixed with anger now flooded the man's eyes. "That wasn't me — I had nothing to do with that. You have to believe me."

"I don't have to believe anything, Mr Shaw. You've just admitted you knew Calvin wouldn't be at home — you now need to tell me why."

All of a sudden, the six-foot wall of muscle opposite Nicki seemed to visibly deflate, as if someone had punctured him with a pin. Nicki knew she needed to keep the pressure on and pulled her laptop towards her. "It won't take us long to see what was on Calvin's laptop and phone — whatever it was you so desperately wanted to hide. But, in the meantime, let's look at this."

She turned the laptop screen towards Shaw. "This is video footage of you calling at Calvin's flat the night his body was found." She pressed 'play' and waited for the images to play out. "You enter the flat at eight forty-five and emerge five minutes later. As you exit, you are carrying the bag currently being analysed in our lab— inside that bag are Calvin's mobile phone and laptop." She paused as the image reel came to an end. "What you now need to do, Mr Shaw, is tell us why you were there. And where you think your stepson was."

CHAPTER TWENTY-SIX

Bury St Edmunds Police Station

Nicki and DS Fox had left Mick Shaw at the Police Investigation Centre. They both hoped the time spent alone, staring at the four bare walls of his cell, contemplating the unholy mess he seemed to have landed himself in, might loosen his tongue the next time they spoke.

As she surveyed the chaos of her desk, she glanced down at her phone and noticed she had several missed calls from Roy. She was about to hit the voicemail button when the man himself burst into her office.

"Good, you're back, boss. You need to see this."

Roy had several pieces of photocopied paper in his hands, plus a plastic evidence bag. "I've been taking a look at the items from Calvin's flat. Nothing stood out to us before, but now . . ."

Nicki noted the gleam in his eyes as he hovered in front of her desk.

Roy continued to grin. "When the evidence was looked at originally, it didn't register with anyone. Everything just seemed normal and run of the mill. But when I took another look, I saw these three unopened letters among the post from the windowsill. From the postmarks, this one was sent first."

Roy held up one of the sheets of paper. "Dated fifteenth of January. This was followed two weeks later by the second letter." Roy waved another piece of paper in the air. "And three weeks later, the third one."

Nicki frowned, unsure where this was heading. "And all returned?"

"Yes. All returned to sender, unopened, using what looks like the same red pen." Roy handed three sheets of photocopied paper across the desk.

Nicki looked down at the papers, noting the red biro scrawling 'RETURN TO SENDER' across the front of each envelope. She was about to question their relevance when Roy beat her to it.

"You'll no doubt notice who all three letters had been addressed to originally. None other than our friend Sir Cecil at Pemberton Hall."

Nicki's eyes widened. "Why on earth would Calvin be writing to him? We've tried to find a link between the two families but there's nothing." She looked up at Roy, noting that the gleam in his eyes was still there. "Don't keep me in suspense, Roy. There's more?"

"There's definitely more, boss. From reading the letters, I discovered something else that I wasn't quite expecting to see." Roy handed across the rest of the photocopied sheets. "It becomes clear, when you read the contents, that Calvin Shaw was under the impression that Sir Cecil Pemberton was his biological father."

* * *

Seymour Street, Bury St Edmunds

In the three or so hours since Mick had been taken away, Heather Shaw had barely moved. Her legs still felt like jelly, every limb trembling, unable to take her weight. Panic engulfed her like a tsunami.

What on earth was happening?
No one was telling her anything.

The very idea that Mick could be responsible for Cal's death brought a wave of acid to her throat, nausea threatening to overwhelm her once again. She knew it wasn't true — why couldn't the police see that too? She'd waved away all offers of tea or other refreshment from the ever-helpful family liaison officer — she knew DC Huntley was only trying to be kind, but right now Heather couldn't stomach a thing.

Her mind churned over the events of that morning. The knock at the door. The police in the house. The unbearable feeling of being suffocated. She wondered how Mick was coping; wondered what they were asking him — *and what he was saying*.

DC Huntley had advised her that the investigation team would most likely want to speak to her in due course, ask her some questions about her husband and Calvin. The thought terrified her. What would she say? Without Mick here to guide her, she started to panic even more.

She clutched her hands together in her lap, digging her fingernails into the backs of her hands. Her mind started to fog, panic rapidly dissolving into confusion. Everything was so hazy now. The past few days had been a blur. None of it felt real. She didn't even know what day it was anymore. All she wanted right now was for it all to go away — for her to wake up from this horrible nightmare, with both Mick and Cal back home where they belonged.

Just then the door opened and DC Huntley slipped inside. "Do you need anything?" The officer wore a sad expression on her face.

Heather shook her head, wiping the tears from her cheeks. "Nothing, thank you. Can I go and see Mick yet? He's been gone ages."

"Unfortunately you won't be able to see him, no. Not while he's under arrest and being interviewed. I can ring the station and find out what's happening, if you like?"

Heather shuddered. "No, it's fine." Part of her didn't want to know. For if she didn't know then none of it was real. "But you can't really think he had anything to do with

Cal — you just can't." Tears welled up once more. "That's not my Mick."

DC Huntley came to sit beside her on the sofa, taking hold of one of her hands. "I'm sure the truth about what happened will come out. Please try not to worry."

* * *

Bury St Edmunds Police Station

"Did he know?" frowned Nicki. "Sir Cecil, I mean. Do we think he knew Calvin thought he was his real dad?" Nicki had brought everyone into the incident room.

"My gut says yes," replied Roy. "The fact that the letters have been returned unopened suggests to me that he knew who they were from, that he already knew what they would say. And he didn't want to read them. I'm guessing there must have been other letters before these — or at least some earlier contact between them. The tone of the letters themselves kind of suggests they've already had that particular discussion — the '*I think you're my real dad*' conversation."

"And do we think it's true?" Nicki cast her gaze expectantly around the room. She was greeted by a variety of murmurs and shrugs. She turned back to face Roy. "Get on to Gemma and see if she's managed to tease anything more out of the wife. Float the idea that one of the potential fathers could be our latest murder victim, Sir Cecil, and see what reaction it gets. But don't say anything about the letters — not yet."

"Will do."

"In the meantime, let's assume Sir Cecil was well aware who Calvin thought he was. I want both sets of phone records analysed for any contact between them. Also, check for any emails now we have Calvin's phone and laptop. Chase up the tech suite."

"On it," replied Roy.

"Graham — let's head back for another chat with our Mr Shaw. See if he's seen sense yet."

CHAPTER TWENTY-SEVEN

Police Investigation Centre, Bury St Edmunds

"I didn't kill him. I couldn't." Mick Shaw took a small sip of water from the plastic cup handed to him. "He was my son."

"If that's the truth, then tell us what did happen." Nicki was starting to lose patience. She checked herself before continuing; she needed to keep her cool. She could feel another headache coming on. "This is your chance to put your side across." She gestured towards the laptop, the screen still facing Shaw. "You've seen the footage. We can place you at Calvin's address on the night of his murder. You've already confirmed that this is you — and that you didn't expect to find him at home that night. You also had items of his in your possession. This is your chance to tell us why." Nicki paused. "You can see what this looks like, can't you? You're a clever man, Mr Shaw. I don't need to spell it out for you."

"But I didn't kill him," repeated Calvin's stepfather, lowering his eyes to the plastic cup. "I didn't kill him."

Beside Nicki, Fox opened a slim manila folder and slipped several sheets of paper out onto the table.

"Let's move on." Nicki cleared her throat while taking hold of the papers. "Tell me about Calvin's real father — his biological father."

The abrupt change of direction brought Mick Shaw's gaze up to meet Nicki's. She noted the immediate look of confusion mixed with unease. With no response forthcoming, she tried again. "Calvin's biological father, Mr Shaw — who is he?"

More neck muscles began to tense. "I don't know who his real father is," Shaw eventually replied. "We've talked about this. Heather doesn't know."

Nicki stared into the man's steel-grey eyes and let a small smile develop. "That's correct — we *did* talk about this before. But I don't necessarily believe the answers you gave. I think you do know who Calvin's real father is. So, let me ask you one more time. Who is he?" Nicki let her hand rest lightly on top of the photocopied sheets that were lying face down on the table. Slowly, she tapped a finger. It had the desired effect. Shaw's gaze darted towards the paperwork, the look in his eyes morphing into something close to panic.

Nicki pressed on. "Calvin knew who his biological father was, didn't he? So did you. And so did your wife. In fact, I think all three of you knew. So why don't we just stop wasting time here. Who is he?"

* * *

Rochdale Police Station

PCs Leonard Foster and Carl Entwhistle pulled out into the late afternoon traffic. Due a well-deserved break, the lure of hot bacon rolls and mugs of tea tantalisingly close, neither had been amused to have been given the task of checking out what sounded like a wild goose chase and a spectacular waste of time.

When they'd been briefed on what it was they were heading towards, both had considered whether today was, in fact, April Fool's Day. The story sounded inconceivable.

"What do you reckon we'll find?" Foster swung the patrol car around the roundabout and headed out of town.

Entwhistle shrugged, gazing through the rain-splattered side window. "My guess is nothing at all. An empty car park. Or it'll be a gang from the Normandy estate laughing at us as we rock up . . ."

Foster had thought much the same himself. "And to think we're missing a bacon roll because of this."

The Stainsby Hotel was only a couple of miles away, and the distance didn't take long to cover. The inclement weather had kept many off the streets — those that had braved the journey to work had cut short their day. Others had merely stayed at home.

Foster pulled the patrol car into the hotel car park, noticing that it was virtually empty, as expected. For a moment he thought the call had, indeed, been a wind-up. But as he continued to make a slow circuit, he spied the vehicle they were looking for. "Give me that registration number again, Carl."

Entwhistle reeled off the vehicle's registration.

"Bingo."

* * *

Bury St Edmunds Police Station

"He's breaking — you can see it." DS Fox handed Nicki the mug of coffee she hadn't asked for but was grateful to receive. "Let's make him sweat for a bit. He'll soon be pleading with us to hear him out." They'd left Mick Shaw in his cell once again and made their way across town to the station for a breather and to reassess the evidence.

Nicki pursed her lips before taking a sip of the strong coffee. "I'm not so sure. I don't think he'll crack that easily. He's a tough one. He might think we're bluffing."

"But we're not bluffing." Fox waved the slim stack of paperwork in the air. "We know Calvin had been writing to Sir Cecil for the last couple of months at least. Most probably longer. The contents of these letters proves that. And it also proves that he thought Sir Cecil was his father."

"Yes, but the letters alone don't actually make it true, do they? All we've got is Calvin *claiming* the man is his real father — Sir Cecil doesn't reply to any of the letters. Or, at least, no letters from him have been found at Calvin's flat. All he's done is return them unopened."

"Then there have to be some earlier letters," countered Fox. "If Sir Cecil is just sending them back unopened, then he must already know what's inside. *And . . .*" He pulled out one of the photocopied sheets that showed the back of one of the envelopes. "He's written Calvin's address on the reverse — he knew where to send them back to. It's different handwriting to that on the front, so it has to be him. Surely this proves he *knew* who was sending the letters — knew what would be inside. He's had letters from Calvin before. We just can't find them."

"That's as maybe, Graham, but we can't *prove* it." Nicki sighed and sank into one of the vacant chairs.

"Maybe we should go back to Pemberton Hall?" volunteered Matt, taking a seat at the back of the incident room. "Take a closer look in case he's stashed them away somewhere? Now we know what we're looking for, we might find something."

It was a good idea and one Nicki had already been considering. Right now they didn't have concrete proof that Sir Cecil was actually Calvin's biological father — just that Calvin thought he was. They could organise DNA testing but that would take time . . . time they didn't necessarily have right now.

"Maybe," she responded, massaging her temples as the headache that had been brewing started to make itself known. "Let's just leave Shaw to stew for a while longer." She glanced up at the clock on the incident room wall. The custody clock was ticking, but they still had time.

Just then, the door to the incident room flew open and DS Carter came charging in, a flustered look on his face. "Boss? Simon down in the tech suite has managed to analyse Calvin's laptop and phone. Guess what he found?"

* * *

Annette had barely moved all day. She'd managed only a fitful night's sleep, ending up back at the window searching for Mason. Larry had told her not to worry — that Mason maybe just needed some time to himself. They'd asked a lot of him over the last few weeks; it was bound to take its toll eventually.

Annette tried her best to believe him. But she couldn't help noticing the doubt creeping into her husband's eyes. He knew something Annette didn't, she was sure of it. And the feeling only increased as the day wore on. Larry had suggested that they move on as planned, leave the hotel and make their way to the next. But Annette could only look at him in horror.

Not leave Mason behind, surely?

She couldn't contemplate going anywhere without him, and Larry had eventually relented. But she could tell he was worried. No matter how many times he reassured her that Mason was fine, and that things would get back to normal soon, she didn't quite believe him.

Peering out into the withering light of the car park, she again searched the shadows for the familiar shape of Mason returning. It was getting late now — almost five o'clock and there was still no word. She saw the police patrol car drive past, her stomach automatically clenching as thoughts of Mason having been involved in an accident filled her head. She was about to call out to Larry, but stopped when she saw the police car drive past the hotel entrance. Relief started to trickle. Mason was OK.

But the relief didn't last long. She watched the police car come to a halt next to the van and two officers exit soon afterwards. A fresh feeling of fear gripped her insides.

"Larry?" she whispered, her eyes still trained on the car park. She cleared her throat and spoke again, louder this time. "Larry? Come and see this."

She heard Larry step out of the bathroom but kept her eyes focused on the window. "What is it?" he replied. "Is it Mason?"

Annette shook her head, her hands gripping the arms of the chair. "No, it's not Mason."

"Then what is it?"

Annette turned her head and blinked. "Two police officers are taking a look at the van."

* * *

Police Investigation Centre, Bury St Edmunds

"Let's try this again, shall we?" Nicki rested a hand on top of the collection of photocopied papers, this time having separated them into two piles. She also had the laptop open again, the screen facing herself on this occasion. "Calvin's biological father, Mr Shaw. You still maintain that you don't know who that is?" The caffeine-laden coffee had sharpened Nicki's senses, and two hastily swallowed paracetamol tablets had banished the emerging headache. With her head now clear, she pressed on. "I think we both know that's not quite true. This is your opportunity to put that right."

Mick Shaw had refused any further refreshment during the enforced break, and now sat with his arms folded across his chest. It was a marked change in posture, and Nicki took it to herald a more defensive attitude. The man had had more than enough time to think — sitting alone in his cell with only his thoughts for company — and his body language suggested that the barriers were rising fast. Nicki knew she probably only had a limited window of opportunity before the words 'no comment' slipped from his mouth.

"Let me help you," she added.

With one hand, she turned over both sets of photocopied papers. With her other hand she swivelled the laptop screen around to face Shaw. "*These* are copies of letters Calvin wrote to the man he believed to be his biological father — the letters themselves were returned to him unopened." Nicki tapped one of the piles of paper. "And *these* are copies of a series of emails we found on Calvin's laptop — emails between Calvin and the same man." Nicki tapped the second pile.

She paused to search Mick Shaw's face for any hint of a reaction. The man stared unblinkingly across the table.

"We also found, as you will no doubt know, a series of texts between yourself and Calvin on your stepson's phone." Nicki locked eyes with Shaw. "I know you know who this man is — the man Calvin had very recently discovered to be his biological father. The evidence is here, as plain as day."

Shaw leaned forward in his seat, arms resting on the edge of the table. His voice was gruff. "If you know who it is, why do you need me to tell you?"

"I don't need you to tell me, Mr Shaw. The text messages are enough. I'm just curious as to why you felt the need to lie about it. In my experience, if someone is lying about one thing, they tend to be lying about other things, too."

Shaw looked as if he was about to say something, but instead sat back in his seat, arms folded across his chest once again. Nicki turned her attention to the laptop. Reaching across, she pressed a button and a series of CCTV images began to play.

"Who do you see there, Mr Shaw?" Nicki paused the footage at the appropriate spot: two figures frozen in time in the centre of the screen. She didn't expect an answer and she didn't get one. "This is you, Mr Shaw — I think we can all see that quite clearly. And the other person is your stepson, Calvin, is it not?" More silence. "This is a recording from Saturday second of March — just five days before Calvin was murdered. You seem to be having an argument in the street, Mr Shaw. Care to tell us what it was about?"

A flicker of unease crossed Shaw's face — it only lasted for a split second, but that was all Nicki needed.

"I think you were arguing about Calvin's real father. There are text messages back and forth between you that day, and to put it bluntly, Mr Shaw, you didn't like him at all, did you? Calvin's biological father?"

Shaw's eyes hardened but he remained silent.

Nicki let a small smile develop as she reached for one of the papers from the second pile in front of her. "And I can't say I blame you. Take this email, for example. He's basically telling Calvin to go away, and that he is — and I quote — '*no son of mine*'. In another email he even goes so far as to say — and again I'm quoting him word for word — '*if I'd known about you at the time I'd have asked the whore that bore you to do the decent thing and get rid of you*'." Nicki paused and looked up. "That's quite a hard thing to read, Mr Shaw — especially about a boy you cared about. I know Calvin sent you these emails — forwarded them on to you. I can see it in the email trail. But it must have hurt you deeply to read them. It must have hurt Calvin to read them, too. So I can understand why they might have provoked anger in you."

"I wasn't angry."

"The CCTV seems to suggest otherwise, Mr Shaw." Nicki gestured towards the laptop screen, which was still showing Shaw and Calvin in the centre. "You look very angry there." Nicki leaned across and started the footage once more. They both watched as Shaw made a grab for his stepson, getting him into a headlock before Calvin managed to break free.

"You don't understand."

"Then make me understand, Mr Shaw. Because right now, what we've got is you turning up at your stepson's flat late at night — somehow knowing he won't be home — and taking away his phone and laptop. Calvin's body is then found some hours later. And now we have another murder — the murder of a man you clearly despise. We know Sir Cecil was Calvin's biological father, let's not beat around the bush any longer on that score. And we know that tensions have been running high between the three of you." Nicki paused and closed the laptop. "You need to start talking, Mr Shaw. And you need to do it now."

CHAPTER TWENTY-EIGHT

Bury St Edmunds Police Station

"Do we really think he's good for both murders?" Matt leaned back in his chair. "Calvin *and* Sir Cecil?"

The air inside the incident room felt electrified. With the evidence from Calvin's laptop and phone, the investigation had taken a startling turn. When they'd picked Calvin's stepfather up earlier that day, Nicki had thought the man was guilty of nothing more than stupidity — that, as suspicious as it looked, there would be some reasonable explanation for him visiting Calvin's flat that night and removing the laptop and phone. And that once they heard his side of things he would be eliminated from the enquiry.

But that wasn't how things had panned out at all.

"Forensics haven't shown up any unaccounted for DNA profiles from either scene yet, have they?" Nicki already knew the answer to the question, but posed it anyway.

"Not yet, boss," confirmed Matt.

She wandered over to the whiteboards. "As galling as it might sound, I do believe we have reason to suspect his involvement in both murders." Nicki tapped the board where details of the investigation into Sir Cecil's killing were displayed. "Especially this one. Sir Cecil might have numerous enemies, but Mick Shaw is high up on that list. He has motive — Sir Cecil basically spurned Calvin in a very humiliating way; said some pretty disgusting things by all accounts. I'm sure the few emails we've seen are just the tip of the iceberg on that front. The man basically called Heather Shaw a whore and told Calvin that he would rather he'd been aborted. Not easy for Calvin to hear, but I'm sure it wasn't easy for Mick Shaw to hear either. I don't think it's too much of a stretch for us to put Shaw in the frame."

"He's a big man, too," added Roy.

"Indeed he is." Nicki's eyes flickered between the first two boards. "He could easily overpower someone like Sir Cecil — and Calvin too."

"Where does he say he was on the nights in question?" asked Duncan.

"On the evening of Calvin's murder, he says he went to Calvin's flat after leaving his wife at home asleep. Then he simply returned home. There's no one to corroborate."

"And Sir Cecil?"

"That's going to be our next line of questioning." Nicki turned away from the whiteboards. "What I'd really like in the meantime is for something from forensics to link Shaw to either scene. Can you chase it up, Roy?" She received a nod in return. "And I'd like his car tracked — see where it went on both nights. Let me know what you get." She turned to DS Fox. "Graham? You ready to go into battle again?"

* * *

Rochdale Town Centre

He could have bought a train ticket, or even got on a coach. But there was something driving him towards hitching that he couldn't quite understand. He'd done it once before when he was seventeen or eighteen, trying to get back home from a party. Larry and Annette had gone ballistic at him, citing all manner of scenarios that could have befallen him — none of them pleasant.

As he turned his collar up against the driving rain, he resumed his walk along the verge at the side of the main road. He needed to feel the danger. He needed to feel *something*. Ever since the discovery of the press cuttings and what was in the back of the van — *who* was in the back of the van — he'd strangely felt nothing. It was as if he'd been rendered completely and utterly numb. So he needed to *feel* — and danger was as good a feeling as any.

His jeans were soaked up to his knees from cars splashing through puddles, but he didn't care. He didn't exactly know where he was heading, all he knew was that he needed to get away. Away from here. Away from whatever this was turning out to be.

Away from Larry and Annette.

Had he been right to alert the police the way he did? He'd considered making an anonymous phone call, but perhaps they would have thought him a time waster that way. But had they taken him any more seriously in person? He was aware of what he looked and sounded like. He hadn't left his name — which one would he have given them anyway? Was he Dean Webster or Mason Browning? They would think him a complete head case if he couldn't even get his name right.

He just hoped he'd told them enough to find the van. Enough to find the real Mason Browning. For whatever he thought about Larry and Annette, Mason deserved better than being carted around the countryside in the back of a transit van.

Looking up, he noted a car pulling into a layby ahead, its indicator flashing. Mason pulled up his collar and ran towards it.

* * *

Police Investigation Centre, Bury St Edmunds

"Michael Shaw. May I remind you that you are still under caution?" Nicki received the briefest of nods in return. "And that you have the right to legal advice?" Another nod. "Are you still happy to continue without the duty solicitor?"

"Let's just get it over with."

Nicki began. "Where were you on the night of Sunday tenth of March?"

"I would have been at home with my wife. We'd just lost our son."

Nicki nodded. "And what did you do that evening?"

Shaw's face was grey — as if all colour had been washed from his existence and what remained was a mere shadow. "Nothing. I imagine we must have eaten something. Watched some TV maybe. Then went to bed."

"You imagine? You don't know?"

"We'd just lost our son — I can't exactly remember every second of every day." A slight edge returned to the man's tone.

"But you definitely didn't go out?"

A shrug followed.

Just then, the door to the interview room opened and a police constable entered. "Sorry to interrupt but there's a message for you."

Nicki took the piece of paper, her eyes widening as she scanned the sparse details. She shot a look across the table. "Are you sure you didn't go out on the night of Sunday the tenth?"

Shaw's body language remained defensive, his mouth shut.

"Because here we have ANPR data telling us that your vehicle was caught leaving the town at around six forty on the evening of Sir Cecil's murder. Where were you going, Mr Shaw?"

More silence.

"It was you driving, wasn't it, Mr Shaw? You didn't lend your car to anyone? Or maybe Mrs Shaw went out that night?"

"Heather can't drive." Shaw's jaw muscles tensed once again. "If anyone was driving it would be me."

"But you can't tell me where you were going? It was only two nights ago, Mr Shaw."

After another lengthy silence, Nicki exchanged a tired look with DS Fox. Shaw wasn't proving easy to break down. Sighing, she began gathering up her paperwork. "Keeping silent won't help her, Mr Shaw. It won't help Heather and it won't help Calvin. You need to tell me where you were going on the night of Sir Cecil's murder."

From the look on Mick Shaw's face, and the continued silence, Nicki knew she was getting nowhere fast and that wasn't likely to change.

"Interview suspended at seven forty-five p.m."

CHAPTER TWENTY-NINE

Wednesday 13 March 2019
Bury St Edmunds Police Station

Nicki often left her car at the station — with limited parking opportunities in the streets around her townhouse, it was just easier that way. But this morning she wished she hadn't. Driving rain pelted from the skies, coupled with a stiff breeze. The threatened hurricane force winds hadn't materialised as promised, but it still made a bleak and soggy journey to work.

Not surprisingly, she hadn't slept much. After leaving Mick Shaw tucked up in his cell, she'd sent the team home, seeing the exhaustion in their eyes. Several had offered to work through the night chasing up results and leads, combing through the evidence again to see what they were missing, but Nicki had stood firm. Their fuel tanks were depleted — soon they would be running on empty and no good to anyone.

As she pushed open the incident room door, she wondered what kind of night Calvin's stepfather had had, and in particular whether he was likely to crack when they started questioning him again. The custody clock would run out around midday, which didn't give them much time. If they wanted to keep him longer, they needed to come up with something.

Late last night, just as Nicki was leaving for home, confirmation had come through from the lab that there was a high probability that the poker found in the pond had been the weapon that killed Sir Cecil. It also matched other similar fireside tools in the drawing room at Pemberton Hall. The tartan rug, however, was too water damaged to carry any useful forensic detail.

Once inside the incident room, she noticed that the team were already assembled. Bleary-eyed, but assembled nonetheless.

"Boss?" Roy swivelled his chair round at the sound of the door opening. "You need to take a look at this."

Nicki hurried across to peer over the detective's shoulder. "What is it, Roy? I need to get cracking with Mick Shaw — we only have him for another few hours."

"Trust me, you'll want to see this. Results are in on the swabs taken from Calvin and Sir Cecil's cheek wounds. DNA profiles were isolated from each and they've both given us the same hit on the database."

Nicki's eyebrows shot up. "What, the same result for both?" Roy nodded. She felt a faint fluttering in the pit of her stomach. "Who is it?" Her hopes that they finally had a forensic link to Mick Shaw were soon shattered.

Roy angled the screen towards her. "Chap by the name of Scott Edgecombe. Age twenty."

"Scott Edgecombe? Why is he on the database?"

Roy cast his eye back to the screen. "Current information says he was arrested and charged in connection with a protest last year outside the council planning offices. Along with a number of other people."

Nicki nodded, vaguely remembering something about it.

"He pleaded guilty to a public order offence and received a fine."

"And where is he now?"

"Last known address puts him as still here in the town — Carnaby Close."

Nicki's brain was rapidly piecing together the dots, then she frowned. "Scott Edgecombe? Why do I know that name?"

Roy gave another grin and gestured towards the whiteboards. "Take a look."

Then she saw it. *Scott Edgecombe* — written in her own handwriting.

Roy continued. "He was the guy we found trolling Calvin Shaw's Facebook profile — posting vicious comments about his plastering business. And then Calvin Shaw clocked him one in the street last summer."

Nicki nodded. Although it wasn't the link she was hoping for, it was a lead they needed to follow up. As much as it pained her, Mick Shaw would have to wait.

"Well, we can't ignore the connection. If his DNA is showing up on both of our murder victims, then we need to talk to him. Get your coat."

* * *

Wednesday 13 March 2019
4 Old Railway Cottages, Dullingham, Nr Newmarket

"Bloody hell." Adrian Browning stared somewhat warily at his brother standing on the doorstep. "The prodigal son returns." He made no move to open the door any wider and stood his ground, his stance wide, his expression cool.

After several seconds of frosty silence, Mason nodded towards the hallway over Adrian's shoulder. "You gonna let me in, or what?"

Adrian remained standing, legs apart, arms crossed in front of him, a sneering smile plastered to his face. "Well, that depends, bro. You gonna tell me where the fuck you guys have been all this time? You up and leave without telling me shit, tell me I've got to stay here, and there's been no word from any of you for months."

"That wasn't my doing, you know that." Mason rubbed his eyes. He'd known Adrian would be pissed off with him just rocking up like this without warning, but he'd been travelling for hours and was dead on his feet.

Dead.

The irony almost made him smile.

Almost.

"Just let me in."

Adrian continued his rock-steady stance for a few more seconds before finally relenting and taking a step back. Mason brushed past, heading straight through to the kitchen.

"You got any beers in?"

Adrian slammed the door and followed his brother. "So you think you're just gonna waltz back in here and start drinking my beer at the crack of dawn as if nothing even happened? Is that how this goes?"

Mason detected the all-too-familiar anger bubbling beneath his brother's skin. It didn't take much. He shook his head wearily. "That's not it at all, Ade. It's just that once I've finished telling you what I know, you're gonna need that drink, whatever time of day it is."

* * *

2 Old Railway Cottages, Dullingham, Nr Newmarket

Benedict Thatcher let the curtain fall back into place. He'd heard the car pull up outside, and knew instantly that it wasn't one that belonged to any of the residents on the street. You live somewhere long enough, take enough interest in your surroundings, and you notice things like that. He'd quickly run upstairs to the bedroom at the front of the house, giving him the best view of the road below.

It hadn't taken him long to recognise the form of Mason Browning exiting the taxi and heading up the garden path next door. Silently cracking the window open a few inches, he'd just been able to overhear the conversation below. One of the advantages of living on a quiet lane, in an equally quiet part of the village, was that sound travelled.

He'd heard the scorn in Adrian's voice from the very beginning — and it was not entirely unexpected. The man was a hothead at the best of times, and he wouldn't have taken kindly to being abandoned by his family and left to fend for himself. The scorn had quickly morphed into anger, and then there was silence before Mason stepped inside the house, the door closing behind him.

Mason Browning.

Back.

He and Nicki had spent the best part of five days trying to find him — and here he was, turning up out of the blue on his own front doorstep.

As he stepped away from the window, Benedict pulled out his phone. He should call Nicki. Any sane person would call her straight away. She had a right to know that her brother had just shown up next door.

But Benedict slipped the phone back into the pocket of his jeans and made his way downstairs. His natural investigative skills began to kick in. He would phone Nicki when he had something else to tell her — in particular, where the hell her brother had been for the last two and a half months.

* * *

Carnaby Close, Bury St Edmunds

Nicki parked the car around the corner from Carnaby Close and she and Roy made the short walk towards Scott Edgecombe's front door. The house looked quiet, with no immediate signs of life from within. Roy rapped on the UPVC front door while Nicki kept an eye on the windows. Nothing moved. No curtains twitched. Roy rapped again.

"If you're looking for the Edgecombes, no one's home."

Nicki whirled round to find a tiny, bird-like woman, standing barely five feet tall, walking across the road towards them. She was dressed in a floral dressing gown, slippers on her feet, wispy white hair tangled on top of her head.

"I'm sorry?"

"The family that live there — the Edgecombes. They're not home. I'm assuming it's young Scott that you're after. You are the police, aren't you?"

Nicki gave a faint nod. She hadn't realised it was so obvious. "Do you happen to know where we might find Scott? It would be most helpful."

"Is he in trouble?" Nicki could hear a tinge of excitement in the old woman's voice.

"If you could just tell us where he is."

"He used to be such a quiet lad when they first arrived — but ever since he got in with those boys from the estate, he plays his music so loud I can hear it from across the street." She gestured to the flats behind her. "Comings and goings at all hours, too. And I'm sure he's responsible for all the graffiti we have on the walls around here . . ." This time she nodded towards a wall that flanked an alleyway at the side of the house. Nicki saw the colourful graffiti tags covering every inch of brickwork. "I've rung up to complain to you so many times, but nothing ever gets done about it. It's his poor mother I feel sorry for. Such a lovely woman."

"Well, I'm sorry about that, Mrs . . . ?"

"Harris," replied the old woman. "Eileen."

"I'll look into it as soon as we get back — but, in the meantime, if you could tell us where to find Mr Edgecombe?"

"I'll tell you the same as I told that young gentleman not ten minutes ago. He was asking about the boy, too. Scott will probably be at work — over at the sugar factory. He took off early this morning, revving that car engine just to be more of a nuisance. That is unless he's slunk off to do some more of that blasted graffiti."

Nicki nodded her thanks and made to turn away. Then she stopped. "What young gentleman?"

CHAPTER THIRTY

British Sugar, Bury St Edmunds

Nicki pulled into the main car park. All the way from Carnaby Close she'd been mulling over what Eileen Harris had said.

'*He was asking about the boy, too.*'

The suggestion that someone else had been asking about Scott's whereabouts had spiked Nicki's interest — and then, when the old woman had gestured towards a car still parked at the end of the street, that interest had turned to concern as she'd recognised the rather battered Peugeot immediately.

What was Jeremy doing sniffing around Scott Edgecombe?

She tried to call him, but Jeremy wasn't answering his phone. After three attempts she sent a text asking him to call her, but for now she had to put him, and whatever he was up to, to the back of her mind.

They headed for the main entrance to the factory and, after showing their IDs and signing in, were shown to a small conference room to wait while someone went to fetch Scott Edgecombe.

"At least it looks like he's here and hasn't done a runner," commented Roy as they waited. After only a few minutes, they heard footsteps and turned to see a tall, muscular man dressed in overalls filling the open doorway, closely followed by another.

"Can I ask what this is about?" enquired the first man.

Nicki's eyebrows lifted. "And you are?"

The man hesitated for a second before extending a hand. "Glenn Clifford. I'm one of the maintenance supervisors. I'm told you want to have a word with young Scott here?"

"You heard correctly, Mr Clifford." Nicki glanced at the proffered hand but instead turned her attention to the young man standing some way behind. "You're Scott Edgecombe?"

The young man nodded, a deep sense of mistrust and defiance crossing his features.

"Is there a problem?" persisted Clifford, lowering his empty hand. "Only we're quite busy at the moment, staff sickness and what have you. I can't really have my staff disappearing for any great length of time."

Nicki plastered the biggest and, she hoped, most patronising smile on her face. "Well, we're kind of busy ourselves, Mr Clifford. But I'll be sure to keep him no longer than absolutely necessary."

"You still haven't said what this is about."

"Correct, Mr Clifford. I haven't." Another condescending smile. "And as you have pointed out, you're *very* busy, so please don't let us keep you any longer. We'll bring Mr Edgecombe back safe and sound once we're finished." Nicki's gaze hardened. She didn't have time for this, not this morning. With the disclosure of Sir Cecil's name in the papers, the pressure was on. It had put them on the back foot before they had even got started. And they still had Mick Shaw stewing in his cell.

Clifford looked like he might reply, but then seemed to think better of it. Nicki watched the man's jaw tense, his eyes hardening. Both he and Scott Edgecombe were of similar build, their sheer bulk filling the door frame. Both wore overalls, and Nicki could see they both sported a well-defined muscular torso beneath, with thick, tree-trunk-like arms.

With one last glance towards Scott, Clifford turned back the way he had come and eventually disappeared from sight.

"Right, Mr Edgecombe." Nicki turned her attention towards Scott. "We've a few questions to ask you about Calvin Shaw and Sir Cecil Pemberton. It won't take long, but I feel it's better done somewhere else, don't you? Away from prying eyes."

Scott came surprisingly willingly, allowing himself to be led to the car. Securing him in the back seat, Nicki turned to Roy as they made their way to the front of the car. The rain had lessened while they'd been inside the factory, but more was coming if the heavy clouds above were anything to go by. Before opening the driver's door, Nicki caught Roy's gaze across the roof of the car.

"After we book him in, I want you to get me everything you can on him. And I mean *everything*. Even his bloody shoe size."

* * *

The Bury Gazette

Jeremy Frost bit his lip. He'd managed to unearth quite a lot about young Scott Edgecombe and none of it was particularly palatable. The more he dug, the more he found — and now there was Nicki to contend with. He'd seen the various calls, and then the text.

'*Why were you at Carnaby Close asking questions about Scott Edgecombe?*'

It was a simple enough question, but one Jeremy was hesitant about answering. How did she know he'd been there? As soon as he asked himself the question, the answer hit him square in the face. *The nosy old woman from across the street.* He hadn't given his name, or disclosed the fact that he was a journalist, but he had left his car parked at the end of the road while he had a walk around the area, getting a feel for where the young man lived. Nicki would have seen it and put two and two together — she wasn't daft.

But then another question reared its head. Why was Nicki looking for Scott Edgecombe? He knew she was investigating the two recent murders in the town — was it connected to that?

He looked down at the handwritten notes he'd made from his research so far. Had Nicki managed to find out exactly who Scott Edgecombe was for herself yet?

Looking back down at the text message, he knew he would have to bite the bullet sooner rather than later.

* * *

Carnaby Close, Bury St Edmunds

Lana Edgecombe rounded the corner to see Eileen Harris hovering on her front doorstep. *Great, that's all I need*, she thought to herself as she put her head down and continued along the pavement towards home. She'd decided to go to the shops along the parade, rather than the large supermarket, hoping it would be quicker and that she would avoid the many looks and stares that often followed her around. She could do without Eileen giving her a lesson in how to raise her son, too.

Scott had sped off to work that morning, on time for a change, barely grunting at her as he departed. At least, she assumed that was where he was going. All she'd heard was the car revving outside, and then he was gone.

The shopping bags weighed heavy in her hands, and she was grateful to put them down outside the front door while fishing for her keys. Eileen Harris wasted no time in hurrying across the street towards her.

"The police were here asking about your boy earlier."

Lana looked up, noticing a glint in the old woman's eyes as she relayed the information. She felt her heart sink.

Police? Not again.

She pulled the set of keys from her bag, not having the time or energy to deal with Eileen Harris right now. "Thank you, Mrs Harris. If I could just get these bags inside."

"But, the *police*. What's he done now?"

Lana saw the glint deepen. The old woman was revelling in it — whatever *it* turned out to be. She shoved the key into the lock and pushed the front door open, grabbing hold of the shopping bags once more. "Good day, Mrs Harris. Thanks again." She tried to keep her voice pleasant-sounding, but relished shutting the door in the old woman's face.

Maybe it was nothing.

But the police and Scott wasn't usually nothing — history told her that much.

* * *

Bury St Edmunds Police Station

"You'd better sit down."

Nicki was pacing the floor of her office. "I don't need to sit down, Jeremy. I'm in the middle of a complex investigation here — I've got two people in custody over at the investigation centre and I need to get back there. The clock is ticking. I don't have time to waste. I need you to tell me what you were doing hanging around Scott Edgecombe's home address. One of the neighbours says you were asking questions about him. Why?" She stopped mid-pace. "Just what are you up to, Jeremy?"

Jeremy Frost again gestured towards the chair behind Nicki's desk. "Honestly — you really do need to sit down for this one."

The urgency in the reporter's eyes made Nicki hesitate, and before she knew what she was doing she was slipping behind her desk. "Go on then — tell me." She fixed him with a stare, noticing the wariness now entering his gaze and deepening with every second that passed. For a moment, Nicki sensed that he was stuck for words, which for Jeremy Frost was almost unheard of. A wave of disquiet started to replace the irritation that had settled in her stomach. Her tone softened. "What is it, Jeremy?"

Jeremy took the seat opposite her and sat stock still for several seconds before finally taking a deep breath. "OK, I admit I've been keeping tabs on your fella back there. Scott Edgecombe. I've watched the house a few times, asked around the neighbours. But . . ." He held up a hand. "I had a good reason. I *have* a good reason."

Leaning forward slightly, he pulled an envelope out of the inside pocket of his jacket. "A story landed on my desk not so long ago. I can't go into too much detail just yet as to how that came about, but the story concerned a young lad — well, a child, really. A child of just eight years old who went by the name of Scott Edgecombe." Jeremy flicked through the contents of the envelope and pulled out a newspaper cutting. "This story ran in 2007." He handed the press cutting across the desk. "There was an incident at an after-school club in North Yorkshire — an incident where another young boy died."

* * *

Thursday 10 May 2007
St Augustus Primary School

He hated going to the after-school club — hated it just about as much as it was possible to hate anything. But that wasn't why he'd done it. He'd done it because he hated *them*, too. And Simon Baxter in particular.

Maybe they would listen to him now.

He'd run away soon after, crawling into the cupboard in Mr Charleston's art room. It smelled comfortingly of paint and plasticine. Sitting in the farthest corner, he pulled his knees up close to his chest. He could feel his heart racing, his breath coming in short, choking gasps.

He felt an odd mix of emotions.

At eight years old he wasn't quite sure what all the emotions were that a human being could feel — certainly not an eight-year-old one anyway. But it still felt like an odd mixture to him. There was fear there, for sure. Cold, hard fear. But there was also exhilaration — something similar to how he'd felt on the rollercoaster at Cleethorpes last summer. That feeling when your stomach leaps into your mouth. You feel scared — but you *like* feeling scared.

That's what he felt like as he hid himself in Mr Charleston's art cupboard.

It wouldn't have happened if Mum hadn't insisted he stay behind after school. *I have to work*, she would always tell him. And he wasn't old enough to walk home on his own — not yet. There were too many big roads to cross, too many strangers prowling the streets. He'd bawled, screamed and cried about how unfair it all was — but to no avail.

So, here he was.

And now look what had happened.

He couldn't blame his mother entirely — even his eight-year-old self knew that. Most of the blame lay with Simon Baxter. The boy was always laughing at him. Teasing and laughing. Kicking sometimes, too.

Well, he wouldn't be laughing any more, would he?

The idea caused a flicker of amusement to join all his other conflicting emotions. What he'd done had been wrong, he knew that. He wasn't a *baby* — no matter how many taunts Simon and the others threw in his direction. He knew right from wrong. He knew good from bad. But he'd needed to do this. For this was the only way to make it stop. To make *them* stop.

He felt a flicker of concern now. Concern at what might happen next. He knew they would find him eventually — and then what?

He still held the rock tightly in his hand. It was lucky that he'd found it when he had. He'd spied it out of the corner of his eye, just sitting there beneath the bush on the edge of the playground. It was as if it had been put there on purpose — so that he could finally do what he had to do. Put an end to it all.

The rock had spoken to him.

Pick me up.
Pick me up.
Pick me up.
So he had.

The rock was covered in blood, as was his hand. Splattered stains decorated his T-shirt, too. Mum would go mad when she saw it. *Blood never comes out*; he could hear her voice already, yelling at him as she scrubbed away at it in vain.

And then there was the blood on Simon's head, and covering his face.

But it wasn't just the blood that stayed with him as he cowered in the corner of the cupboard.

The crunch of Simon's skull as he had pounded it with the rock would be something he would never forget.

* * *

Wednesday 13 March 2019
Bury St Edmunds Police Station

Nicki let the cutting fall back to the desk. "You're saying . . ."

Jeremy nodded. "The kid who battered this Simon Baxter to death in 2007 is none other than your Scott Edgecombe. He was only eight at the time, so he was below the age of criminal responsibility. He couldn't be arrested or charged with anything. He openly admitted what he'd done, and why he'd done it — but there was nothing anyone could do." Jeremy gathered up the cutting and slotted it back inside the envelope. He then pulled out a copy of a small, passport-sized photograph. "This was him back then. Aged eight." He passed the photograph across the desk. "Social services understandably got involved, plus a multitude of other organisations, but after a while the family just seemed to drop out of sight. They moved away from the area. My source tells me that Edgecombe hasn't been in trouble with the law since, but . . ."

Nicki took hold of the photograph and studied it. "But once a killer, always a killer," she muttered. After a moment or two she looked up. "And you're sure? This is definitely him?"

"One hundred per cent. My source is genuine — knew the family back then and knows them now."

"Who is your source?"

"You know I can't tell you that. Not yet, anyway. This lad might not be your killer."

"That's very true — but his DNA is on both of my bodies." Nicki looked sharply across the desk. "Which is information you are going to keep strictly to yourself, Jeremy Frost." She shouldn't really have divulged such information to anyone — and definitely not to the press. Jeremy might be a friend, but he was also a journalist.

The reporter's eyes widened. "DNA?"

"Which you are going to keep to yourself," repeated Nicki. She received a nod in response. "I'll go and check this out — if what you say is true then he'll be on our system. Don't go anywhere."

CHAPTER THIRTY-ONE

Bury St Edmunds Police Station

Roy stood at the third whiteboard, where a fresh mugshot had already been tacked. "This is Scott Edgecombe. Aged twenty. As mentioned before, he had a conviction for a public order offence last year after a protest at the local planning offices." He added the brief details to the board next to the image of Edgecombe. "Lives with his mother in a house on Carnaby Close. Works as an apprentice at British Sugar — has done for the last twelve months. Other than that one conviction, he hasn't shown up on our radar before. Except . . ."

Roy dashed a look towards Nicki who was standing at the back of the incident room. She nodded at him to continue.

"As soon as we fed Scott Edgecombe into the system, he came up with a hit for a PVP." Roy added the details to the whiteboard.

Various eyebrows were raised around the room.

Roy continued. "The Protecting Vulnerable People tag was entered because of an incident when Scott Edgecombe was eight years old."

Over the next five minutes, Roy filled the rest of the team in on Scott Edgecombe's violent history.

Nicki joined Roy at the whiteboard. "So, as you can see, Scott Edgecombe is a major person of interest for both of our current investigations. He has a proven history of violent behaviour — albeit when he was under the age of criminal responsibility — and his DNA has been linked to both victims. We have him in custody right now, and Graham and I will be heading over to interview him shortly."

DS Fox got to his feet, shrugging into his jacket. "We know he's linked to Calvin Shaw with the assault — what about Sir Cecil?"

Roy went back to his desk and checked his notes. "As far as I can tell, the Edgecombe family only moved into the area eighteen months ago. Before that, they lived in Hastings. Before that, North Yorkshire. Like you say, we already know Edgecombe is the one who trolled Calvin Shaw on social media, and Shaw punched him in the altercation outside the Grapes last summer. But as far as I can tell, that's their only link to each other. As far as Sir Cecil is concerned . . . I can't find anything to say they've ever met."

"We've also got to be mindful that the kill methods on both murders were different," added Nicki. "And the body disposals, too. But if we are thinking there's just the one killer, then there has to be something linking the two cases. They're too random otherwise."

"We also have the CCTV from the DIY store car park." Roy shook the mouse to wake up his computer monitor. "Remember the guy we saw?" He brought up the still image from the car park. "It's not great quality, but . . ." He angled the screen so the others, who were now crowding round his desk, could see. "I think it could be him — Edgecombe."

Nicki was the closest to Roy's monitor. "It's not the greatest quality, like you say. It's possible, though."

"What about Mick Shaw?" Fox hovered by Nicki's shoulder. "His custody clock is about to run out any moment."

Nicki grimaced and headed for the door, gesturing for Fox to follow. "Let's go and see Scott Edgecombe — I'll worry about Mick Shaw on the way."

* * *

Benedict had known that phoning the taxi company wouldn't get him very far. He'd noted the company name emblazoned on the door of the Lexus before it pulled away from the kerb. He'd given them a call, pretending to be a police officer investigating a missing person case. He was suitably vague, and to begin with the woman who'd answered the phone was taken in. For a few minutes at least.

Nicki would string him up if she found out, but it was a risk he was prepared to take. If Dean had returned alone, that meant Larry and Annette were still out there somewhere. And so was the body of the real Mason Browning.

All he'd managed to glean from the taxi company was that Dean had been picked up that morning in Newmarket town centre. It didn't help him much. He'd asked for the name of the driver who'd driven Dean home, at which point the woman became more guarded and mentioned having to check with her supervisor.

At that point Benedict cut the call.

If he wanted to know where Larry and Annette were, he was just going to have to ask the man himself.

CHAPTER THIRTY-TWO

Nicki rubbed her eyes as she went through the preliminaries once again. Another suspect; another custody clock ticking.

Mick Shaw was about to be released from his cell. She'd intended to re-interview him this morning — tie up a few loose ends, put the ANPR evidence to him — but the recent DNA results had thrown a rather large spanner in the works. There were still many unanswered questions bouncing around inside her head as far as Calvin's stepfather was concerned, but right now she had to focus on Scott Edgecombe. And specifically why his DNA had turned up at both crime scenes. With his violent past, it couldn't be ignored. So Mick Shaw was being allowed to walk.

"Mr Edgecombe, just to remind you that you are being interviewed under caution. And that this interview is being recorded." She gestured towards the video camera blinking high up on the ceiling, and the audio recording equipment by her side. Scott merely blinked in response, his expression blank. "You've been arrested on suspicion of murder. I'll remind you again that you do not have to say anything, but it may harm your defence if you do not mention when questioned something which you later rely on in court. Anything you do say may be given in evidence. Do you understand?"

More blinking was then followed by a short nod.

"Let's start by finding out where you were on the night of the seventh of March. It was last Thursday." Nicki stared across the table. At first she wasn't quite sure if he'd heard the question, but then he spoke, his voice steady, if a little monosyllabic.

"I don't remember."

"It was only six days ago, Mr Edgecombe. Try again."

Scott made a face and shook his head. "Nope. Can't think."

Nicki gazed down at the brief notes she'd compiled before entering the interview room. "What about the night of Sunday the tenth? What were you doing then?"

The same blank expression met her gaze from across the table, followed by a shrug. "I can't remember."

Nicki bit her tongue. "You seem very forgetful, Mr Edgecombe. We'll come back to that. Let's try something else. How well do you know Calvin Shaw?"

A faint frown registered on the man's brow before he replied, "I'm not sure that I do."

"You don't think you've met before?"

Another shrug. "Doesn't ring a bell — should it?"

"Do you remember an incident last summer. You were involved in an altercation in the street just outside the Grapes."

"Aah." Slowly a shadow of realisation crossed Scott's features. "That."

"Yes, *that*."

"Was he the guy who thumped me?"

"He was the young man that assaulted you, yes."

Scott nodded. "OK, yes, I've met him, then. But I still don't know what you're getting at."

"You've not met since?"

Scott shook his head. "Nope. Should we have?"

"Do you read the papers at all, Mr Edgecombe?" The vacant look gave Nicki the answer she needed. "Not been looking at the news online?" Another shake of the head followed. "Let's come back to that one, too. How about Sir Cecil Pemberton? How do you know him?"

"Who says that I do?"

"Just answer the question, Mr Edgecombe."

"Well that's easy — he's the guy that lived in that big mansion just outside the town. Everybody knows that."

"Lived?" Nicki flashed a look across the table. "Why do you say he 'lived' in the big mansion? Does he not still live there?"

Scott hesitated, the vacant look now sporting a faint wariness. "Because he's dead, isn't he?"

"How do you know that, Mr Edgecombe?"

"It's all over the news, isn't it? You can't miss it."

"I thought you didn't look at the news? I think that's what you just said."

Another hesitation followed by another shrug. "Maybe I caught a bit of that. It's everywhere."

"Tell me more about Sir Cecil. How do you know him?"

"I don't — but he was the guy they were all moaning about at the residents' meeting."

"Residents' meeting? Where and when was that?"

Scott started to shrug, then seemed to change his mind. "Sometime last week, I think. It got quite nasty towards the end — lots of people seemed to hate the guy."

Nicki watched Fox make a note on his pad, after which they exchanged a look. "Interview suspended at eleven fifty-nine a.m. We'll come back and see you in a bit, Mr Edgecombe. Don't get too comfortable."

* * *

Bury St Edmunds Police Station

"So, what's your first impression of him, boss?" DS Fox followed Nicki into her office.

"I'm not sure." She gestured for Fox to take a seat opposite her desk. "I can't place him. He seems completely

238

unconcerned about being arrested on suspicion of murder — *two* murders, in fact. It's almost like he finds it amusing, that he's completely unconnected to reality."

Fox dutifully sat down. "That's what they say though, isn't it? About psychopaths? That they have no empathy at all — no ability to connect with others or show emotion. They don't have any kind of conscience and don't accept any form of responsibility for their actions."

Nicki raised a tired eyebrow.

Fox grinned. "I did a course once. Psychopaths versus sociopaths, and how to tell the difference. It was very interesting, as it goes. And our friend Scott ticks *all* the boxes for a psychopath in my book."

Great, thought Nicki. *That's all we need. A psychopath.* "Let's leave him to marinate for a little while — in the meantime, we need to find out all we can about this so-called residents' meeting — if there even was one. If Sir Cecil was the focus of the discussion, I'd like to know what was said — and by who. Can you go and see if Roy is free to make some enquiries?"

"Will do." Fox made to get up. "Did you see the latest lab report just come in? The can of spray paint found under the sideboard at Pemberton Hall has thrown up a match for Edgecombe's fingerprints."

Nicki nodded. She'd seen the report just moments before. "Something else to put to him when we re-interview."

Fox reached the door and half-turned. "What about Mick Shaw? Has he been released?"

Nicki pinched the top of her nose between her thumb and forefinger. Another headache was brewing. "I didn't have much choice, I had to cut him loose. Let's deal with Edgecombe first; we'll come back to Mick Shaw as and when we need to."

After Fox left to go in search of DS Carter, Nicki swallowed two more paracetamol tablets and prayed for her headache to abate.

Mick Shaw.

Scott Edgecombe.

Both names were thumping their way around her head. There was definitely something about Edgecombe that unnerved her. The initial interview hadn't thrown up much — except for how calm and collected he seemed to be. Graham's suggested diagnosis of him being a psychopath only added to her disquiet. But the detective was certainly right about the man's character traits: a complete absence of empathy, zero emotion, completely unconcerned about the reason for his arrest. His calmness wasn't normal. Guilty or innocent, people were generally edgy when being interviewed, but she'd seen nothing of the sort in Scott Edgecombe's behaviour.

And then there was Mick Shaw. There was still something not quite right about him, but she just couldn't put her finger on it. The man was hiding something, that was abundantly clear. But what was it? Both Shaw and his wife had lied about not knowing who Calvin's real father was — and when people lied it was usually because they had something to hide.

With recent reports suggesting cameras had picked up Shaw's car leaving the town on the night of Sir Cecil's murder, it raised more questions than answers. But the cameras alone weren't enough to keep him in custody — there was nothing to prove he'd been anywhere near Pemberton Hall that night. So her hands were tied on that front and she'd had to release the man under investigation, as much as it irked her.

They'd brought back some sandwiches for lunch, but Nicki's appetite had waned. Glancing at her watch, she decided to leave Scott a while longer — long enough for him to start to get concerned about his predicament. She also needed time to figure out how she would approach his past violent behaviour — what questions she would ask to unsettle him enough to start talking. She'd give it an hour — maybe two. Then she'd hit him with Simon Baxter.

CHAPTER THIRTY-THREE

Sinclair Avenue, Bury St Edmunds

It hadn't taken Roy long to track down details of the residents' meeting. A member of staff who worked in the canteen lived near Carnaby Close and knew the person who'd organised it all. A man by the name of Morris Skinner. She even had a contact number for him. One quick phone call had been all it took to get Roy an invite to the man's house.

"Can you run me through what these residents' meetings are all about? How often you have them?" Roy seated himself on an armchair next to a three-bar electric fire. The small living room was cosy, to the point of being suffocatingly warm. He eased the tie from around his shirt collar.

The chairman of the residents' association sat opposite, in another identical floral armchair. Roy noted that he was a small man — *small-boned*, his grandmother would have called him. An angular jaw, prominent cheekbones, wide forehead with receding hairline, Morris Skinner blinked behind a set of round-rimmed spectacles.

"We meet once a month usually — occasionally there's an emergency meeting if needed. But the last time that happened was a few years ago when we had Storm Angus — several residents suffered flooding and other damage to their homes." Morris nudged at his spectacles. "I do hope this storm doesn't bring a repeat." He gave a small, nervous laugh, gesturing towards the window and the rattling wind outside.

"Quite," replied Roy. "And what kind of things do you discuss at these meetings?"

"Oh, it can be anything really, but I do try to keep to an agenda. It's not meant to be a free for all. Residents must email me seventy-two hours before a meeting if they want a topic included for discussion."

"And when was the last meeting you had? I believe it was sometime last week?"

Morris nodded. "Friday night. The eighth."

"And what was on the agenda for that evening?"

Morris Skinner reached for a slim A4 diary that he had balanced on the arm of his chair. Nudging again at his spectacles, he opened it and flicked to the appropriate page. He nodded quietly to himself. "I keep copious notes, detective. I don't feel you can run something like this without being organised." Inside the diary were two sheets of folded A4 paper. "My wife Marjorie types up the minutes for me — I keep notes as the meeting progresses and she types them up the following day." Morris proceeded to unfold one of the A4 sheets. "On that date, the agenda was mostly concerning the proposed housing development at Pemberton Hall. There were a couple of other items at the beginning of the meeting — wheelie bin collections and the never-ending graffiti that seems to blight many of the open spaces on the estate. And we briefly mentioned that awful business over at the heath. The body?"

Roy nodded but remained silent. He wasn't here to talk about Calvin Shaw.

Realising he wasn't about to get any salacious inside information, Morris continued. "We despatched those topics quite quickly and turned to the main issue of Pemberton Hall." The chairman looked up over the rim of his spectacles. "I'm assuming that is what you've come to discuss, detective?" His gaze slid sideways to a copy of the *Daily Express* folded up on a side table. "I couldn't help but see the news about Sir Cecil."

"Indeed." Roy gave a curt nod. "What kind of things were said about the development, and Sir Cecil?"

"Well, it all got rather heated towards the end, I can tell you that much. I pride myself in running a tight ship, detective — keeping the discussions within the bounds of decency and respect. Everyone has a right to an opinion and to express that opinion openly, but I don't tolerate any threatening behaviour or bad language."

Roy didn't doubt it for a second. "How did things get out of hand?"

"Well, let's just say there are a couple of residents who are well known for canvassing their opinions at these meetings, and they can often clash heads, especially if it's a particularly heated discussion."

"Do you have their names?"

"Oh, I have the names of everyone who attended the meeting, detective. You can never be too careful these days." Morris gave another nervous chuckle and pulled out the second sheet of A4 paper. "They're all listed here." He rose from his chair and passed the paper across the small hearth towards Roy. "The two residents I mentioned are Erin Fletcher and Glenn Clifford. They often clash, but that night they did even more so than usual."

* * *

Police Investigation Centre, Bury St Edmunds

"I must remind you that you are still under caution, Mr Edgecombe." Nicki resumed her seat opposite Scott Edgecombe in the interview room. "I also remind you of your right to legal representation, and that this interview is being recorded." She paused. There was no reply or reaction from across the table, so she pressed on. While Roy was off following up details of the residents' association meeting, Nicki had decided to turn up the heat on Scott.

"Tell me what happened with Sir Cecil Pemberton."

"Nothing happened."

"You're sure about that?" Nicki thought she saw a small flicker of doubt edge into Scott Edgecombe's eyes. But then it was gone, if it had even been there to begin with.

"Have you ever been to Pemberton Hall?"

Scott hesitated before shaking his head. "No."

"Never?"

"Never."

"What about Calvin Shaw? Have you seen him recently?"

Another shake of the head. "Not since he thumped me last summer."

"OK. We'll come back to that. How do you explain your DNA showing up on both our victims' bodies?" Nicki let the question sink in. "You do know what DNA is, don't you, Mr Edgecombe?" Another flicker of doubt. "This means we can put you in close proximity to both Calvin Shaw and Sir Cecil Pemberton at the time of their deaths — your DNA is on both of them. I need you to explain to me why that is."

Nicki watched as Scott's gaze lowered to his lap, where he began to pick at his fingernails. It was almost as if he hadn't heard the question.

"Mr Edgecombe? I need you to explain why that would be. This is your chance to tell me."

Still nothing.

"We know you threatened Calvin online — posted some malicious comments on one of his business threads." Nicki selected a sheet of paper from the pile in front of her. She passed it across the table. "Why did you do that?"

A faint shrug accompanied the continued silence.

"Were you jealous of him? He had a thriving business and you were just working in a factory?"

Scott continued to pick at his fingernails, barely blinking.

"Your life not quite working out the way you wanted it, so you thought you'd try and mess with someone else's?"

Nicki tried to hide her annoyance at the lack of response. "And this is what then led to your altercation outside the Grapes last summer?"

Nothing.

"Let's fast forward to now. Did you still harbour some animosity towards Mr Shaw? Decided that you wanted to exert your revenge for the assault?"

Scott barely flinched.

Nicki acknowledged the continued silence. "Let's come back to that, shall we? Do you enjoy DIY, Mr Edgecombe?"

The question seemed to momentarily confuse, and Nicki saw Scott's brow creasing.

"Not really," came the eventual response.

"Do you ever visit any DIY stores? Buy anything to fix things around the house maybe?"

More brow creasing and a shrug. "No. Not really."

"I want to show you something." Nicki activated her laptop screen and turned it around. "For the purposes of the tape, I'm showing Mr Edgecombe a copy of CCTV footage taken from the car park of a DIY store some two weeks ago." Nicki noticed this elicited more of a reaction. Scott lifted his gaze to look at the screen just as she pressed 'play'.

"This footage shows someone I believe to be you returning to your car, having purchased a coil of blue polypropylene rope. We have confirmation of the sale from the store's checkout. Why did you buy the rope, Mr Edgecombe?"

The flicker of doubt from earlier returned — and stayed longer this time. Nicki pressed ahead. "A very similar section of rope was found not only in Sir Cecil's drawing room after his murder, but also close to his body when it was pulled from the pond. It was also used to string Calvin Shaw's body from a tree on the heath. Why would that be so, Mr Edgecombe?"

Scott continued to stare at the laptop screen but remained mute.

"Any reason you can think of why you would be seen buying a very similar, if not identical, coil of rope just two weeks before both of these murders?" Nicki wasn't expecting a reply and she didn't get one. "Do you like art, Mr Edgecombe?" She decided to change tack. "Drawing? Painting?"

Scott's gaze remained fixed on the laptop, but Nicki could clearly see the confusion swirling. After a while he gave a faint nod. "Sure."

"Ever use spray cans? Spray paint?"

A guardedness entered Scott's voice. "Maybe."

Nicki slid another piece of paper from the pile and passed it across the table. "This can of spray paint was found in Sir Cecil's drawing room — does it belong to you?"

A faint shake of the head together with a shrug.

"Then can you explain to me why we found your fingerprints on it, Mr Edgecombe, if it isn't yours and you claim never to have been to Pemberton Hall? You're lying, aren't you, Mr Edgecombe?" Nicki paused, just long enough to see the fresh unease cross Scott's features. "You need to stop lying to us. We can clearly put you at the scene of Sir Cecil's murder — your DNA and fingerprints are there, despite you saying you've never been. Your DNA is also on Calvin Shaw's body, despite you saying you haven't seen him since, and I quote, '*he thumped me last summer*'." Nicki's gaze hardened. "Why are you lying, Mr Edgecombe?"

Nicki stared into Scott Edgecombe's eyes. She knew she was looking into the eyes of a killer — but was he the killer of Calvin and Sir Cecil? She decided to keep pressing. It was time to bring up the past.

"Can you tell me what happened at St Augustus Primary School in 2007, Mr Edgecombe?"

The words got a reaction almost before they left Nicki's mouth. Scott's eyes narrowed and hardened. He blinked slowly, his mouth tense.

"How about you tell me what happened to a young boy named Simon Baxter?"

CHAPTER THIRTY-FOUR

Sinclair Avenue, Bury St Edmunds

Roy scanned the list of names on the sheet. He'd recognised Glenn Clifford's name as soon as Morris Skinner had said it, remembering him from the visit to the British Sugar factory earlier that morning. Scott Edgecombe's name was also on the list.

"Can you elaborate for me what exactly was said about Sir Cecil and Pemberton Hall? Why was there such a heated discussion?"

Morris leaned forward in his chair, his bony hands knitted in his lap. "Everyone at the meeting was very much of the same opinion about the proposed plans at Pemberton Hall — nobody wants that monstrous development on their doorstep, detective. The increase in traffic, the pressure on GP surgeries and schools, and all the other facilities, too. The area just can't cope with such a sudden influx. And then there is the effect on the local wildlife and countryside as a whole. The proposals have angered a lot of people."

Roy nodded. "So I can see. But if everyone was of the same opinion, why was the debate so heated? That's how I think you put it . . ." Roy made a point of looking back in his notebook.

"It wasn't so much that people disagreed over the development as such, it was more a disagreement over what to do about it. Erin is very much one of your old-school protesters — if you can even call her that anymore. Her heart is in the right place — she just doesn't support the use of violence to get the point across, or to get people to listen."

Roy raised an eyebrow. "And other people do?"

The chairman's cheeks coloured. "Of course I don't support violence, detective. Let's make that very clear. Violence has no place in a civilised society."

"Quite. What else can you tell me about Erin Fletcher and Glenn Clifford clashing? Anything in particular that was said? Any direct threats towards Sir Cecil from either of them?"

"Glenn is a little more hot-headed than Erin. He can be quite challenging at times, especially when he gets a bee in his bonnet about something. And he was very worked up about Pemberton Hall, encouraging more 'direct action', I think he calls it. That was what he and Erin came to blows over. She wants a more peaceful protest, petitions and such like, whereas he . . . well." Morris paused. "He can often come across as aggressive — but his bark is definitely worse than his bite."

Roy thought back to the man standing in the doorway at the British Sugar factory. He didn't look like someone you wanted to mess with. "How do you mean? Do you have any evidence that his bark is worse than his bite?"

"Well, no, but . . ." The chairman's cheeks pinked even further. "But I can't see him mixed up in anything like this." Once more, his gaze drifted towards the folded newspaper on the side table.

Roy turned his attention back to the list. "What about Scott Edgecombe? What can you tell me about him? He was there, yes? His name appears on the list."

A frown crossed Morris's flat forehead. "Well, yes — yes he was. Along with the others in his gang from the estate. They often come, but never really take part in any discussions. I think they come for the free biscuits."

"So he didn't join in the discussion at all?"

"No, none of them did. They just fidgeted about at the back of the hall. I kept my eye on them in case they were there to cause trouble, but they behaved."

"What made you think they might be there to cause trouble?"

"Nothing specific — it's just that they're well known around the estate. General antisocial behaviour, that sort of thing. We're all certain they're responsible for the increase in graffiti we've seen lately. They hang around street corners, bus stops, anywhere they can cause a nuisance and leave litter in their wake."

Roy nodded. "And what can you tell me about Scott Edgecombe in particular?" he repeated. "Do you know him?"

The chairman's narrow shoulders shrugged. "He's a quiet lad. Lives with his mother over on Carnaby Close. I'm not sure how long they've been living here — I don't know them too well, to tell you the truth. He can look a bit intimidating — he's quite well-built. I certainly wouldn't want to meet him in a dark alley, anyway." Morris tried to inject some humour into his tone.

Roy scribbled some final notes into his book. "Is it OK if I take this list with me?" He waved the sheet of A4 paper in the air.

"Of course."

"Anything else you can tell me about that night? Anything that stands out in your memory?" Roy slipped the list of names into his notebook.

The chairman began to shake his head, then stopped. "Well, now I come to think about it, there was one thing. As I was leaving, walking to my car, the lads were all hanging about in the car park. It's another of their regular hangouts you see. It smelled like they were smoking something — not tobacco, if you get my meaning. Anyway, Glenn was standing with them. He seemed to be quite worked up about something — maybe he was just carrying on with his little tirade from inside, I don't know. There's certainly no love lost between him and Sir Cecil, I can tell you that much. But I just left them to it. Got in my car and came home."

Roy nodded as he rose to his feet. "Thank you, Mr Skinner. You've been most helpful."

As Morris began to show Roy out of the stuffy living room, a small woman came through from the kitchen.

"Shall I make some tea?"

* * *

4 Old Railway Cottages, Dullingham, Nr Newmarket

Dean eyed Adrian Browning across the kitchen table, his brother's face a mixture of emotions.

Should he even be calling Adrian his brother now? Everything seemed so strange — so surreal.

Adrian stared down at the wooden table, eyes blinking rapidly. Eventually he spoke. "Well, you're not wrong there."

Dean raised his eyebrows. "Not wrong about what?"

Adrian reached for another beer from the six-pack on the table between them. "Me needing a drink." He pushed a can across the table, but Dean shook his head and left it untouched. His head was already swimming. "So, how long have you known?"

Dean had shown Adrian the newspaper cuttings he'd taken from the hotel — plus a snapshot he'd taken with his phone in the back of the van of Mason Browning's headstone. It had taken his brother a while to digest, sinking a can of beer before he even spoke.

"Literally just yesterday. I think it was yesterday, anyway. I've no idea about time at the moment — everything's a blur. Maybe it was the day before." Dean rubbed his eyes, his head banging. He felt like he'd been travelling for days. The sleepless hours on the night bus were catching up with him fast.

"What do you plan to do?"

Dean had thought of nothing else during the long journey back to Suffolk. The series of drivers who'd been good enough to stop and give him a lift had tried their best at small talk, but after only getting the barest of grunts in response, they had left him to his thoughts.

What *was* he going to do?

Before he was forced to give the question any more thought, there was a loud rapping at the door. Both Dean and Adrian looked up, their eyes raking towards the hall-way. Dean wondered if the same thought was going through his brother's head. Was that Larry and Annette? Had they tracked him down?

They both sat in silence while the rapping continued. Eventually, with an irritated sigh, Adrian got up and lum-bered towards the front door. Dean got to his feet but hung back in the doorway. He had no idea what he would say to them if they came face to face right now. He had plenty of questions, but wasn't sure he wanted to ask them. He might not like the answers.

Adrian pulled open the door. Relief crossed Dean's face when he saw it wasn't Larry or Annette — it was just the man from next door.

"Adrian? Do you have a moment?" Benedict Thatcher hovered on the doorstep.

Adrian's frown deepened while he watched his neigh-bour's gaze travel over his shoulder and into the house.

"I'd like to have a word with your brother, if that's OK?" Benedict paused. "A word with Dean?"

* * *

Bury St Edmunds Police Station

"The meeting was on the Friday — the day *after* Calvin was killed. And two days before Sir Cecil's murder. I've got a list of all the people who attended." Roy passed the list Morris Skinner had given him across Nicki's desk.

"You're sure it was the Friday? Not the Thursday?"

Roy shook his head. "Definitely the Friday."

"So this still doesn't give our Mr Edgecombe an alibi for Calvin's murder, then, does it? What else did you find out?"

"The main topic of conversation seems to have been the proposed development at Pemberton Hall. By all accounts it got rather heated and almost ended in fisticuffs. Our friend Scott Edgecombe is on the list — he was telling the truth about that, at least — but you'll also find another name there that you'll recognise. Remember that fella in the sugar factory — the one who said he was Edgecombe's supervisor?"

Nicki scanned the list, her gaze coming to rest on a name near the bottom. "Glenn Clifford."

"Yep. That's him. Apparently, he was one of the main ones getting all fired up about Sir Cecil. Him and a woman called Erin Fletcher. They both banged heads during the discussion. Then, after it was all over, Clifford was seen outside talking to Edgecombe and the gang he hangs around with, again quite heatedly."

Nicki sank back in her chair. Her head throbbed and she felt as though she was being pulled in all manner of directions. She was still reeling from what Jeremy had told her about Scott Edgecombe's violent past. She couldn't help but think that if he was capable of something like that aged eight, what would he be capable of now? Especially taking into account the size of him. When she'd brought up the subject of Simon Baxter at the end of the last interview, Scott had merely stared her out. He'd made no comment at all, barely even flinched.

Was Graham right and they were dealing with a psychopath here? He seemed to have most of the traits, if not all of them. She sighed and turned back to the list.

"If Matt and Duncan are free, ask them to go and talk to the two you mentioned — Glenn Clifford and Erin Fletcher. Just to get another angle on what happened. See if either of them are acquainted with our Mr Edgecombe. Meanwhile, I'll go back and resume my chat with him."

CHAPTER THIRTY-FIVE

Police Investigation Centre, Bury St Edmunds

"Let's go back to Simon Baxter." Nicki took her seat in the interview room. As she looked across the table towards Scott Edgecombe, she detected a slight change in his demeanour. Gone was the disinterested, almost vacant expression in his eyes. This time he fidgeted in his seat before giving a small nod.

"OK, look, I was there. At Pemberton Hall that night. But I didn't kill him." Scott reached for a plastic cup of water, which he gulped down in three mouthfuls. "And I didn't kill the other one either."

Nicki sat back in her chair. "Why don't you tell us what you *were* doing at Pemberton Hall, then, Mr Edgecombe?"

* * *

Thursday 7 March 2019
7.45 p.m.
Pemberton Hall

Slinging the rope over his shoulder, Scott scaled the eight-foot-high brick wall with ease. The man wasn't exactly making it difficult for him; security was non-existent as far as he could see. To get to the wall that surrounded Pemberton Hall, he'd run across the fields from the woods that flanked the estate, with very little to stop him.

The wall had a '*PRIVATE PROPERTY — KEEP OUT*' sign bolted on, with a picture of two ferocious-looking Dobermann dogs next to it, but it looked neglected and rusty. After dropping down on the other side of the wall, he quickly ran through the landscaped gardens. There were no security lights springing into action, and no sound of the aforementioned dogs, either.

Pemberton Hall slumbered on.

When the others had put him forward for the job, he'd initially been a little hesitant. It wasn't that he didn't think he was capable of doing it — he was. More than capable. He just wasn't sure he could be bothered. Then he'd sensed the others in the group questioning his loyalties; questioning his ability to push the boundaries.

He grinned beneath his balaclava. They didn't know who they were dealing with. He wasn't called '*The Edge*' for nothing. He didn't think about Simon Baxter all that much these days, but for some reason the boy's face flickered into his mind as he ran. He found himself smiling again. He'd never really been all that honest with the multitude of social workers who had flocked around him afterwards — never told them how much he had actually *enjoyed* crushing Simon Baxter's skull to dust. He suspected it might have raised an eyebrow or two.

Heaving the small rucksack higher onto his back, he bent down low and approached the house. The closer he got, the better he could see the crumbling brickwork, the loose guttering. The general air of abandonment.

None of which particularly bothered Scott Edgecombe.

He gave the main entrance a wide berth, knowing it was unlikely he would be able to get inside that way. But these old houses were full of windows and doors — he was sure there would be another way in. He just needed to find it.

Skirting around the side of the house — east wing, west wing, he had no idea, having been dismal at geography at school — he started heading towards the back. Although there were security lights embedded in the brickwork, none activated. Everything was quiet. Everything was still. Not a breath could be heard other than his own. To anyone on the outside, the place looked deserted.

Maybe Sir Cecil wasn't even at home?

The thought had flickered through Scott's head as he'd scaled the outer wall and seen the house swamped in darkness. If Sir Cecil wasn't at home, then this whole escapade would be a spectacular waste of time. But as he crept along the rear of the house, he saw a muted light coming from one of the windows on the ground floor. Cautiously, he peered inside, seeing a faint glow from a table lamp. Beyond it was the entrance to a kitchen.

Turning his attention to the window itself, he noted the rotten frames. Swinging his rucksack from his back, he slipped the crowbar out and wedged it between the rotting wood. It wasn't long before a welcome splitting sound could be heard, but the surrounding silence soon swallowed it whole.

Replacing the crowbar inside his rucksack, he edged the window up — high enough to pull himself through the gap, dropping soundlessly to the floor on the other side. Pausing, he listened to the quiet — still nothing.

Leaving the window open for his escape, he padded as silently as his heavy boots allowed on the flagstone floor towards the kitchen. A large wooden table took up most of the space, the far wall housing a range cooker and two Butler sinks.

Not an expert in large stately homes, even Scott could imagine the room being the hub of the house — warm and inviting, the aroma of baking filling the air. But, right now, it had a forgotten feel to it. The cooker emitted no heat — and by the looks of it, it hadn't seen a flicker of a flame for some time. A tap hanging over one of the Butler sinks was dripping, the only sound filling the otherwise silent room — a steady drip-drip, drip-drip.

Scott continued his journey deeper into the house. *Where would he be?*

It didn't take him long to find out.

The stone passageway led him towards a heavy oak door, with soft light spilling from around its edges. As Scott inched closer, he heard the sound of classical music and thought he could smell the odd wisp of cigar smoke even through his balaclava. A faint ripple of anticipation entered his bloodstream.

It was time.

* * *

Wednesday 13 March 2019
Police Investigation Centre, Bury St Edmunds

"So, you admit you broke into Pemberton Hall?" Nicki saw the faintest of nods from the other side of the table. "For the purposes of the tape, Mr Edgecombe is nodding. What happened after you entered the Hall?"

Scott replaced the empty plastic cup on the table. "I found him."

"You found who?"

"The posh guy that lives there — Sir Cecil."

"And what did you do when you found him?"

* * *

Thursday 7 March 2019
7.55 p.m.
Pemberton Hall

"What the devil do you think you're doing?" Sir Cecil sprang out of his Chesterfield armchair, dropping his half-smoked cigar onto the rug as he did so. "Stop right there."

Scott gripped the crowbar in his hand. He felt another rush of adrenaline course through him, the familiar *buzz* as Simon Baxter flickered into his thoughts once more. He fixed his eyes on the man's expression — seeing fear and surprise in equal measure. But there was something else, too. An unmistakable look of entitlement — a condescension that only the landed gentry could pull off.

Scott took in the man's long, narrow nose and pointed chin — reminding him a little of Mr Burns from *The Simpsons*. But he was clearly tall, and sported broad shoulders beneath a well-cut but ageing suit. He wouldn't be a pushover — so Scott swung the crowbar in front of him and moved another step closer.

Sir Cecil peered haughtily down his nose. "I thought I told you to stay where you were. Someone will be along here any minute. I have security, you know."

But the threat was an empty one — something they both knew.

Scott continued advancing, placing the rucksack on the back of an armchair, but not once taking his eyes off Sir Cecil. The man might be getting on in years, but he could still make things difficult if he wanted to. Unzipping the rucksack, he pulled out the coil of polypropylene rope and several cans of spray paint.

"I don't have any money in the house, if that's what you want." Sir Cecil's pale eyes widened as he saw the rope, his gaze shifting sideways towards the fireplace — and the cast-iron poker resting against the brickwork.

"Don't even think about it," Scott growled. "You stay right where I can see you."

* * *

Wednesday 13 March 2019
Police Investigation Centre, Bury St Edmunds

"I hit him, but I didn't kill him." Scott Edgecombe's voice was firm.

"You hit Sir Cecil?" repeated Nicki evenly. "With what?"

"I had a crowbar — to help me get into the house."

"Whereabouts did you hit him?"

Scott shrugged. "I dunno. On his body maybe. He put his arms up — I probably hit his arms."

"And then what happened?"

"He fell over — by the fireplace. He was reaching for one of those pokers, so I hit him again."

"You hit him again?"

Scott nodded. "Yes. I took my gloves off — I couldn't grip the crowbar properly. He was getting to his feet so then I punched him in the face. Maybe twice, I can't remember."

Nicki paused. That could account for the DNA on Sir Cecil's cheek wound. "And then what happened?"

"I tied him up with the rope."

Nicki's eyebrows hitched. "You tied him up?" As far as she knew, Sir Cecil hadn't been found with any bindings when they'd pulled him out of the pond, although some rope was later found at the bottom by the divers. It was something she would have to check. "Go on."

"I used the rope to tie him up, then did what I went there to do."

Nicki frowned. "Which was what, exactly?"

Scott frowned. "The spray paint, obviously. The graffiti. I was only there to scare him. Nothing else. I've told you, I didn't kill him."

Nicki felt her confusion deepen just as DS Fox passed her a handwritten note.

Date? it said, simply.

Nicki looked back up at Scott. "What date did you break into Pemberton Hall and assault Sir Cecil?"

A blank look crossed Scott's face. "It was the Thursday. Last week. I don't know what time — it was dark."

"Thursday? You're sure about that?"

Scott nodded. "Positive. The night before that stupid meeting."

Nicki flashed a look towards Fox. Sir Cecil didn't die until Sunday evening. Something here didn't add up.

"Tell me what happened next . . ."

* * *

Scott stepped away from the sideboard to admire his handi-work. It wasn't his best, but he was under pressure. The old guy was wriggling around on the floor by the fireplace, trying to shout for help. Scott wasn't bothered about the noise — he knew they were alone in the huge house, despite what the man had said about security — but Sir Cecil was starting to irritate him.

He picked up the can of green spray paint and started to put the final touches to his artwork.

'*Burn in hell.*'

As he did so, the drawing room door crashed open. Scott whirled round, dropping the spray can, which rolled under-neath the sideboard and disappeared from sight. Maybe the old guy had been telling the truth about having security after all. He lunged for the rucksack that housed the crowbar.

"Help me, Calvin!" Sir Cecil turned towards the figure in the doorway. "Help me!"

Calvin Shaw rushed into the drawing room, pushing roughly past Scott as he did so. Sir Cecil was lying on his side on the rug, his hands tied behind his back, his legs tied together at the ankles.

"Help me," Sir Cecil repeated.

"Stay where you are!" barked Scott, holding the crowbar out in front of him. "Don't come any closer!"

"Have you hurt my dad?" Calvin ignored Scott and took a step closer to Sir Cecil. "Because if you have . . ."

Dad? Scott frowned beneath his balaclava. It was then that he recognised the man who'd disturbed them. It was the prick who'd thumped him last summer. Calvin Shaw. But since when was Sir Cecil Pemberton this bloke's father? Scott shook his head. It mattered not to him who he was. What did matter was getting the job done and getting out of there smartish, without the cops being called. The posh

259

bloke he could deal with — especially now he'd got him tied up. But the other guy looked like he could handle himself. Scott remembered the punch he'd taken outside the Grapes.

But Calvin Shaw didn't seem to be getting the message. Scott watched as he bent down and started to untie Sir Cecil. Ramming the crowbar back in his rucksack, Scott took several confident strides forward. The only weapons he needed were his fists. "Get away from him!"

His fist connected with Calvin's left cheek. He thought he heard something crack and crunch beneath his knuckles, but he couldn't be sure. He'd left his gloves off to use the spray cans, and the force of the blow stung his hand. While he watched Calvin's legs shake beneath him, he pulled his arm back and landed another blow in the same place. This one knocked Calvin from his feet.

Scott saw a smear of blood on his knuckles. He wasn't sure if it was his own or Calvin's, and he wasn't about to hang around and find out. Just as Calvin crumpled to the ground, Sir Cecil seemed to find some inner strength from somewhere and shrugged off the rope that had now been pulled loose. The man pulled himself to his feet and lunged towards Scott.

"Get out of my house!" he thundered, eyes blazing. Staggering forward, he walked right into it — Scott's fist, that is; the same fist that had knocked Calvin's lights out only moments before.

Scott watched Sir Cecil fall backwards, landing heavily on the rug in front of the fireplace. He glanced at the wall, and the graffiti he'd managed to decorate it with. He wasn't quite finished but it would have to do. Calvin was stirring, and it wouldn't be long before the guy was back on his feet, baying for blood.

Scott pulled his gloves back on, his hand now bleeding from its contact with Sir Cecil's cheekbone. He snatched his rucksack, stuffed the spray cans back inside and bolted for the door.

* * *

"That's all I did, I swear."

Nicki's head was spinning — and by the look on DS Fox's face, so was his. The interview with Scott Edgecombe wasn't going quite the way she'd expected — *if* the man was telling the truth, that was. Everyone knew psychopaths could show a tendency towards the pathological — but was Scott Edgecombe really a psychopath? Or had his past, the killing of another child as an eight-year-old, been just a tragic mistake? Could someone really come back from that and lead a normal life thereafter?

Thoughts continued to tumble through Nicki's head. "I think we'll take a break. Interview suspended at three thirty p.m."

Nicki drove in silence as she and Fox headed back to the station. As they entered the incident room, Matt was the first to grab her attention.

"I didn't get much from Erin Fletcher. She didn't know Edgecombe, other than being a face she saw occasionally around the estate. She seemed genuine. Although she didn't particularly like Sir Cecil or his proposed development, I can't see her being involved. She didn't seem to know Calvin Shaw at all."

Duncan added, "Same with Glenn Clifford. He's a fairly formidable character — certainly strong enough by the size of his biceps, but I didn't get the '*killer*' vibe from him. Knew Calvin by sight only — knows Edgecombe a lot better as they obviously work together at the sugar factory. Told me Edgecombe was a quiet lad on the whole. Other than that, not much use really."

Nicki stood by the whiteboards. "Thanks, both. While you've been out we've had a bit of a development with our Mr Edgecombe." For the next fifteen minutes she outlined what had been said during the interview.

"So," pondered Roy, "if he's to be believed, he went to Pemberton Hall on the night of Thursday the seventh, leaving Calvin and Sir Cecil both alive and well. He admits to punching both in the face, which could account for leaving his DNA behind."

Nicki nodded. "It would appear so, yes. Edgecombe was very firm on the date — it was definitely the Thursday evening. And we know that Calvin's body was found later that same night. The only logical explanation is that Sir Cecil killed Calvin." Nicki let the statement sink in.

"Killed his own son?" Roy's eyebrows shot up. "Not that he really considered him to be his son, if the contents of the letters are anything to go by. And the emails especially. But still . . ."

"It's not such a bold suggestion. Has anyone taken a look at the writing on the reverse of those envelopes?" Duncan jumped to his feet and strode over to one of the whiteboards, where the photocopies of the three envelopes sent back to Calvin Shaw were tacked up. He tapped one of them. "See the block capitals here? Nice and neat, uniform height?" He then turned to a copy of the supposed suicide note that had been left in Calvin's pocket on the heath. "Writing look familiar to anyone?"

Nicki stepped closer. "Well, I'll be damned. It's virtually identical. Good spot, Duncan."

"So, on that basis, we're convinced Sir Cecil killed Calvin." Matt frowned. "Which means we don't have the same killer after all, and the cases *aren't* connected? If Sir Cecil killed Calvin, then who killed Sir Cecil?"

Fox joined Nicki at the whiteboards. "We might have two different killers, but our cases could still be linked — just maybe not how we originally thought."

"I agree," replied Nicki. "It seems too much of a coincidence otherwise."

"But what was Calvin doing at Pemberton Hall that night?" asked Roy. "I don't think it's very likely that Sir Cecil invited him over for a family get together, do you?"

"Unfortunately, I doubt we'll ever find out the answer to that one." Nicki turned away from the boards. "But, as

Matt says, what we need to ask ourselves now is who killed Sir Cecil three days later?" She posed the question more to herself than anyone else.

"Although Sir Cecil didn't have that much of a fan club," mused Roy, "I can't see many people going to the extreme of killing him just over some proposed land development."

Nicki nodded. "My thoughts exactly. On that basis, I think we can rule out Erin Fletcher and Glenn Clifford. But there *is* someone else who might have borne a grudge so deep-rooted it was worth killing over." Before she could elaborate further, the door to the incident room opened and a lone PC's head appeared around the frame.

"Message from the front desk. Michael Shaw has presented himself and wants to talk to you."

"Bingo," beamed Nicki. "Just the person I was thinking about."

CHAPTER THIRTY-SIX

Police Investigation Centre, Bury St Edmunds

"Michael Shaw. Although you have attended voluntarily, I am placing you under arrest for the murder of Sir Cecil Pemberton. You do not have to say anything, but it may harm your defence if you fail to mention when questioned something that you later rely on in court. Anything you do say may be given in evidence. Do you understand?"

Nicki received a nod from across the table. It was just after half past four and Scott Edgecombe had been returned to his cell. They had until the morning to make a decision on what to do with him. So, for now, Mick Shaw was her sole focus.

"You came to the station voluntarily, Mr Shaw. What is it that you would like to say?"

Mick Shaw stared down into his lap, eyes almost closed. For a moment, Nicki wondered if the man had changed his mind. But then he took in a deep breath, raised his gaze and began to speak.

"I killed him — Sir Cecil. I admit that. But I didn't lay a finger on Cal."

Nicki gave a slow nod. "Why don't you just tell us what happened?"

Shaw took in another shuddering breath. "A week before he died, I took Cal over to Pemberton Hall. He'd worked out Sir Cecil was his father a while back — how he found that out I have no idea. He never said. He came to me a few months ago — asked me what I knew about the man. I told him not much, which was the truth." Pausing, Shaw stared into Nicki's eyes. "Then, a week before he died, Cal came to me to say he wanted to go up to Pemberton Hall, have it out with Sir Cecil. He showed me some of the emails — you've seen them, they were vile. I tried to talk him out of it initially, told him I wouldn't help him. That I wouldn't take him to see the man. But Cal was insistent, and I knew he would just drive up there on his own if I refused. So I agreed — I figured it was better that I was around."

Nicki made some hurried notes on her pad. "Did Heather know anything about this? Did she know that Calvin had found out about his biological father?"

Shaw shook his head. "Cal just confided in me." He paused, and once more locked his gaze with Nicki's. "So I took him."

* * *

Friday 1 March 2019
7.00 p.m.
Pemberton Hall

"You OK?" Mick Shaw killed the engine and looked across to the passenger seat. "We can just as easily turn around and go back."

Calvin shook his head fiercely. "No. I want to see him. I need to see him."

Mick saw the fire in his stepson's eyes and knew there was no point in trying to dissuade him any further. The boy would do this, with or without him. "OK. Then I'll wait here."

"You don't have to. I can make my own way back."

"I know I don't have to — I want to. I'll wait for you. Just don't do anything stupid in there. If the man doesn't want anything to do with you, then that's his loss."

"He called her a whore." Calvin's hand hovered over the car door handle, his voice taut. "He called Mum a whore."

Mick could only nod. "The man's a prick, what else can I say? You get over there and say your piece if you want to, but come straight back. You hear me?"

Calvin took in a deep breath, released his seatbelt and exited the car.

Mick watched him disappear into the night. Was he doing the right thing in bringing him here? But what other choice did he have? Cal was a sensible lad but could be stubborn and hot-headed at times. Mick would need to be there for him when it all came crashing down around him, which it inevitably would.

As he sat waiting, he wondered what Heather would say if she knew. He hated lying to her, going behind her back like this. But he would do anything for Cal. The boy was like flesh and blood to him. He would go to the ends of the earth and beyond to protect him from people like Sir Cecil bloody Pemberton. And he would do anything to protect Heather, too; the bond he had with her was unbreakable.

Time ticked by slowly, but eventually Mick felt the car sway as Calvin wrenched open the passenger door and launched himself inside. He was out of breath, chest heaving — the hall was a good mile away across the fields — and his face was flushed.

"You OK?" Mick glanced warily towards the passenger seat as Calvin slammed the door behind him. "How did it go?"

Calvin didn't reply at first, just nodding towards the steering wheel. "Just drive."

Mick reversed the car out of the narrow track and headed for the road back to town. A couple of minutes into the journey, Calvin spoke.

"He threw me out, Dad. Literally got me by the collar and chucked me out. He didn't want to know."

Mick sighed. "I did say nothing good would come of it, Cal. You need to leave it be now. People like that — you just can't talk to them. It's impossible. You can't reason with them." He glanced towards the passenger seat and made a face. "This ends here and now, right?" He had to wait a few moments before Cal gave a small nod. "Good. Don't give the weasel another thought."

* * *

Wednesday 13 March 2019
Police Investigation Centre, Bury St Edmunds

"Cal came out raging. Said Sir Cecil had literally thrown him out — telling him that he would call the police if he didn't leave right away."

"How did Calvin get in? Did Sir Cecil *invite* him in?"

"Cal told me he went in through an unlocked door at the back, but . . ." Shaw sighed. "I don't know. Maybe he broke in. I can't see Sir Cecil welcoming him inside with open arms, can you?"

"Quite."

"But Cal wasn't a bad lad — he wouldn't have wanted any trouble. Not after what happened last year. He was trying to build a solid business and wouldn't have wanted any more damage to his reputation." Shaw took another sip from the plastic cup of water Nicki had nudged across the table.

"What else did Calvin tell you about that night?"

"Sir Cecil thought Cal was after his money — his fortune. Because that's what people like him always think, isn't it? That everything revolves around money. He told Cal that no child of that whore would ever get a single penny from him. Like I said, Cal was raging. He wasn't after the man's money, he just wanted . . . Hell, I'm not really sure what it was that he wanted, but it sure wasn't money." He looked up once again and met Nicki's gaze. "I knew it was a complete waste of time, but what could I do? I had to be there to support him."

"And that was the week before Calvin died? What happened afterwards?"

"Cal was still obsessed with it all — kept saying that he wanted to go back again, and that this time he wouldn't leave until he'd said everything he wanted to say. Again, I tried to talk him out of it. Heather was beginning to notice the tension between us. That was what you saw on the CCTV — us arguing in the street. Cal was telling me he was going back to Pemberton Hall. I was just . . . I was just trying to stop him. Make him see sense." Shaw's head drooped, his eyes half-closing. "But what was I meant to do? I couldn't let him go back there again — not alone."

Nicki's eyebrows hitched. "So you did go back?"

Shaw nodded, pulling his gaze up once more. Nicki could see the pain etched deep in the man's eyes. "If I hadn't taken him back that night, he'd still be alive, wouldn't he? I have to live with that."

"And this was the night of Thursday the seventh?"

More nodding. "We argued all the way over. I was still trying to talk him out of it, but it was no use. I dropped him where I did the first time — it's about a mile through the fields to the hall. But I . . ." Shaw's voice cracked. "But I didn't wait for him this time. We'd argued — like I said — and we exchanged quite a few heated words during the journey there. I told him that if he got out of the car and went ahead with it, then he was on his own." Shaw hung his head. "Last time I saw him he was running across the fields towards Pemberton Hall."

"What did you do next?"

"I was still angry at him — and at Sir Cecil. At the whole bloody situation. I decided to swing by Cal's flat and pick up his laptop and phone. I thought it was time we showed Heather what had been going on — she deserved to know. I felt bad that we'd done this all behind her back. That's why I took them. I wanted her to see the poison the man had been drip-feeding Cal."

"But Cal never made it home . . ."

Shaw shook his head. "No, he didn't. But I didn't know that until the next day. If I'd never taken him there that night . . ." He stopped and swallowed back the rest of the words. "But I'm not stupid. Cal would have gone whether I took him or not. Doesn't make it any easier to live with, though."

"And Sir Cecil? What happened with him?"

Shaw took in a deep breath before replying. "I killed him."

* * *

Sunday 10 March 2019
8.00 p.m.
Pemberton Hall

He sensed it before he heard it. That feeling that something wasn't quite right.

The house was old, but not so old that Sir Cecil didn't recognise the usual creaking and groaning from the aged brick and woodwork. The house had its own sounds as the temperature dropped and it began to settle itself down for the night — but this was different.

And after the intruders he'd had a few nights ago, he was especially sensitive to the noises.

He pursed his thin lips and put down his brandy glass. Maybe it was the alcohol. He stared into the dying embers of the ornate fireplace, their warmth long-since burnt out. On the outside it looked like he lived the life of the landed gentry. But that was only because people didn't look closely enough — they only saw what they wanted to see.

They saw the big house, the expensive cars, the well-land-scaped gardens and fountains. They saw the racks of expensive wine in the cellar. What they didn't notice was the roof that needed immediate repair, the window frames starting to rot, the ancient heating system that needed an urgent upgrade. He'd taken to living in just one section of the house now, leaving the rest to freeze over during the winter.

Pushing himself to his feet, he crossed the rug to stoke the embers in the grate. It wasn't that he didn't have the money for the repairs — he did. He had various investments around the globe, but often they were tied up in so much red tape that they weren't easy to access. His father had left him a small fortune; just about the only decent thing daddy dearest had done for him. But that was the thing about money — once you had it, you wanted to keep it. And then you wanted more.

Hence the deal with the developers. There was far more land around Pemberton Hall than he needed, so why shouldn't he sell some of it off and make a few quid on the side? So long as the houses couldn't be seen from his own windows, and the great unwashed who ended up living there never bothered him or came within walking distance of his gates, why should he care?

He knew there'd been various protests in recent weeks — people shouting about ripping up the landscape, destroying vital habitats for wildlife, how additional building would put strain on an already beleaguered infrastructure. Blah. Blah. Blah. It was all white noise to Sir Cecil. He'd stopped listening a long time ago.

There it was again.

Sir Cecil stopped prodding the embers with the poker and strained his ears, expecting more sounds to follow. But there was nothing. Maybe it was the house after all, or the wind outside. The storm they'd all been promised hadn't come to much in the end — but the wind was still whipping strongly across the fields. The brandy swirled in his stomach. He hadn't eaten any dinner, unable to summon up the enthusiasm to venture down to the cold, stone-floored kitchen and see what was left in the larder. Before his father's death, the house was blessed with a cook, a housekeeper, a landscape gardener, a butler and a general handyman. All were gone now — now he just paid for Clarence to keep the gardens trim once a fortnight.

He replaced the poker on a stand next to the fireplace and crossed over to the huge bay window that looked out onto the expanse of front gardens. It was too dark to see much, but as far as he could tell, nothing seemed out of place.

Yet everything did.

The noise came again. A creak to accompany the tension now seeping into the air of the drawing room. Sir Cecil knew each and every creaky wooden floorboard in the house, and he knew this could only be caused by someone on the other side of the door.

Someone who shouldn't be here.

Again.

Silently, he crossed back to the fireplace and grabbed the poker. He wasn't going to be caught off-guard this time. Although concerned as to the sound of the creaking floorboard, he wasn't particularly scared. More irritated, if anything. For a fleeting moment, an image of the board game *Cluedo* flashed into his mind — it was Sir Cecil, in the drawing room, with the poker. A tense smile flickered onto his taut face.

He edged towards the oak-panelled door just as it began to creak open.

"You?" Sir Cecil didn't attempt to hide his surprise. He lowered the poker. "How did you manage to get in?"

* * *

Wednesday 13 March 2019
Police Investigation Centre, Bury St Edmunds

"So, you got inside Pemberton Hall. How did you manage that?" asked Nicki.

"I found one of the doors around the back was open."

"An open door? That was convenient."

Shaw merely shrugged. "It brought me in by the kitchen."

"Why kill him? Sir Cecil — why did you want him dead?"

"I don't think you really need to ask that question, do you? You must have worked out by now that he killed my boy."

"How did you know Sir Cecil was responsible for Calvin's death? You weren't there — you didn't see it happen."

Shaw gave a rueful smile. "I didn't need to see it. I just *knew*. I took Calvin to Pemberton Hall that night, and a few hours later he's dead. Doesn't take Einstein to work that one out. Anyway — he squealed like a pig eventually, admitted it himself."

"That may be so, but it doesn't entitle you to take the law into your own hands, Mr Shaw. Why didn't you just call us? Tell us what you knew?"

"You don't think I haven't asked myself that question a thousand times? After it happened — when they found Cal's body — I didn't want Heather knowing I'd taken him there myself. That I'd played a part in putting Cal in harm's way."

"How did you kill him? Sir Cecil?" Nicki noticed a brief hesitation flash across Mick Shaw's face before he replied.

"With the poker. I hit him around the head with it."

Nicki gazed down at the paperwork in front of her before glancing at her watch. "Is there anything else you would like to say, Mr Shaw, before we charge you?"

Shaw paused before finally shaking his head. "No. Only that I'm sorry for what happened — and for what it will do to Heather. But I don't regret what I did. Not for one single second."

CHAPTER THIRTY-SEVEN

Thursday 14 March 2019
Bury St Edmunds Police Station

The aroma of strong coffee and pastries quickly filled the incident room. The morning briefing had been put back to ten thirty to allow the team a more relaxed start following several intense days with the Calvin Shaw and Sir Cecil Pemberton investigations. Even so, most of the team slid into their seats much earlier, bleary-eyed and craving caffeine but with an unmistakable hint of satisfaction in their eyes.

We did it.

Nicki surveyed the room, clutching her mug emblazoned with '*BOSS*', savouring the warm, coffee-scented steam wafting towards her nose. They'd finished late last night, wrapping up the interviews with Mick Shaw and Scott Edgecombe, and she hadn't got home until after midnight, much to Luna's intense displeasure. But, despite her exhaustion, Nicki managed to snatch only a few hours' sleep, dragging herself out of bed at six a.m. for a run to clear her head.

"Thanks to everyone here, the investigations into the deaths of Calvin Shaw and Sir Cecil Pemberton have reached their conclusion." Nicki paused to take a mouthful of her coffee. "Searches at Pemberton Hall resumed early this morning, and reports say a vehicle stored in one of the garages has tested positive for potential blood in the boot. Samples have been taken for further analysis to confirm that it is blood, and whose it may be. We are, of course, suspecting it will be Calvin's. The rest of the house is being re-processed in the light of what we learned yesterday — we now suspect it to be the crime scene for not just Sir Cecil's death, but also that of Calvin Shaw.

"Following Michael Shaw's confession, he has been charged with the murder of Sir Cecil Pemberton. He'll be appearing at the Magistrates Court later today and no doubt remanded in custody." Nicki paused. Despite the team solving both murders, she knew nobody felt particularly elated. Sir Cecil's actions had been abhorrent — killing his own son and trying to pass it off as a suicide; that would never sit easy with anyone — but Mick Shaw? She knew she wasn't alone in having some degree of sympathy for the man's actions: killing the man responsible for ending the life of his stepson. But, although those actions were somewhat understandable and driven by grief, murder was still murder. A life had been taken.

"Do you think the judge will go easy on him, assuming he pleads guilty when it eventually gets to court?" Matt was halfway through a breakfast sausage roll. "Give him a lesser sentence?"

Nicki swallowed another mouthful of coffee, eyeing up the freshly baked croissants. "I hope so. That family has seen enough grief over the last few days to last them a lifetime. But you know as well as I do, Matt, provocation is no defence to murder. He might get it knocked down to manslaughter, but . . ." She shrugged. "It gives a reason for his actions, but it's not a defence."

"What about Edgecombe?" DS Fox was munching his way through his own sausage roll, pastry flakes littering his customary crumpled shirt.

Nicki sighed. "Scott Edgecombe has been charged with burglary and false imprisonment. I'm satisfied he played no part in either murder. It just so happened he chose that particular night to break into Pemberton Hall; the same night Calvin Shaw turned up and met his death at the hands of Sir Cecil. He's still in custody and will also be making an appearance before the magistrates later today."

"It's the wife I feel sorry for." Roy bit into his croissant. Despite the late night, Nicki noted that the detective looked bright and alert, freshly shaven, and immaculately presented in a well-fitting suit. She couldn't help smiling to herself as DS Fox brushed the pastry flakes from his shirt and from his unshaven chin. Polar opposites, the pair of them.

"Gemma is remaining with Heather Shaw for the time being — the woman will definitely need some degree of support going forward. She's lost both her son and husband in the space of a week. Plus, Calvin's biological father — although she may not grieve so much for that one. It's certainly a lot for one person to process, anyway."

Various nods and murmurs circulated the room.

"That Edgecombe fella," mused Fox, wiping his mouth with a serviette. "He might not have killed anyone this time around, but it won't be long — I'm sure of that. He'll get caught up in something similar before he's much older. He was so cold, so detached. People with psychopathic tendencies are like that." He shrugged and threw his serviette in the bin. "I don't think they ever go away."

Just then, the incident room door flew open and DC Darcie Butler breezed in.

"Hi everyone, I'm back!" She stopped and took a look at everyone's exhausted faces. "Wow, what did I miss?"

* * *

Police Investigation Centre, Bury St Edmunds

He hadn't slept much — but he hadn't really expected to. All he could think about was Heather.

And Cal.

275

Mick stood up from the hard, unforgiving mattress and stretched his arms above his head, feeling the bones in his shoulders and neck crunch. He was a big man, not made for small spaces like this.

While counting down the hours overnight, he'd had plenty of time to think — about the past, but also about the future that now stretched out in front of him. It wasn't the kind of future he'd planned, but it was the one he was being dealt.

Mostly he thought about Heather.

He hoped she was bearing up and that she had someone there for her. After the final interview, he'd asked the detective inspector to pass a message to her — to tell her to phone one of her friends, ask someone to be with her in the coming days. He couldn't bear the thought of her being on her own. Whether the message would reach her, he had no idea.

He'd been treated well, considering. They had fed and watered him, and checked on him during the night to make sure he was OK. He didn't feel like he particularly deserved it, but it was appreciated all the same. When he was taken to the desk to be formally charged by the custody sergeant, he thought he'd detected a faint glimmer of compassion in the man's eyes as he read out the charge.

Murder.

It made him shudder.

Such a cold word; a blunt word.

Murder.

But Mick Shaw didn't regret his actions — he didn't regret anything about that night. If he had to do it all over again, he would. The time had come for him to step up, so he'd made his confession in a steady and controlled voice. He'd done it for Cal.

He would do anything for that boy. *Anything.*

But even more so, he would do anything for his beloved Heather.

* * *

Mick Shaw switched off the engine, his eyes trained on the steering wheel. Silence filled every inch of the car. Eventually he drew in a deep breath.

"You're sure you want to do this?" He turned to face his wife in the passenger seat.

Heather stared resolutely out of the windscreen ahead. He noticed the red circles around her eyes, joining the black ones that had been there for a while now. It had been three days of intense pain since Cal's death, and he could see each and every minute etched into his wife's face. He watched her nod.

"I'll come in with you, then."

"No." Heather's voice was stern, belying her fragile state. "I have to do this alone."

They had driven to Pemberton Hall in silence, Mick failing to push thoughts of Cal out of his head as he drove. He'd made this exact same journey twice with Cal — and now he was doing it with Heather. Déjà vu overwhelmed him with every mile.

But this time they weren't hiding.

Mick had driven the car straight through the unlocked gates of Pemberton Hall and up the gravel drive towards the main entrance, coming to a stop adjacent to a rather ostentatious fountain. His hands still gripped the steering wheel as the engine died.

"But what if he—"

Heather cut him short. "He won't. I just want him to look me in the eye and tell me what he did to Cal. And then I want to tell him what I think of him — to his face."

Mick had heard virtually the same words escape Cal's mouth from the same passenger seat not three days before. And look how that had ended. The man inside this building was a murderer.

277

"But—"

"But nothing." Heather leaned across and placed a hand on Mick's arm, giving it a faint squeeze. "I'll be fine. But I have to do this. And I have to do it alone." With that, she exited the car and headed around the side of the house.

Mick felt a gnawing sensation in the pit of his stomach. None of this felt right. He'd come clean to Heather about Cal visiting Pemberton Hall. There was no way he could keep it from her, not after losing Cal so horrifically. So, after they'd been to the mortuary to view Cal's body and ended the day looking through the family photo albums, reliving Cal's childhood page by painful page, tears streaking both their cheeks, he planned to tell her everything. Before he could do so, Heather confirmed she already knew Cal had discovered who his biological father was. She didn't enlighten him as to how she knew — somehow it didn't matter anymore. So, instead, he'd told her how he'd taken Cal to visit Sir Cecil — how he'd taken their boy to his death.

Then he'd shown her the emails on Cal's laptop and watched his wife crumble before his very eyes.

They had then spoken at length about Cal — and about his biological father. Mick saw the pain and hatred intensify in his wife's eyes as the story unfolded. He'd grabbed her hand and let her sob onto his shoulder as she recounted how Sir Cecil had forced himself upon her all those years ago — raped her in the back of his car.

'*I was too weak to do anything about it, Mick — too weak to tell anyone what he had done. I made a promise to myself that that man would never have anything to do with Cal. Not ever.*'

And now here he was at Pemberton Hall — *again.*

Mick stared out of the side window. How long had she been gone? Five minutes? Ten? More? It still didn't sit right with him — leaving her to confront the man who'd killed her son all on her own. But she had been so insistent; he could see where Cal got his stubbornness from.

He sighed and rubbed his eyes. Why hadn't he just called the police after Cal's body was found? It wasn't the first time he'd asked himself that question. And after coming clean to Heather, they'd both agreed who was responsible. They knew it was Sir Cecil. Why hadn't they just told the truth and let the police deal with it?

His hand gravitated towards his pocket and the mobile phone inside. He could call them now. Tell them what he knew. It wasn't too late. Surely there would be some evidence inside, something to prove what Sir Cecil had done? His hand hovered over his pocket.

But he knew he wouldn't call them. Not yet anyway. Heather needed to do this — to say whatever it was she needed to say. After that the police could come and do whatever they wanted to do. But for now, Heather needed to come first. So, instead of making the call, he pulled a pair of leather gloves from the glove box and climbed out of the car. He wasn't going to let Heather confront the man alone — despite what she'd said. He wanted to be there, too. He *needed* to be there, too.

Because he would do *anything* for Heather.

CHAPTER THIRTY-EIGHT

Sunday 10 March 2019
8.00 p.m.
Pemberton Hall

Mick stood frozen in the doorway of the drawing room of Pemberton Hall.

"It's done." Heather's voice was barely audible. She was standing by the side of the fireplace, one of Sir Cecil's cast-iron pokers in her gloved hand. Sir Cecil himself lay motionless on the rug by her feet.

Mick's eyes widened. "Heather? What have you done?" It wasn't really a question, and he didn't expect her to answer. It was obvious to Mick what had happened — he could see it with his own shocked eyes.

Sir Cecil lay face down, his body crumpled awkwardly beneath him. A large, gaping bloodied wound was visible on the back of his head, more blood covering his face. Mick's mind started to race. He noted his wife's gloved hands, similar to his own. A quick glance around the drawing room showed nothing particularly out of place; nothing to suggest the violent tussle that had ensued within its walls. The only evidence of that lay on the rug at Heather's feet.

"Put the poker down," he instructed, stepping slowly into the room. He watched Heather drop the poker next to Sir Cecil's still body. "Now step away and mind the . . ." Mick's voice caught. "Mind the blood."

Heather did as she was told, inching carefully around the body and making her way to her husband's side. Her face was ashen, almost ghost-like, her eyes glazed. She reached for his hand. "I had to," she whispered. "I had to."

Mick nodded. "I know." He noted his wife's hand was trembling in his own. He wanted to pull her close and embrace her, but he thought better of it. They needed to get out of here without leaving any trace of themselves behind — and that could take some time. He didn't know how long they had. "Have you touched anything? In here?"

Heather shook her head. "No — just the . . . just the poker." Looking up, her glassy eyes searched his. "He was laughing at me, Mick. Laughing at Cal. I—" She broke off at the mention of her son's name. "I just snapped. He turned his back on me and told me to get out. I . . . I caught him by surprise. He didn't see it coming."

"Go out and wait in the car." Mick turned his wife in the direction of the door. "Don't touch *anything* on your way out. I'll be there soon."

Heather lowered her gaze and began retracing her steps. Mick noted how small she looked, with her narrow shoulders hunched forward as she made her way from the room. She looked completely broken. How on earth had she managed to . . .

Mick wrenched his thoughts away from Heather. It didn't matter how she'd managed it — she had. *She'd killed him.*

With Heather now safely out of sight, he edged across the carpet and picked up the poker. He gave Sir Cecil a prod to make sure he was dead.

Dead.

He wasn't quite sure how that made him feel.

He should feel relieved. Pleased, even.

Maybe he did.

Dropping the poker back to the rug, he remained hovering by the still body. Other than his own ragged breathing, there was complete silence, the only sound the gentle tick-ticking of the mantelpiece clock. He glanced down at his hands.

At least he'd had the foresight to wear gloves.

But he didn't need the clock to tell him that he needed to act quickly. That he needed to get out of there.

With another glance at the dead body by his feet, he made his way over to the window that looked out onto the landscaped gardens beyond. He knew no one could possibly see inside — there was no one around for miles. But it still made him shiver. He glanced back at Sir Cecil's body and a form of clarity and order started to return.

He needed to get rid of the body.

His mind started to race.

Although he knew the house to be empty, he didn't want to stay a second longer than he needed to. It didn't look like there had been too much disruption to the drawing room itself — the chairs were still upright, the man's brandy glass still sitting on the fireside table.

But he needed to get rid of the body.

Dead bodies began to smell after a while — and who knew what visitors made it up to Pemberton Hall these days. He couldn't guarantee they wouldn't get disturbed and he couldn't risk the man being found too soon. He'd watched enough of those true crime TV shows to know that clues were always left behind, no matter how careful you think you might have been. *Every contact leaves a trace*, wasn't that what they said?

Pulling a tartan rug from one of the high-backed armchairs next to the fire, he laid it on the floor next to Sir Cecil and began to roll up the body like a stick of rock. The cast-iron poker, with what looked like blood on its tip, lay by Sir Cecil's side. He picked it up with a gloved hand and tucked it inside the blanket.

Sweeping the room through squinted eyes, he saw nothing else particularly out of place. The contest had clearly been brief and very one-sided, Sir Cecil quickly brought to his knees after the first blow from the poker. In some ways, he wished it had lasted longer — that more pain and suffering had been inflicted on the man now lying at his feet, wrapped up in a tartan rug. But it was too late for that now. What was done was done.

As he bent down to grab hold of the rug, his eyes caught the graffiti on the wall above the sideboard. A smile teased his lips — it was good work. And, by the looks of it, nothing short of what the man deserved. Maybe some of it would look good on his headstone — if anyone ever found him.

There was some evidence of an unsuccessful attempt by Sir Cecil to clean the paint from the walls. He clearly hadn't called the police; the man probably didn't want cops traipsing through the place where he'd murdered his own son. He might be a particularly distasteful human being, but he wasn't stupid.

Grabbing the end of the rug, Mick pulled the body towards the door.

* * *

Thursday 14 March 2019
Police Investigation Centre, Bury St Edmunds

Mick heard various doors banging and clattering, their sound echoing along the corridor. He'd often said he would do anything for Heather — and he'd meant it. She wouldn't last five minutes in a place like this — and as for prison? The thought made him shudder. Mick would survive incarceration — he was strong. And knowing Heather would be waiting for him on the outside would enable him to cope. He could do his time.

He just hoped Heather would cope without him. She had a resilience that belied her small frame, he knew that much. When they'd left Pemberton Hall that night with Sir Cecil's body in the boot of the car, her face had been set like stone. But there was also a peacefulness about her — as if she had finally righted a wrong after so many years of suffering.

No, Heather would be fine.

And as for himself? Nothing would take away the grief he felt at losing Cal, but the sight of Sir Cecil's body lying bleeding out onto his own rug had brought him a curious sense of satisfaction.

Yes — he could survive this.

He would do anything for Heather.

* * *

Carnaby Close, Bury St Edmunds

Lana heaved the suitcases down from the loft, letting them tumble onto the landing. She almost fell from the ladder with the effort. She knew she would need more than just a couple of suitcases, but it was a start. She'd booked the removals company for next week, but she couldn't just sit around and wait. She had to do something. Keep busy.

There was no question now that she would need to leave the house and move on. The lease was due for renewal in a couple of months anyway — but there was no way she could stay.

Not now.

Scott was appearing in court today, but she wasn't going to go. She couldn't bring herself to see him, or listen to whatever it was he'd got himself caught up in. Not today. She would let him get settled into whichever prison he was remanded to — for she was certain he wouldn't be given bail — and then she would visit.

But for now she needed to box her life up and move on. Again.

She wiped a smudge of dirt from her cheek as she clambered down the last few remaining steps of the ladder. There was so much to pack up — twenty years of her and Scott's life together to be rammed into wooden crates and cardboard boxes.

And where would she go?

Anywhere.

Anywhere that wasn't here.

She'd taken a call from a journalist that morning — she'd already forgotten the man's name, but it was written down somewhere on a piece of paper — so she knew what was coming.

The bombshell.

She'd always known it would only be a matter of time before the past finally caught up with them. And here it was. In some ways she was surprised it had taken this long. Scott may very well be heading to prison for something entirely different, but was it karma finally dishing out the punishment he'd managed to avoid when he was a boy? Once the truth was out about Simon Baxter, she knew many people around here would form that opinion — and maybe there was a part of her that thought it, too. She'd never really forgiven Scott for what he'd done.

Edging around the suitcases on the landing, she hovered outside Scott's bedroom door. Predictably it was locked — she would need to break it open if she was to pack up any of his things.

But not yet.

She couldn't face that today.

CHAPTER THIRTY-NINE

The Nutshell, Bury St Edmunds

Nicki placed the pint of beer down in front of Roy, slipping back into her own seat. At 6 p.m. the pub was full to capacity — which didn't take much. At just fifteen by seven feet in area, it was cosy to say the least. She took a sip of her orange juice.

"You're not having a drink?" Roy gestured towards his own pint glass before lifting it from the table.

Nicki shook her head. "I'm meant to be going out to dinner tonight — I'll maybe have a glass or two later."

Roy took a mouthful of his beer, then asked, "Do you think she knew? The wife, I mean."

Nicki frowned. "Heather?"

Roy nodded. "She told us quite early on that she didn't know who Calvin's real dad was — but that was a blatant lie. She clearly did know. I can't help wondering what else she was keeping quiet about. Did she know what her husband had done?"

Nicki had to admit it had crossed her mind once or twice as both cases came to their respective conclusions. Had Heather known about Calvin visiting Sir Cecil? Did she know more about her son's death than she was prepared to admit? And Sir Cecil's? Anything was possible — goodness knows — but as much as Nicki tried, she couldn't quite see it.

"I'm not so sure," she eventually replied. "She seemed genuinely shocked — both at the news about Calvin, and also about Mick's part in it all. I don't think she knew about Mick and Sir Cecil."

"Maybe." Roy placed his pint glass down. "I still can't help thinking about it, though. Killing the man — Sir Cecil, I mean — it's quite an extreme reaction, even to the murder of someone you considered to be your own flesh and blood. I don't know why, but there's something niggling at me that we might not have been told the whole story."

It was a feeling Nicki knew well. She gave a non-committal shrug. "We often don't find out everything, Roy — you know that as well as I do. There will always be something hidden away, buried so deeply that not even the greatest investigation team in the world would be able to uncover it. It's just the way it is sometimes."

They passed the next few minutes in companionable silence, sipping their drinks and watching the world go by from the window. Nicki took a sly glance across the table and noticed her detective sergeant's pensive look.

"You OK, Roy?"

For a moment she didn't think he'd heard her. Then he turned and gave a nod. "I contacted Ellis's dad earlier today." He paused, then gave a sad smile. "He seemed genuinely pleased to hear from me. It'll be ten years this year — since Ellis died. It seems like yesterday."

Nicki lowered her gaze to her glass. She knew how that felt right enough. "You handled yourself well in this investigation, Roy. Despite the ghosts it must have resurrected for you."

"I'm kind of sad we didn't get justice for Calvin; not really, anyway. Sir Cecil might be dead, but he didn't get to suffer for what he did to that family. That bugs me a little."

Roy drained the rest of his pint. "I've said I'll go and see them — Ellis's parents. We didn't really speak much after the funeral. It'll be nice to catch up after all this time."

"Good idea." Nicki glanced at her watch. Damn. She was meant to be going out to dinner but she really didn't feel like it. All she wanted to do was run a hot bath and unwind. She got to her feet. "I'm going to have to go, Roy. You stay and finish your pint. I'll see you in the morning."

* * *

College Lane, Bury St Edmunds

"Thanks. Sorry I'm not feeling up to going out." Nicki eyed the two takeaway carrier bags sitting on her kitchen worktop. "But how many people are you planning on feeding?"

Jeremy smiled and gestured towards the bags. "I couldn't decide — one's Indian and the other Chinese. Whatever we don't eat tonight, you can have tomorrow."

Nicki headed for the fridge and the bottle of Pinot Grigio she knew was inside. "Well, it's much appreciated. Sorry again for making you change your plans."

Jeremy shrugged and plucked two plates from the draining board. "It's no problem. I cancelled the restaurant reservation and swung by the takeaway instead. To be honest, a quiet night in suits me fine. This week has been a bit manic."

Nicki poured them both a large glass of wine. "I didn't like to say, but you do look a bit rough." She handed Jeremy his glass and ducked out of the way of the playful shove she knew would be heading in her direction.

"Now, now, Miss Hardcastle, there's no need for that. I'm a very sensitive person."

Nicki grinned and started loading up her plate with food. "*That* I very much doubt — you've got skin as tough as rhino hide."

Their plates full, they made their way over to the sofa.

"So, when's it going live?" Nicki scooped up a forkful of chicken bhuna. "Your piece about Scott Edgecombe?"

Jeremy swallowed a mouthful of pilau rice before answering. "Still under review with my editor at the moment — but I'm hopeful it'll get the green light soon. They're making sure we won't land ourselves in hot water, legally speaking."

Nicki nodded, washing down some rice with a mouthful of wine. "Are you sure it's something that needs to be published? I mean, hasn't his mother gone through enough?"

Jeremy's fork hovered over his plate. It was a conversation they often had — his hunger for chasing the next big story, Nicki's quest for compassion and doing what was right. It was always a good-natured discussion, though; they simply saw things from different perspectives.

"To be honest, there's no guarantee it will be. I'm hopeful, of course, it's a great story, but with Edgecombe now charged we'll have to tread carefully over what we write about him." He stabbed a piece of chicken with his fork. "But I still think it's a story that needs to be told."

Nicki knew better than to force the issue, plus she was too tired. After the morning briefing when she'd confirmed both Scott Edgecombe and Mick Shaw had been charged, she'd slumped behind her desk and let the weariness of the last seven days envelop her. The DCI had called by to congratulate the team on wrapping up both investigations, and he'd even stopped long enough to partake in a few of the delicacies that Darcie had brought back from her travels. Nicki had made her excuses, saying she had piles of paperwork needing her attention, and slipped away to the sanctuary of her office.

In reality, she'd been thinking about Deano.

Both investigations had side-tracked her thoughts for a while, but now he was at the forefront of her mind again.

"You OK?"

Nicki felt herself jolt, blinking rapidly to see Jeremy's concerned expression.

"You zoned out there for a minute or two."

"Sorry, dog tired." Nicki gave a faint smile and buried her face behind her wine glass. It was then, as she looked over the rim, that she spied the photographs still on the mantel-piece. Colour flooded her cheeks and she felt her heart rate quicken. She'd forgotten to put them away after her parents' visit at the weekend. Caz had been round since, but her friend hadn't seemed to notice them. Or, if she had, she'd decided not to say anything.

Deano's cheeky smile grinned out at her.

She saw Jeremy's gaze follow her own — and then the frown that followed. "Who's the little fella?"

The chicken bhuna instantly began to churn inside Nicki's stomach. Damn — she'd always worried that this might happen. That she would forget to put the photographs away. And now she had. While desperately thinking of something — *anything* — to say, she took another mouthful of wine. As she did so, her mobile chirped with a message.

Glad of the interruption, Nicki grabbed it from the table. *'You need to come now. It's about your brother.'*

* * *

2 Old Railway Cottages, Dullingham, Nr Newmarket

"Are you going to enlighten me as to what's going on?" Nicki noted Jeremy's deepening frown as he pulled the car to a stop. "This is all rather weird."

Nicki released her seatbelt, the mixture of wine and Indian food sloshing around inside her stomach making her feel queasy. Benedict's message had unnerved her. She'd dashed off a reply, asking what he meant and had anything happened — but he merely repeated that she needed to get herself over to Dullingham.

Fast.

She knew she owed Jeremy an explanation — the man had been good enough to drive her when she had felt too wired and full of wine to get behind the wheel herself — but her tongue tied itself up in knots every time she tried to find the words. Where would she start?

Finally, she found her voice. "I will, I promise. I just need to do this first."

She climbed out of the car just as Benedict opened his front door. She hurried up the short garden path, Jeremy following on a few steps behind, the bemused expression still decorating his face.

"What's happened?" Her voice was taut, and as soon as Benedict stepped back to usher her inside, she saw the small rucksack on the floor. "Where are you going? Is it Deano?"

Benedict caught Nicki's eye but looked away quickly, shaking his head. "No. I have to go away for a while — for work. I mentioned that job? Well, I need to leave tonight."

Nicki's face dropped. "But . . . what about Deano? We still need to find him. Now these two investigations are more or less wrapped up, I might be able to take some more time off. We can go—"

Benedict stepped closer, placing a hand on Nicki's arm to silence her. "Hey, calm down." He could feel her quivering beneath his touch. "It's good news. We don't need to go back on the road to look for him." Benedict paused, holding Nicki in his gaze. "Because he's right next door."

THE END

MESSAGE FROM THE AUTHOR

There are many people I need to thank for helping get the latest DI Nicki Hardcastle book on to the shelves.

First, I must thank Detective Inspector Steve Duncan and Police Sergeant Rebecca McCarthy for once again being on the end of my often weird and vague-sounding questions. Your help is much appreciated, and if there are any remaining procedural inaccuracies, then I can assure you that they are mine and mine alone!

I must also thank Karen Pinches for the background information regarding British Sugar, and both Jim Parker and Ella Webb for the loan of their names!

My good friend Sarah Bezant always deserves a special mention — you have the most amazing hawk eye when it comes to plot holes, typos and missing words. I really appreciate everything you do for me.

And, of course, I must thank everyone involved at my publishers, Joffe Books — and especially Kate Lyall Grant for believing in me and making my writing the best it can be.

Thanks must go to Charlie Dorner and Sylvia Smith from the Moreton Hall Pub for always making me feel so welcome (and for making sure I always get the best table). Your support of my writing and offering to host book signings is very much appreciated.

And, finally, to you — the readers! Without you, none of these books would ever see the light of day. I thank each and every one of you.

To keep up to date, there are various ways to get in touch: www.michellekiddauthor.com — join my author newsletter for information on future releases and special offers. I also give away free downloads, content not available anywhere else!

www.facebook.com/michellekiddauthor
Twitter @AuthorKidd
Instagram @michellekiddauthor

THE JOFFE BOOKS STORY

We began in 2014 when Jasper agreed to publish his mum's much-rejected romance novel and it became a bestseller.

Since then we've grown into the largest independent publisher in the UK. We're extremely proud to publish some of the very best writers in the world, including Joy Ellis, Faith Martin, Caro Ramsay, Helen Forrester, Simon Brett and Robert Goddard. Everyone at Joffe Books loves reading and we never forget that it all begins with the magic of an author telling a story.

We are proud to publish talented first-time authors, as well as established writers whose books we love introducing to a new generation of readers.

We won Trade Publisher of the Year at the Independent Publishing Awards in 2023. We have been shortlisted for Independent Publisher of the Year at the British Book Awards for the last four years, and were shortlisted for the Diversity and Inclusivity Award at the 2022 Independent Publishing Awards. In 2023 we were shortlisted for Publisher of the Year at the RNA Industry Awards.

We built this company with your help, and we love to hear from you, so please email us about absolutely anything bookish at feedback@joffebooks.com

If you want to receive free books every Friday and hear about all our new releases, join our mailing list: www.joffebooks.com/contact

And when you tell your friends about us, just remember: it's pronounced Joffe as in coffee or toffee!

ALSO BY MICHELLE KIDD

DI NICKI HARDCASTLE SERIES
Book 1: MISSING BOY
Book 2: THE TROPHY KILLER
Book 3: THE HARDWICK HEATH KILLER

DI JACK MCINTOSH SERIES
Book 1: SEVEN DAYS TO DIE
Book 2: FIFTEEN REASONS TO KILL
Book 3: SIXTEEN CARVED PIECES
Book 4: TWENTY YEARS BURIED
Book 5: THREE BROKEN BODIES

Milton Keynes UK
Ingram Content Group UK Ltd.
UKHW010728110724
445512UK00004B/86